The Orange Tree

BOOKS BY CARLOS FUENTES

Carlos Fuentes

THE ORANGE TREE

Translated from the Spanish by
Alfred Mac Adam

HarperPerennial
A Division of HarperCollins*Publishers*

Contents

The Orange Tree

The Two Shores

TO JUAN GOYTISOLO

*Like the planets in their orbits, the world of ideas
tends toward circularity.*
—AMOS OZ, *Late Love*

Combien de royaumes nous ignorent!
—PASCAL, *Pensées*

[10]

ALL this I saw. The fall of the great Aztec city in the
moan of the conch shells, the clash of steel against
flint, and the fire of Castilian cannon. I saw the burnt water
of the lake where stood this Great Tenochtitlán, two times
the size of Córdoba.

The temples fell, the standards, the trophies. The very
gods themselves fell. And the day after the defeat, using
the stones of the Indian temples, we began to build the
Christian churches. Anyone curious —or who happens to
be a mole—will find at the base of the columns of the
Cathedral of Mexico the magic emblems of the God of
Night, the smoking mirror of Tezcatlipoca. How long will
the new mansions of our one God, built on the ruins of
the not one but thousand gods last? Perhaps as long as the
name of these: Rain, Water, Wind, Fire, Garbage . . .

To tell the truth, I don't know. I just died of buboes.
A horrible death, painful, incurable. A bouquet of plagues
bestowed upon me by my own Indian brothers in exchange

3

for the evils we Spaniards visited on them. I am shocked to see this city of Mexico populated by faces scarred by smallpox, as devastated as the causeways of the conquered city—all in the twinkling of an eye. The water of the lake heaves, boiling; the walls have contracted an incurable leprosy; the faces have forever lost their dark beauty, their perfect profile: for all time, Europe has marked the face of this New World, which, in fact, is older than the European face. Although to tell the truth, from this Olympian vantage point death has given me, I see everything that's happened as the meeting of two old worlds, both millenarian—the stones we've found here are as old as those of Egypt, and the destiny of all empires was written for all time on the wall at Balthazar's feast.

I saw it all. I'd like to tell it all. But my appearances in history are rigorously limited to what's been said about me. The chronicler Bernal Díaz del Castillo mentions me fifty-eight times in his *True History of the Conquest of New Spain*. The last thing known about me is that I was already dead when Hernán Cortés, our commander, embarked on his ill-fated expedition to Honduras in October of 1524. That's how the chronicler describes it, and he soon forgets about me.

True, I do reappear in the final parade of ghosts, when Bernal Díaz lists the fates of the comrades of the conquest. The writer possesses a prodigious memory: he remembers every name, doesn't forget a single horse or who rode it. Perhaps he had no other recourse but memory to save himself from death. Or from something worse: disillusion and sadness. Let's not fool ourselves. No one escaped unscathed from this venture of discovery and conquest—neither the conquered, who witnessed the destruction of their world, nor the conquerors, who never achieved the total satisfaction of their ambitions, suffering instead endless injustices and disenchantments. Both should have built a new world after their shared defeat. I can know that because I've already died; the chronicler from Medina del Campo didn't know it very well when he wrote his fabulous history, which is why he's got more than enough memory and not enough imagination.

Not a single comrade of the conquest is missing from his list. But the vast majority are dispatched with a laconic epitaph: *He died his death*. It's true that some, very few, are singled out because they died "in the power of the Indians." The most interesting are those who had a singular, almost always violent, fate.

Glory and abjection are equally evident in this affair of the conquest. Cortés sentenced Pedro Escudero and Juan Cermeño to the gallows because they tried to escape to Cuba on a boat, while he only ordered their pilot, Gonzalo de Umbría, to have his toes cut off. Maimed and all, this Umbría had the effrontery to appear before the King and complain, obtaining thereby rents paid in gold and Indian townships. Cortés must have regretted not having hanged him as well. Observe then, readers, listeners, penitents, or whatever you are as you approach my tomb, how decisions are made when time presses and history suppresses. Things could always have happened exactly opposite to the way the chronicle records them. Always.

But it also tells you that in this undertaking there was a bit of everything, from the personal pleasures of a certain Morón who was a great musician, a man named Porras with bright red hair who was a great singer, or an Ortiz who was a great cittern player and dancing master, to the disasters of Enrique something-or-other, a native of Palencia, who drowned from fatigue, the weight of his weapons, and the heat they caused him.

There are crossed destinies: Cortés marries Alfonso de

Grado to no less a personage than Doña Isabel, daughter of the Aztec emperor Moctezuma; at the same time, a certain Xuárez, called the Old Man, ends up killing his wife with a corn-grinding stone. Who wins, who loses in a war of conquest? Juan Sedeño came with a fortune— merely his own ship, a mare and a black to serve him, bacon, a good supply of cassava bread—and made more here. A certain Burguillos, on the other hand, acquired wealth and good Indians, but he gave it all up to become a Franciscan. Most returned from the conquest or stayed on in Mexico without saving a single *maravedí*.

So what can one more destiny—my own—matter in this parade of glory and misery? I'll merely say that in this matter of destinies, I think that the wisest of all of us was the man called Solís, "Behind-the-Door," who spent his time in his house behind the door watching the others pass by in the street, not meddling with anyone and not being meddled with by anyone. Now I think that in death we're all like Solís: behind the door, watching people pass by without being seen, and reading what's said about us in the chronicles written by the survivors.

About me, then, this is the final statement:

Another soldier, whose name was Jerónimo de Aguilar, passed; I include Aguilar in this account because he was the man we found at Catoche Point, who was being held by Indians and who became our translator. He died crippled with buboes.

[9]

I have many final impressions of the great business of the conquest of Mexico, in which fewer than six hundred valiant Spaniards subdued an empire nine times larger than

Spain in territory and three times larger in population. To say nothing of the fabulous treasure we found here, which, shipped to Cádiz and Seville, made the fortune not only of Spain but of the whole of Europe, for all time, right until today.

I, Jerónimo de Aguilar, look at the New World before closing my eyes forever, and the last thing I see is the coast of Veracruz and the ships setting sail filled with Mexican treasure, guided by the most trustworthy of compasses: a sun of gold and a moon of silver, both simultaneously hanging over a blue-black sky that is stormy on high but bloody as soon as it touches the surface of the water.

I want to bid farewell to the world with this image of power and riches in the background of my vision: five well-stocked ships, a large number of soldiers, and many horses, shot, shotguns, crossbows, and all sorts of weapons, piled up to the masts and stored in the holds as ballast; eighty thousand pesos in gold and silver, infinite jewels, and the entire wardrobe of Moctezuma and Guatemuz, the last Mexican kings. A clean conquest operation, justified by the treasure a bold captain in the service of the Crown sends to His Majesty, King Charles.

But my eyes don't manage to close in peace, thinking above all about the abundance of protection, arms, men, and horses that accompanied the gold and silver of Mexico back to Spain—a cruel contrast to the insecurity, slim resources, and small number of soldiers with which Cortés and his men came from Cuba in the first moment of this dubious exploit. And yet, just look at the ironies of history.

Quiñones, captain of Cortés's personal guard, sent to protect the treasure, crossed the Bahamas but stopped at the island of Terceira with the booty of Mexico. He fell in love with a woman there, and was stabbed to death because of it; while Alonso de Dávila, who led the expe-

7

dition, crossed the path of the French pirate Jean Fleury, whose nickname among us is Juan Florín, who stole the gold and silver and imprisoned Dávila in France, where King Francis I had declared again and again, "Show me the clause in Adam's testament in which the king of Spain is given half the world," to which his corsairs answered in chorus: "When God created the sea, he gave it to all of us without exception." And as a moral to the story: Florín or Fleury was himself captured on the high seas by Basques (Valladolid, Burgos, the Basque Country: the Discovery and Conquest finally united and mobilized all Spain!) and hanged in the port of Pico . . .

And the thing doesn't end there, because a certain Cárdenas, a pilot born in the Triana district of Seville and a member of our expedition, denounced Cortés in Castile, saying that he'd never seen a land where there were two kings as there were in New Spain, since Cortés took for himself, without any right to it, as much as he sent to His Majesty. For his declaration, the King gave this man from Triana a thousand pesos in rents and a parcel of Indians.

The bad thing is that he was right. We were all witnesses to the way our commander took the lion's share and promised us soldiers rewards at the end of the war. May it be long in coming! So we were left, after sweating our teeth out, without a pot to piss in . . . Cortés was sentenced and deprived of power; his captains lost their lives, their freedom, and, what's worse, the treasure, which ended up scattered to the four corners of Europe . . .

Is there any justice, I ask myself, in all this? Did we do nothing more than give the gold of the Aztecs a better destiny by pulling it out of its sterile occupation and spreading it around, distributing it, conferring on it an economic purpose instead of an ornamental or sacred one, putting it into circulation, melting it down the better to see it melt away?

[8]

From my grave, I try to judge things calmly; but one image forces itself on my thoughts again and again. I see before me a young man, about twenty-two years old, of clear, dark complexion, of a very noble disposition, both in body and in facial features.

He was married to one of Moctezuma's nieces. He was called Guatemuz or Guatimozín and had a cloud of blood in his eyes. Whenever he felt his vision blur, he lowered his eyelids, and I saw them: one was gold and the other silver. He was the last emperor of the Aztecs, after his uncle Moctezuma was stoned to death by the disillusioned mob. We Spaniards killed something more than the power of the Indians: we killed the magic that surrounded it. Moctezuma did not fight. Guatemuz—let it be said to his honor—fought like a hero.

Captured with his captains and brought before Cortés on August 13, at the hour of vespers on Saint Hippolytus Day in the year 1521, Guatemuz said that in the defense of his people and vassals he'd done everything he was obliged to do out of honor and (he added) also out of passion, strength, and conviction. "And since I've been brought by force, a prisoner," he said then to Cortés, "before your person and power. Take that dagger you wear on your belt and kill me with it."

This young, valiant Indian, the last emperor of the Aztecs, began to weep, but Cortés answered him that for being so brave he should come in peace to the fallen city and govern in Mexico and in its provinces as he had before.

I know all this because I was the translator of the interview between Cortés and Guatemuz, who could not understand each other alone. I translated as I pleased. I didn't communicate to the conquered prince what Cortés really said, but put into the mouth of our leader a threat: "You will be my prisoner; today I will torture you by burning your feet and those of your comrades until you confess where the rest of your uncle Moctezuma's treasure is (the part that didn't end up in the hands of French pirates)."

I added, inventing on my own and mocking Cortés: "You'll never be able to walk again, but you'll accompany me on future conquests, crippled and weeping, as a symbol of continuity and the source of legitimacy for my enterprise, whose banners, raised on high, are gold and fame, power and religion."

I translated, I betrayed, I invented. Right then and there, Guatemuz's tears dried, and instead of tears, down one cheek ran gold and down the other silver, cutting a furrow in them as a knife would, leaving a permanent wound in them which, may it please God, death has healed.

Since my own death, I remember that vespers of Saint Hippolytus, recorded by Bernal Díaz as an eternal night of rain and lightning, and I reveal myself before posterity as a falsifier, a traitor to my commander Cortés, who instead of making a peace offering to the fallen prince offered him cruelty, continued oppression without mercy, and eternal shame for the conquered.

But since things happened as I'd said, my false words becoming reality, wasn't I right to translate the commander backwards and tell the truth with my lies to the Aztec? Or were my words perhaps a mere exchange and I nothing more than the intermediary (the translator), the mainspring of a fatal destiny that transformed trick into truth?

On that Saint Hippolytus night, playing the role of translator between the conquistador and the conquered, I merely confirmed the power of words: I used them to say the opposite of what Cortés said only to express what he actually did. I'd acquired a knowledge of the soul of my commander, Hernán Cortés, a dazzling mix of reason and folly, will and weakness, skepticism and fantastic naïveté, good luck and bad, gallantry and jest, virtue and malice —all those things went into the man from Estremadura, the conqueror of Mexico whom I'd followed from Yucatan to Moctezuma's court.

The powers of folly and foolishness or malice and good fortune when they're not in harmony, when they're only words, can turn our intentions upside down. The story of the last Aztec king, Guatemuz, ended with him not in the place of power promised by Cortés, not in the honor with which the Indian surrendered, but in a cruel comedy, the very one I'd invented and made inevitable with my lies. The young emperor was the king of fools, dragged without feet by the victor's chariot, crowned with cactus, and finally hanged upside down from the branches of a sacred silk-cotton tree like a hunted-down animal. What happened was exactly what I had lyingly invented.

For that reason I don't sleep in peace. Possibilities not carried out, the alternatives of freedom all rob me of sleep.

A woman was to blame.

[7]

Among all the prodigies produced by my captain Don Hernán Cortés to impress the Indians—fire from harquebuses, steel swords, glass beads—none was so important as the horses of the conquest. A shotgun blast fades in smoke; a Spanish blade can be overcome by a two-handed

Indian sword; glass may fool people, an emerald as well. But the horse exists, stands there, has a life of its own, moves, possesses the combined power of nerve, gloss, muscle, foaming mouth, and hooves. Those hooves, links to the earth, makers of thunder, twins of steel. Hypnotic eyes. The rider who gets on and off adds to the perpetual metamorphosis of the beast seen now but never before imagined, not, certainly, by the Indians, not even by a single one of their gods.

Could the horse be the dream of a god who never communicated his secret nightmare to us?

An Indian could never overcome an armed Castilian on horseback, and this is the true secret of the conquest, not any dream or prophecy. Cortés exploited his meager cavalry to the limit, not only in attacks or fights in open country but in specially prepared seaside cavalcades where the chargers seemed to shake the waves—so much so that even we Spaniards imagined that if the horses were not there, these coasts would be as calm as a mirror of water.

We stared in astonishment at the unthought-of fraternity between the sea foam and the foam on their dewlaps.

And in Tabasco, when Captain Cortés wanted to astonish the envoys of the Great Moctezuma, he paired off a stallion with a mare in heat and hid them, instructing me to make them whinny at the right moment. The king's envoys had never heard that sound and succumbed in shock to the powers of the *Teúl*, or Spanish God, as the Indians called Cortés from that moment on.

The truth is that neither I nor anyone else had ever before heard such a whinny come out of the silence, devoid of a body, and reveal animal desire, bestial lust, with such crude force. My captain's theatrics far surpassed his intentions and even shocked us Spaniards. It made all of us feel a bit like beasts . . .

But the emissaries of the Great Moctezuma had also seen all the portents of that year prophesied by their magicians concerning the return of their blond and bearded god. Our marvels—the horses, the cannon—only confirmed what they already carried in their eyes: comets at midday, water in flames, fallen towers, nocturnal shrieking of wandering women, children carried away by the wind . . .

And lo and behold, Don Hernán Cortés arrives at that precise moment, as white as winters in the Gredos mountains, as hard as the earth in Medellín and Trujillo, and with a beard older than he was. So they wait for the return of the gods and instead get people like the hunchback Rodrigo Jara or Juan Pérez, who killed his wife, known as the Cowherd's Daughter, or Pedro Perón de Toledo, of turbulent descendancy, or a certain Izquierdo from Castromocho. Some gods! Even in the grave I cackle to think of it.

One image cuts off my laughter. The horse.

Even Valladolid, "the Fat Man," looked good on horseback; I mean he inspired respect and awe. The mortality of the man was saved by the immortality of the horse. Cortés was right when he told us from the first moment: "We shall bury the dead at night and in secret. That way our enemies will think us immortal."

The rider fell; never the charger. Never; not Cortés's bay, not Alonso Hernández's silver-gray mare that ran so well, not Montejo's sorrel, not even Morán's splayfooted, spotted nag. So it wasn't just men who entered the Great Tenochtitlán on November 3, 1520, but centaurs: mythological beings with two heads and six feet, armed with thunder and dressed in stone. And besides, thanks to the coincidences of the calendar, we'd been confused with the returning god, Quetzalcoatl.

Appropriately, Moctezuma received us on foot, halfway along the causeway that linked the valley to the city built on a lake, saying: "Welcome. You are home. Now rest."

No one among us had ever seen a city more splendid than Moctezuma's capital, neither in the Old World nor in the New: the canals, the canoes, the towers and wide plazas, the well-stocked markets and the novel things to be seen there, things never seen by us, things not mentioned in the Bible: tomatoes, turkeys, chili, chocolate, maize, potatoes, tobacco, agave beer, emeralds, jade, gold and silver in abundance, featherwork, and soft, mournful chanting . . .

Beautiful women, well-swept rooms, patios full of birds, and cages stuffed with tigers; gardens and albino dwarfs to serve us. Like Alexander in Capua, we were threatened by the delights of triumph. We were rewarded for our efforts. The horses were well taken care of.

Until one morning. Moctezuma, the great king who had received us with such hospitality in his city and in his palace, was in a royal chamber surrounded by all of us, when something happened that changed the course of our enterprise.

Cortés's lieutenant, Pedro de Alvarado, bold and gallant, cruel and shameless, had red hair and a red beard, which made the Indians call him *Tonantío*, which means the Sun. Likable and brazen, Tonantío had been amusing King Moctezuma with a game of dice—another novelty for these Indians—and for the moment the monarch was distracted, incapable of guessing his fortune beyond the next toss of the dice, even when he was being cheated, as he was at that moment by the irrepressible Alvarado. The king looked irritated, because he usually changed clothes several times a day, and either his serving maids were late or his tunic smelled or itched, who knows what . . .

Just at that moment, four *tamemes*, or Indian bearers, walk into the chamber followed by the usual din of our guards, and with impassive expressions drop in front of Cortés and the emperor the severed head of a horse.

It was then that the conquistador's second translator, an enslaved princess from Tabasco baptized Doña Marina but nicknamed La Malinche, quickly interpreted the messengers who'd come from the coast with news of an uprising of Mexicans in Veracruz against the garrison left there by Cortés. The Aztec troops had killed Juan de Escalante, head constable of the port, and six Spaniards.

Most important, they'd killed the horse. Here was the proof.

I noticed that Alvarado stood stock-still with his hand filled with dice in the air, staring at the half-open, glassy eyes of the horse as if he'd seen himself in them and as if in the flint-cut neck, slashed as if in rage, the enraged and red-haired captain had seen his own end.

Moctezuma lost interest in the game, shrugging his shoulders a bit, and stared fixedly at the horse's head. His eloquent eyes, however, silently told us Spaniards, "So you're gods? Well then, behold the mortality of your powers."

Cortés, on the other hand, stood staring at Moctezuma with such a face of betrayal that I could only read in it what our captain wanted to see in the king's countenance.

I have never felt that so many things were said without a word being spoken. Moctezuma, approaching the horse's head in a devout, almost humiliated fashion, said, without saying anything, that just as the horse died so could the Spaniards die if he decreed it. And he would decree it, if the foreigners did not withdraw in peace.

Without saying a word, Cortés warned the king that it would not be advisable for him to start a war that would ultimately destroy both him and his city.

Pedro de Alvarado, who knew nothing of subtle discourses, spoken or unspoken, violently threw the dice against the face of the horrifying divinity that presided over the chamber, the goddess named for her skirt of serpents. Before Moctezuma could say anything, Cortés stepped forward and ordered the king to abandon his palace and come to live in the one occupied by the Spaniards.

"If you sound an alarm or shout, you will be killed by my captains," Cortés said in an even tone, impressing Moctezuma more by that than Alvarado had with his physical fury. Nevertheless, after his initial shock and dismay, the king responded by removing from his arm and wrist the seal of Huichilobos, the god of war, as if he were going to order our slaughter.

But all he did was excuse himself: "I never ordered the attack in Veracruz. I shall punish my captains for having done it."

The handmaidens entered with the fresh clothes. They seemed flustered by the low tavern brawl they'd stumbled upon. Moctezuma recovered his dignity and said he would not leave his palace.

Alvarado then confronted Cortés: "Why are you wasting so many words? Either we take him prisoner or we run him through."

Once again, it was the interpreter Doña Marina who decided the struggle, forcefully advising the king: "Lord Moctezuma, what I recommend is that you go with them now to their dwelling without making a sound. I know they will honor you as the great lord you are. If you do otherwise, you will be put to death."

You understand that the woman said these things to the emperor on her own initiative, not translating Cortés but speaking Moctezuma's Mexican language fluently. The king looked like a cornered animal, but instead of shifting around on four legs he staggered on his own two feet. He offered his sons as hostages. He repeated these words several times: "Do not dishonor me in this way. What will my principal men say if they see me taken prisoner? Anything but this dishonor."

Was this pusillanimous creature the great lord who had subjugated all the tribes from Xalisco to Nicaragua through terror? Was this the cruel despot who one day ordered that those who dreamed about the end of his reign be put to death so that the dreams would die with the dreamers? I can only understand the enigma of Moctezuma's weakness before the Spaniards by using words as an explanation. Called *Tlatoani*, or Lord of the Great Voice, Moctezuma was slowly but surely losing his control over words—more than his control over men. I think that novelty disconcerted him, and Doña Marina had just proven, by arguing with him face to face, that the words of the king were no longer sovereign. Therefore, neither was he. Others, the foreigners, but also this treacherous woman from Tabasco, owned a vocabulary forbidden to Moctezuma.

In this second opportunity that stood between things said, things done, and the unforeseeable consequences of both, I saw my own opportunity. That night, under a mantle of secrecy, I spoke to the king in Mexican and told him privately about the dangers threatening the Spaniards. Did Moctezuma know that the governor of Cuba had sent an expedition to arrest Cortés, whom he considered a vile rebel who acted without authorization and who was worthy of being imprisoned instead of making a prisoner of such a great lord as Moctezuma, the equal only of another king, Don Carlos, whom Cortés, with no credentials, sought to represent?

I repeat these words as I said them, in one rush, without taking a breath, with no shade of meaning, no subtlety, hating myself for my betrayal but, above all, for my inferiority in the arts of dissimulation, trickery, and dramatic pauses, in which my rivals, Cortés and La Malinche, were masters.

I ended as abruptly as I'd begun, getting, as they say, right to the point: "This expedition against Cortés is led by Pánfilo de Narváez, a captain as bold as Cortés himself, but with five times as many men."

"Are they also Christians?" asked Moctezuma.

I said they were, and that they represented King Carlos, from whom Cortés was fleeing.

Moctezuma patted my hand and offered me a ring as green as a parrot. I gave it back and told him that my love for his people was reward enough. The king looked at me without understanding, as if he himself had never understood that he led a group of human beings. I asked myself then and I ask myself now, what kind of power did Moctezuma think he had and over whom? Perhaps he was only acting out some pantomime in front of the gods, wearing himself out in an effort to hear them and to be heard by them. But what was exchanged there was neither jewels nor pats on the hand but words, words that could give Moctezuma more power than all the horses and harquebuses the Spaniards possessed, if the Aztec king would only decide to speak to his men, his people, instead of speaking to the gods, his pantheon.

I told the king the secret of Cortés's weakness, just as Doña Marina had given Cortés the secret of Aztec weakness, the discord, the envy, the struggle between brothers, which affected Spain just as much as Mexico: one half of the country perpetually dying of the other half.

[6]

Thus I associated myself with the hope of an Indian victory. All my acts, you've already guessed and I can tell you right from my intangible shroud, were directed toward that goal: the triumph of the Indians over the Spaniards. Once again, Moctezuma let opportunity slip through his fingers. He got ahead of events, boasting in the presence of Cortés that he knew Cortés was threatened by Narváez instead of hastening to join forces with Narváez against Cortés, to defeat the man from Estremadura, and then to turn the Aztec nation against the fatigued regiment of Narváez. In that way, Mexico would have been saved . . .

I must say at this point that Moctezuma's vanity was always stronger than his cunning, although even stronger than his vanity was his feeling that everything was foretold, which was why the king had only to carry out the role set for him by religious and political ceremonial. In the soul of the king, fidelity to forms was its own reward. It had always happened that way, wasn't that the truth?

I didn't know how to say it wasn't, to argue with him. Perhaps my Mexican vocabulary was insufficient, and I didn't know the subtlest forms of Aztec philosophic and moral reasoning. What I did want was to frustrate the fatal plan, if such a thing existed, by means of words, imagination, lies. But when words, imagination, and lies jumble together, the result is the truth . . .

The Aztec king was hoping Cortés would be beaten by the punitive expedition sent by the governor of Cuba, but he did nothing to hasten the defeat of our captain. His certainty was understandable. If Cortés, with only five hundred men, had defeated the chiefs of Tabasco and Zempoala as well as the fierce Tlaxcaltecs, wouldn't more than two thousand Spaniards also armed with fire and horses defeat him?

But the cunning Cortés, accompanied by his new Indian allies, defeated Narváez's people and captured their leader. Observe the irony of this matter: now we had two prisoners of importance, one Aztec and the other Spanish, Moctezuma and Narváez. Was there any limit to the number of our victories?

"The truth is, I don't understand you," the Great Moctezuma, sequestered but quite at his ease being bathed by his beautiful handmaidens, said to us.

But did we understand him?

This question, reader, obliges me to pause and reflect before events once again rush to their conclusion, always more swiftly than the pen of the narrator, although this time he writes from death.

Moctezuma: Did we understand exactly how alien to him treacherous political machinations were, and how natural, by contrast, was the proximity of a religious world impenetrable to Europeans? Impenetrable for having been forgotten: our contact with God and His primary emanations had been lost for a long, long time. In that, Moctezuma and his people were indeed alike, though neither knew it: the clay of creation, the nearness of the gods, still moistened them.

Did we understand him, sheltered as he was in another time, the time of origins, which for him was current, immediate time, portentous as both refuge and threat?

I compared him to a cornered animal. Instead, this refined man seems to me, now that death has made us equal, not only like the scrupulous individual of infinite courtesies we met when we entered Mexico but like the first man, always the first, amazed that the world exists and that the light advances every day before fading into the cruelty of every night. His obligation consisted in always being, in the name of all, the first man to ask: "Will the sun come up again?"

This was a more urgent question for Moctezuma and the Aztecs than knowing whether Narváez defeated Cortés, Cortés defeated Narváez, the Tlaxcaltecs defeated Cortés, or if Moctezuma would fall before all of them: as long as he didn't fall before the gods.

Would it rain again, would the maize grow again, the river run, the beasts roar?

All the power, the elegance, the very distance of Moctezuma was the disguise of a man recently arrived at the regions of the dawn. He was a witness to the first shout and the first terror. Fear of being and gratitude for being were mixed within him, behind the paraphernalia of plumed headpieces and collars, handmaidens, tiger knights, and bloody priests.

It was a woman, Marina, an Indian like him, from his own land, who actually defeated him, although she did use two tongues. It was she who revealed to Cortés that the Aztec empire was divided, that the peoples subjugated by Moctezuma hated him and hated each other as well, and that the Spaniards could grasp opportunity by the forelock; it was she who understood the secret uniting our two lands: fratricidal hatred, division—I've already said it: two nations, each one dying of the other . . .

Too late. I communicated to Moctezuma that Cortés was also hated and beset on all sides from an imperial Spain as contentious as the Mexican empire he was conquering.

I forgot two things.

Cortés listened to Marina not only as an interpreter but

as a lover. And as translator and lover, she paid attention to the human voices of this land. Moctezuma listened only to the gods; I wasn't one of them, so the attention he paid me was one more manifestation of his courtesy, as rich as an emerald but as evanescent as the voice of a parrot.

I, who also possessed the two voices, European and American, had been defeated. I had two homelands, which perhaps was more my weakness than my strength. Marina, La Malinche, bore the deep pain and rancor but also the hope of her condition; she had to risk everything to save her life and have descendants. Her weapon was the same as mine: her tongue. But I found myself divided between Spain and the New World. I knew both shores.

Marina didn't; she could give herself entirely to the New World, not to her subjugated past, true enough, but to her ambiguous, uncertain, and therefore unconquered future. Perhaps I deserved my defeat. I could not save the poor king of my adoptive country, Mexico, by telling him a secret, a truth, an infidelity.

Then came the defeat I've already told of.

[5]

Doña Marina and I fought, truly fought, in the drama of Cholula. I didn't always possess the Mexican language. My initial advantage was knowing Spanish and Maya after the long time I spent among the Indians in Yucatan. Doña Marina—La Malinche—spoke only Maya and Mexican when she was given to Cortés as a slave. So for a while I was the only one who could translate into the language of Castile. The Mayas of the coast told me the things I would translate into Spanish or say them to La Malinche, but she depended on me to communicate them to Cortés. Sometimes, the Mexicans would tell the woman things she would say to me in Maya and I would translate them into Spanish. And although in those instances she had an advantage— she could invent whatever she wanted in passing from Nahuatl to Maya—I went on being the master of language. The Castilian translation that reached the ears of the conquistador was always mine.

Then we reached Cholula, after the vicissitudes of the coast, the founding of Veracruz, the taking of Zempoala and its fat chieftain, who revealed to us, huffing and puffing from his litter, that the conquered peoples would unite with us against Moctezuma. We arrived after our fight against the haughty Tlaxcaltecs, who, even though they were mortal enemies of Moctezuma, did not want to exchange the power of Mexico for the new oppression of the Spaniards.

For centuries, people have said that the Tlaxcaltecs are to blame for everything; pride and betrayal can be faithful companions, each one covering up for the other. The fact is that when we—Cortés and our small band of Spaniards, along with the battalions of fierce Tlaxcaltec warriors— drew up outside the gates of Cholula, we were stopped by the priests of those holy places, because Cholula was the pantheon of all the gods of these lands. As in Rome, they were all admitted, with no distinctions made about their origin, into the great, collective temple of divinities. To that end, the people of Cholula erected the greatest pyramid of all, a honeycomb of seven structures one inside the other, all linked together by deep labyrinths of red and yellow reverberations.

I already knew that in this land everything is governed by the stars, the Sun and Moon, Venus, who is her own precious twin at dawn and dusk, and a calendar that provides a precise account of the agricultural year and its 360 bountiful days plus 5 unlucky days: the masked days.

It must have been on one of those days that we Spaniards arrived here, because after sending the Tlaxcaltec host ahead we ran into a blockade of popes, priests dressed in black—black tunics, black hair, black skin, all as black as the night wolves of these lands, with one single flash emblazoned on their hair, eyes, and togas: the shine of the blood, like a sticky, brilliant sweat, that was proper to their office.

Loud and firmly did these priests speak, forbidding admittance to the violent Tlaxcaltecs. Cortés yielded to their demand, on condition that the Cholulans quickly abandon their idols.

"They haven't even entered, and they're already asking us to betray the gods!" exclaimed the popes in a tone difficult to define, between a lament and a challenge, between sigh and fury, between fatality and dissimulation, as if they were ready to die for their divinities, but resigning themselves at the same time to give them up for lost.

All this did La Malinche translate from Mexican into Spanish, while I, Jerónimo de Aguilar, the first of all the interpreters, remained in a kind of limbo, waiting for my turn to translate into Castilian, until I realized, perhaps stupefied by the unbearable stench of muddy blood and incense, shit from Andalusian horses, excessive sweat from the soldiers, conflictive cooking of chili and bacon, of garlic and turkey, all indistinguishable from the sacrificial cooking that wafted its smoke and chanting from the pyramid, I realized that Jerónimo de Aguilar was no longer needed. The diabolical female was translating everything, this bitch of a Marina, this whore who learned to speak Spanish. This scoundrel, this trickster, this expert in sucking, the conquistador's concubine, had stolen my professional singularity away from me, the function where there was no substitute for me, my—to coin a word—my *monopoly* over the Castilian language . . . La Malinche had pulled the Spanish language out of Cortés's sex, she'd sucked it out of him, she'd castrated him of it without his knowing it, by disguising mutilation as pleasure . . .

This language was no longer mine alone. Now it belonged to her, and that night I tortured myself in my own sheltered solitude within the clamor of Cholula, whose people had crowded into the streets and onto the terraces to watch us pass with our horses and shotguns and helmets and beards; I tortured myself imagining the nights of love of the man from Estremadura and his whore, her body, hairless and cinnamon-hued, with the excitable nipples these women use to attack and the secret and deep sex they hide, sparse in hair, abundant in juices, between their wide hips. I imagined the incomparable smoothness of the thighs of Indian women, used to having water flow over them to wash away the crusts of time, the past, and the pain that clot between the legs of our Spanish mothers. Female smoothness, I imagined her in my solitude, hidden holes in which my lord Hernán Cortés has poked his fingers, tongue, phallus, his fingers adorned with festive rings and wrapped in gauntlets when time came for war: the hands of the conquistador, between jewels and steel, metal nails, fingertips of blood, and lines of fire—luck, love, intelligence in flames, guiding toward the perfumed medlar of the Indian woman first his sex sheathed in a pubic beard which must be as ascetic as the vegetation of Estremadura, and a pair of balls which I imagine tense, as hard as the shot of our harquebuses.

But Cortés's sex was ultimately less sexual than his mouth and beard, that beard which seemed too old for a thirty-five-year-old man, as if he'd inherited it from the times of Viriatus and his fields of hay set afire against the Roman invaders, from the times of the besieged city of

Numantia and its squadrons dressed in mourning, from the times of Pelayo and his lances made from pure Asturian mist: a beard older than the man on whose jaws it grew. Perhaps the Mexicans were right, and a beardless Cortés wore, borrowed, the extremely long beard of that very same god Quetzalcoatl, with whom these natives confused him . . .

The most terrible, the most shocking thing was not Cortés's sex, but that from the depth of the forest, from the mourning, from the mist, would emerge his tongue, which was the conqueror's true sex, and that he would stick it into the Indian woman's mouth with more power, more seed, and more pregnancy—my God, I'm delirious! I'm suffering, Lord!—with more fecundity than his sex. Tongue-phallus-whip, thrashing, hard, and ductile at the same time: poor me, Jerónimo de Aguilar, dead all this time, with my tongue split up the middle, fork-tongued like the plumed serpent. Who am I, of what use am I?

[4]

The Cholulans said we could enter without the Tlax-caltecs. They could not renounce their gods, but they would obey the King of Spain with pleasure. They said it through La Malinche, who translated it from Mexican into Spanish while I stood there like a royal ninny, mulling over what my next step would be to recover my tattered dignity. (I'm not going far enough: language was more than dignity, it was power; and more than power, it was the very life that animated my plans, my own program of discovery, unique, surprising, unrepeatable . . .)

But since I couldn't go to bed with Cortés, I thought I'd be better off giving the devil her due and decided that at least for now there was no sense crying over spilt milk.

During the first days, the Cholulans gave us abundant food and feed. But soon enough they began to stint on the food. Then they grew obstinate and remiss, and I started looking at Doña Marina with suspicion, while she stared back at me, immutable, firmly supported by her carnal intimacy with our captain.

A perpetual cloud ominously hung over the sacred city; the smoke became so thick we couldn't see the tops of the temples or the stones under our feet. Cholula's head and feet dissolved in mist, though it was impossible to know if it came, as I said when we arrived, from the different levels of the pyramid, from the horses' assholes, or from the bowels of the mountains. The strange thing is that Cholula stands on level ground, but now nothing was level here and instead seemed unfathomable and craggy.

Observe how words transformed even the landscape: Cholula's new landscape was nothing more than the reflection of the sinuous struggle of words, sometimes as deep as a ravine, at other times craggy, like a mountain of thorns; whispering and soothing like a great river, or stirred up and raucous like an ocean dragging loose stones: a shrieking of mermaids wounded by the tide.

I told the popes: "I lived in Yucatan for eight years. That's where I have my true friends. If I abandoned them, it was to follow these white gods and find out their secrets, because they have not come to be your brothers but to conquer this land and smash your gods.

"Listen carefully to me," I said to the priests. "These foreigners really are gods, but they are enemies of your gods."

I said to Cortés: "There is no danger. They're convinced we're gods and honor us as gods."

27

Cortés said: "Why then are they refusing us food and fodder?"

Marina told Cortés: "The city is full of sharpened stakes to kill your horses if you use them to attack; take care, sir; the roofs are piled high with stones, they've built protective screens of adobe bricks, and the streets are blocked with thick logs."

I told the popes: "They are evil gods, but they are gods. They don't have to eat."

The popes replied: "How can it be they do not eat? What kind of gods can they be? The *teúles* eat. They demand sacrifices."

I insisted: "They are different *teúles*. They don't want sacrifices."

I said it and bit my tongue because I saw in my argument a justification of the Christian religion I hadn't noticed before. The popes exchanged looks, and a chill ran down my spine. They realized what I realized. The Aztec gods demanded the sacrifice of men. The Christian God, nailed to the cross, sacrificed himself. The popes stared at the crucifix raised at the entrance to the house taken over by the Spaniards and felt their minds collapse. In that moment, I would have been delighted to change places with the crucified Jesus, accepting His wounds if this nation did not make the invincible exchange between a religion that demanded human sacrifice and another that allowed divine sacrifice.

"There is no danger," I said to Cortés, knowing there was danger.

"There is danger," Marina said to Cortés, knowing there was none.

I wanted to destroy the conquistador so he would never reach the gates of the Great Tenochtitlán: I wanted Cholula to be his tomb, the end of his daring exploits.

Marina wanted to make an example of Cholula to preclude future betrayals. She had to invent the danger. As proof, she brought in an old woman and her son who swore that a great ambush was being prepared against the Spaniards and that the Indians had prepared their cooking pots with salt, chili, and tomatoes to boil us so they could stuff themselves with our flesh. Is it true, or did Doña Marina invent as much as I did?

"There is no danger," I said to Cortés and Marina.

"There is danger," Marina said to all of us.

That night, after a shotgun was fired, the Spanish massacre fell on the City of the Gods, and those who did not die pierced by our swords or blasted to pieces by our harquebuses were burned alive. When the Tlaxcaltecs entered, they poured through the city like a savage pestilence, stealing and raping without our being able to stop them.

In Cholula, not one idol was left standing, not one altar unscathed. The 365 Indian temples were whitewashed to banish the demons and dedicated to 365 saints, virgins, and martyrs from our book of saints' lives, passing forever into the service of God Our Lord.

Cholula's punishment was soon known in all the provinces of Mexico. In doubt, the Spaniards opted for force.

My defeat, less known, I declare here today.

Because I understood then that, in doubt, Cortés would believe La Malinche, his woman, and not me, a fellow Spaniard.

[3]

It wasn't always that way. On the coasts of Tabasco, I was his only interpreter. I remember with joy our landing at Champotón, when Cortés depended totally on me, and our rafts plied the river opposite the Indian squadrons lined up on the shores. Cortés proclaimed in Spanish that we had come in peace, as brothers, while I translated into Maya, but also in the language of shadows:

"He's lying! He's come to conquer us, defend yourselves, don't believe him."

What impunity I had, how I delight in remembering it from the bed of an eternity even more ominous than my betrayal!

"We are brothers!"

"We are enemies!"

"We come in peace!"

"We come in war!"

No one, no one in the thick forest of Tabasco, its river, its jungle, its roots sunk forever in the darkness where only the macaws seemed touched by the sun, Tabasco of the first day of creation, cradle of silence broken by the screech of the bird, Tabasco, echo of the initial dawn: no one there, I say, could know that by translating the conquistador I lied. And yet, I spoke the truth.

Hernán Cortés's words of peace, translated by me into the vocabulary of war, provoked a rain of Indian arrows. Taken aback, the captain saw the sky wounded by the arrows and reacted by engaging in battle on the very banks of the river . . . As he disembarked, he lost a sandal in the mud, and because I recovered it for him, I was hit by an arrow in the thigh; fourteen Spaniards were wounded, thanks to me in great measure, but eighteen Indians fell dead . . . We slept there that night, after the victory I didn't want, with large torches and sentinels, on the wet ground, and if my dreams were unquiet—the Indians I had induced to fight had been defeated—they were also pleasant, because I proved my power to decide peace or war thanks to my ownership of words.

Poor fool: I lived in a false paradise where, for an instant, language and power coincided with my luck, because when I joined the Spaniards in Yucatan, the former interpreter, a cross-eyed Indian named Melchorejo, whispered into my ear, as if he guessed my intentions: "They're invincible. They speak with the animals."

The next morning, Melchorejo disappeared, leaving his Spanish clothing hung from a silk-cotton tree which Cortés, to indicate Spanish possession, had slashed three times with his knife.

Someone saw the first interpreter flee naked in a canoe. I was left thinking about what he'd said. Everyone would say that the Spaniards were gods and that they spoke with gods. Only Melchorejo divined that their power was to speak with the horses. Was he right?

Days later, the defeated chiefs of this region delivered twenty women as slaves for the Spaniards. One of them caught my eye, not only because of her beauty but because of her arrogance: she overawed not only the other slaves but the chiefs themselves. She had what's called a lot of presence, and her orders brooked no disagreement.

We exchanged looks, and without speaking I said to her, "Be mine, I speak your Maya tongue and love your people, I don't know how to combat the fatality of all that's happening, I can't stop it, but perhaps you and I together, Indian and Spaniard, can save something if we come to an agreement and above all if we love each other a bit . . .

"Do you want me to teach you to speak Castilla?" I asked.

When I came near her, my blood pounded; one of those times when mere seeing provokes pleasure and excitation. It was perhaps augmented because I'd gone back to using Spanish breeches for the first time in a long time, after having worn a loose shirt and nothing underneath it, allowing the heat and the breeze to ventilate my balls freely. Now the cloth caressed me, and the leather squeezed me, and my eyes linked me to the woman I saw as my ideal partner for confronting what was to happen. I imagined that together we could change the course of events.

Her name was Malintzin, which means "Penitence."

That same day, the Mercederian Olmedo baptized her Marina, making her the first Christian woman in New Spain.

But her people called her La Malinche, the traitor.

I spoke to her. She didn't answer me. However, she did allow me to admire her.

"Do you want me to teach you to speak . . . ?"

That evening in March of the year 1519, she disrobed before me in the mangrove swamp, while a simultaneous chorus of hummingbirds, dragonflies, rattlesnakes, lizards, and hairless dogs broke loose around her transfigured nakedness. In that instant, the captive Indian woman was svelte and massive, heavy and ethereal, animal and human, sane and insane. She was all that, as if she were not only inseparable from the earth that surrounded her but also its summary and symbol. And also as if she told me that what I was seeing that night I would never see again. She disrobed to deny herself to me.

I dreamed all night about her name, Marina, Malintzin, I dreamed about a son of ours, I dreamed that together she and I, Marina and Jerónimo, owners of the languages, would also be owners of the lands, an invincible couple because we understood the two voices of Mexico, the voice of men and the voice of the gods.

I imagined her rolling around in my sheets.

The next day, Cortés chose her as his concubine and his interpreter.

I was already the latter for the Spanish captain. I could not be the former.

"You speak Spanish and Maya," she said to me in the language of Yucatan. "I speak Maya and Mexican. Teach me Spanish."

"Let your owner teach you," I answered in rancor.

From my tomb, I assure you, we see our rancor as the most sterile part of our lives. Rancor (and envy, which is sorrow over someone else's well-being) closely follows resentment as a sorrow that wounds the person suffering it more deeply than it does the person who provokes it. Jealousy doesn't do that: jealousy may be the source of exquisite agonies and incomparable excitations. Vanity doesn't do that either: vanity is a human trait that links us to everyone else, the great equalizer of poor and rich, strong and weak. In that, it resembles cruelty, which is the best-distributed thing in the world. But rancor and envy: how was I going to triumph over those who provoked them in me, he and she, the couple of the conquest, Cortés and La Malinche, the couple she and I might have been? Poor Marina, ultimately abandoned by her conquistador, burdened with a fatherless child, stigmatized by her people with the mark of betrayal, and, nevertheless, because of all that, mother and origin of a new nation, which perhaps could only be born and grow against the charges of abandonment, illegitimacy, and betrayal . . .

Poor Malinche, poor rich Malinche as well, who with her man shaped history, but who with me, the poor soldier killed by buboes and not by Indians, would not have passed from the anonymity that surrounded the Indian concubines of Francisco de Barco, native of Ávila, or Juan Álvarez Chico, born in Fregenal . . .

Am I humiliating myself too much? Death authorizes

me to say that it seems little compared to the humiliation and failure I felt then. Deprived of the desired female, I substituted the power of the tongue for her. But you've already seen how La Malinche took even that away from me even before the worms dined on it forever.

Cortés's cruelty was refined. He ordered me, since she and I spoke the Indian languages, to take it upon myself to communicate to her the truths and mysteries of our holy religion. The devil has never had a more unfortunate catechist.

[2]

I mean to say that I speak Spanish. It's time to confess that I had to relearn it, because after eight years among the Indians I almost lost it. Now with Cortés's troops, I rediscover my own language, the one that flowed toward my lips from my Castilian mother's breasts. And I quickly learned Mexican, so I could speak to the Aztecs. La Malinche was always one step ahead of me.

The persistent question, nevertheless, is a different one: Did I rediscover myself when I returned to the company and language of the Spaniards?

When they found me among the Indians of Yucatan, they thought I was an Indian.

This is how they saw me: dark, hair cropped short, an oar on my shoulder, wearing ancient sandals long beyond repair, an old, ruinous shirt, and a loincloth to cover my shame.

Thus they saw me then: sunburned, my long hair a tangle, my beard shaved off with arrows, my sex old and uncertain under my loincloth, my old shoes, and my lost tongue.

Cortés, as was his custom, gave precise orders to overcome any doubt or obstacle. He ordered me dressed in shirt and doublet, breeches, pointed cap, and hemp sandals, and ordered me to tell how I came to that place. I told him as simply as I could:

"I was born in Ecija. Eight years ago, fifteen men and two women, making our way from Darien to the island of Santo Domingo, got lost. Our captains fought each other over money matters, since we were carrying ten thousand gold pesos from Panama to La Española, and the ship, with no one at the helm, smashed against some reefs in Los Alacranes. My comrades and I abandoned our incompetent, unfaithful leaders, taking the lifeboat from the wrecked ship. We thought we were heading toward Cuba, but the heavy currents pushed us far from there toward this land called Yucatan."

At that instant, I could not keep from looking toward a man whose face was tattooed, and whose ears and lower lip were pierced with plugs, surrounded by his wife and three children, whose eyes were begging me for what I already knew. I went on, turning my eyes back to Cortés and seeing that he saw everything.

"Ten men reached this place. Nine were killed, and only I survived. Why did they leave me alive? I'll go to my grave not knowing. There are mysteries it's better not to inquire into. This is one of them . . . Imagine a shipwrecked man, almost drowned, naked, and washed up on a beach as hard as mortar, with a single hut and in it a dog that did not bark when it saw me. Perhaps that saved me, because I sought protection in that shelter while the dog went out to bark at my shipmates, provoking the alarm and attack of the Indians. When they found me hidden in the hut, with the dog licking my hand, they laughed and joked. The dog wagged his tail with joy, and I was taken, not with honors but with camaraderie, to the cluster of

primitive huts erected next to the great pyramidal con-
structions now covered with vegetation . . .

"Ever since, I've been useful. I've helped to build. I've
helped them plant their poor crops. But I also planted the
seeds of an orange tree that came, along with a sack of
wheat and a cask of red wine, in the lifeboat that tossed
us up on these shores."

Cortés asked me about my other comrades, staring
fixedly at the Indian with the tattooed face accompanied
by a woman and three children.

"You haven't told me what happened to your comrades."

In an attempt to distract Cortés's insistent gaze, I went
on with my story, which I didn't want to do, finding myself
obliged to say what I then told.

"The chiefs in the area divided us among them."

"There were ten. I see only you."

Again I fell into the trap: "Most were sacrificed to the
idols."

"And what about the women?"

"They died. The Indians made them grind corn, and
they weren't used to spending that much time on their
knees in the sun."

"And what about you?"

"They kept me as a slave. All I do is bring in firewood
and weed the cornfields."

"Want to come with us . . . ?"

Cortés asked me that, again staring at the Indian with
the tattooed face.

"Jerónimo de Aguilar, born in Ecija," I blurted out
hastily to distract the captain's attention.

Cortés walked over to the Indian with the tattooed face,
smiled at him, and patted the head of one of the children,
who had curly blond hair despite his dark skin and black
eyes. "Cannibalism, slavery, and barbarous customs," said

Cortés, staring directly at my unrecognizable companion.
"Do you want to stay in this life?"

My only concern was to distract him, capture his attention. As luck would have it, in my old mantle I'd kept one
of the oranges, the fruit of the tree Guerrero and I planted
here. I showed it to him as if for a moment I was the King
of Coins in our Spanish playing cards: I had the sun in
my hands. Could any image verify a Spaniard's identity
better than the sight of a man eating an orange? I sank
my teeth avidly into the skin until they found the hidden
flesh of the orange, her flesh, the woman-fruit, the feminine
fruit. The juice ran down my chin. I laughed, as if saying
to Cortés, What better proof could you want that I'm a
Spaniard?

The captain didn't answer me, merely expressing his
pleasure that oranges could grow here. He asked me if *we*
had brought it, and I, to distract his attention, which was
fixed on the unrecognizable Guerrero, said we had, but
that in these lands the oranges were larger, not as highly
colored, and more bitter, almost like grapefruit. I told the
Mayas to gather a sack of orange seeds for the Spanish
captain, but he insisted on asking that same question again,
staring fixedly at the imperturbable Guerrero: "Do you
want to stay in this life?"

He said it to the man with the tattooed face, but I quickly
answered that I didn't, that I renounced living among these
pagans and would be delighted to join the Spanish troops
to wipe out all abominable customs or beliefs and to implant
our Holy Religion here . . . Cortés laughed and stopped
patting the child's head. He told me then that since I spoke
the language of the natives and a bad but comprehensible
Spanish, I would join him as his interpreter to translate
from Spanish to Maya and from Maya to Castilian. He
turned his back on the Indian with the tattooed face.

I had promised my friend Gonzalo Guerrero, the other survivor of the shipwreck, that I wouldn't reveal his identity. It was, in any case, difficult to discern. His tattooed face and pierced ears. His Indian wife. And the three mestizo children Cortés patted on the head and stared at with such prolonged curiosity.

"Brother Aguilar," Guerrero said when the Spaniards arrived. "I'm married, I have three children, and among these people I'm a chief and captain in war. You go your way, but my face is tattooed and my ears pierced. What would the Spaniards say if they saw me this way? And you can see how adorable my children are, and how sweet my woman is . . ."

She scolded me angrily, telling me to go away with the Spaniards and to leave her husband in peace . . .

I had no other intention. It was indispensable that Gonzalo Guerrero remain here so that my own grand enterprise of discovery and conquest be carried out. Ever since we'd arrived here eight years before, Guerrero and I had taken great pleasure in seeing the great Mayan towers at night, when they seemed to come back to life and reveal in the moonlight the exquisite carved script that Guerrero, who came from Palos, said he'd seen in Arab mosques and even in the recently reconquered Granada. But during the day, the sun whitened the great structures to a blinding degree, and life concentrated in the minutia of fires, resin, dyes, and washing, the crying of children, the savory taste of raw deer meat: the life of the village that lived right next to the dead temples.

We entered into that life in a natural way. It's true, of course, that we had no other prospects, but most of all it was the sweetness and dignity of these people that conquered us. They had so little and yet wanted no more. They never told us what had happened to the inhabitants of the splendid cities that resembled biblical descriptions of Babylon and watched over the details of everyday life in the village; we felt it was a kind of respect reserved for the dead.

Only little by little did we learn, connecting bits and pieces of stories here and there as we acquired the language of our captors, that once there were great powers here, which, like all great powers, depended on the weakness of the people and needed to fight other strong nations to convince themselves of their power. We were able to deduce that the Indian nations destroyed each other while the weak people survived, stronger than the strong. The greatness of power fell; the small lives of the people survived. Why? We'll have time to understand why.

Guerrero, as I said, married an Indian and had three children. He was a seaman and had worked in the Palos shipyards. So when the expedition led by Francisco Hernández de Córdoba came to this land a year before Cortés, Guerrero organized the Indian counterattack that caused the calamitous defeat of the expedition right on the coast. Thanks to that, he was raised to the rank of chief and captain, becoming part of the defensive organization of these Indians. Thanks to that as well, he decided to stay among them when I left with Cortés.

Why did Cortés leave him when he'd guessed—his facial expressions all revealed it—who Guerrero was? Perhaps, I later thought, because he didn't want to bring a traitor along. He could have killed him right then and there: but then he couldn't have counted on peace and the good will of the Catoche Mayas. Perhaps he thought it was better to abandon Guerrero to a destiny devoid of destiny: the barbarous wars of sacrifice. But it's also true that Cortés liked to postpone revenge, just to enjoy it more.

In any case, he brought me with him without suspecting

that I was the real traitor. Because if I went with Cortés and Guerrero stayed behind in Yucatan, it was by mutual agreement. We wanted to ensure, I with the foreigners and Guerrero among the Indians, that the Indian world would triumph over the European world. I will tell you briefly, with the little breath left to me, why.

While I lived among the Maya, I remained celibate, as if I were waiting for a woman who would be perfectly mine, who would complement my character, passion, and tenderness. I fell in love with my new people, with their simple way of dealing with the matters of life, letting the daily necessities of life take care of themselves naturally but without diminishing the importance of serious things. Above all, they took care of their land, their air, their precious, scarce water hidden in deep wells: this plain of Yucatan has no visible rivers but is crisscrossed by underground streams.

Taking care of the land was their fundamental mission; they were the servants of the land—that's why they'd been born. Their magic stories, their ceremonies, their prayers, I realized, had no other purpose than to keep the land alive and fertile, to honor the ancestors who had in their turn kept it alive, inherited it, and had passed it quickly on, abundant or scanty, but alive, to their descendants.

Endless obligation, long succession, which at first could have seemed to us an eternally repetitive labor of ants, until we realized that doing what they did was its own reward. It was the Indians' daily offering: in serving nature, they created themselves. It's true: they lived in order to survive; but they also lived so the world would go on feeding their descendants when they died. Death for them was the price for the life of their descendants.

Birth and death therefore were equal celebrations for these natives, events equally worthy of joy and honor. I shall always remember the first funeral ceremony we attended, because in it we discerned a celebration of origins and the continuity of all things, identical to what we celebrate when born. Death, proclaimed the faces, gestures, musical rhythms, is the source of life, death is the first birth. We come from death. We cannot be born unless someone dies for our sake, for us.

They owned nothing, but held everything in common. But there were wars, rivalries incomprehensible for us, as if our innocence deserved only the bounty of peace and not the cruelty of war. Guerrero, spurred on by his wife, decided to take part in the wars among the nations, admitting he did not understand them. But once he'd shown his ability as a shipwright in repelling Hernández de Córdoba's expedition, his desire and mine—the art of making boats and the art of ordering words—joined forces and silently swore an oath, with a shared intelligence and a definite goal . . .

[1]

Little by little—it took us eight years to discover it— Gonzalo Guerrero and I, Jerónimo de Aguilar, gathered enough information to divine (we'd never know it for certain) the destiny of the Mayan peoples, the proximity of fallen grandeur and surviving misery. Why did greatness collapse, why did misery survive?

During those eight years, we saw the fragility of the land and wondered, both of us after all sons of Castilian or Andalusian farmers, how the life of the great abandoned cities could be sustained by such meager soil and such impenetrable forests. We had the answers of our own ancestors: Exploit the riches of the forest lightly, exploit the riches of the plains well, and take care of both. This had been the behavior of the peasants since time immemorial. When it coincided with the behavior of the dynasties, Yucatan lived. When the dynasties put the greatness of power above the greatness of life, the thin soil and the thick forest could not produce enough to meet the demands of kings, priests, warriors, and bureaucrats. Then came wars, the abandonment of the land, the flight to the cities at first and then from the cities later. The land could no longer sustain power. Power fell. The land remained. Those who remained had no power other than the land.

Words remained.

In their public ceremonies, but also in their private prayers, they incessantly repeated the following story:

The world was created by two gods, one named Heart of Heaven and the other named Heart of Earth. When they met, between them they made all things fertile by naming them. They named the earth, and the earth was made. Creation, as it was named, dissolved and multiplied, calling itself by turns fog, cloud, or whirlwind of dust. Named, the mountains shot from the depths of the sea, magic valleys formed, and in them grew pines and cypresses.

The gods filled with joy when they divided the waters and caused the animals to be born. But none of this possessed the same thing which had created it: language. Mist, ocelot, pine, and water: silent. Then the gods decided to create the only beings capable of speaking and of naming all things created by the word of the gods.

And so people were born, with the purpose of sustaining divine creation day by day by means of the same thing that brought forth the earth, the sky, and all things in them: language. When we understood these things, Guerrero and I understood that the real greatness of these people was not in their magnificent temples or their deeds in war but in the most humble vocation of repeating in every minute, in every activity in life, the greatest and most heroic thing of all, which was the creation of the world by the gods.

From then on, we strove to strengthen that mission and to restore to our native Spanish earth the time, beauty, candor, and humanity we found among these Indians . . . Language was the double power shared by gods and men. We found out that the fall of the empires liberated language and men from a falsified servitude. Poor, clean, owners of their words, the Maya could renew their lives and those of the entire world beyond the sea . . .

In the place called Bay of the Bad Fight, the very place where Gonzalo Guerrero's knowledge allowed the Indians to defeat the Spaniards, forests were leveled, planks sawed, hardware manufactured, and the frameworks raised for our Indian fleet . . .

From my Mexican tomb, I encouraged my comrade, the other surviving Spaniard, to answer conquest with conquest. I failed in my attempt to make Cortés fail; you, Gonzalo, must not fail. Do what you swore to me you would do. Look: I'm watching you from my bed in the ancient lake of Tenochtitlán, I the fifty-eight times named Jerónimo de Aguilar, the man who was the transitory master of words who lost them in an unequal fight with a woman . . .

[0]

All this I saw. The fall of the great Andalusian city in the moan of the conch shells, the clash of steel against flint, and the fire of Mayan flamethrowers. I saw the burnt water of the Guadalquivir and the burning of the Tower of Gold.

The temples fell, from Cádiz to Seville; the standards, the towers, the trophies. And the day after the defeat, using the stones of the Giralda, we began to build the temple of the four religions, inscribed with the word of Christ, Mohammed, Abraham, and Quetzalcoatl, where all the powers of imagination and language would have their place, without exception, lasting perhaps as long as the names of the thousand gods of a world suddenly animated by the encounter of everything forgotten, prohibited, mutilated . . .

We committed a few crimes, it's true. We gave the members of the Holy Inquisition a taste of their own medicine, burning them in the public plazas, from Logroño to Barcelona and from Oviedo to Córdoba . . . We also burned their archives, along with the laws about purity of blood and being "old Christians," and if some convents (and their tenants) were violated, the ultimate result was an increased mixing of bloods—Indian and Spanish but also Arab and Jew—that in a few years crossed the Pyrenees and spread over all of Europe . . . The complexion of the old continent quickly became darker, as that of southern, Arabian Spain already was.

We revoked the edicts of expulsion for Jews and Moors. They returned with the frozen keys of the houses they'd abandoned in Toledo and Seville in order to unlock once again the wooden doors and to put back into their clothespresses, with burning hands, the old prayer of their love for Spain, the cruel mother who expelled them and whom they, the children of Israel, never stopped loving despite all her cruelties . . . And the return of the Moors filled the air with songs sometimes deep, like a sexual moan, sometimes high, like the voice of the muezzin punctually calling the faithful to prayer. Sweet Mayan songs joined those of the Provençal troubadours, the flute joined the cittern, the flageolet joined the mandolin, and from the sea near the Port of Santa María emerged sirens of all colors who had accompanied us from the islands of the Caribbean . . . All those of us who contributed to the Indian conquest of Spain immediately felt that a universe simultaneously new and recovered, permeable, complex, and fertile, had been born from the contact among the cultures, frustrating the fatal, purifying plan of the Catholic Kings, Ferdinand and Isabella.

But don't think the discovery of Spain by the Maya was an idyll. We could not restrain the religious atavism of some of our captains. The fact is, however, that the Spaniards sacrificed at the altars of Valladolid and Burgos, in the plazas of Cáceres and Jaén, had the honor of dying in a cosmic rite and not in one of those street fights so common in Spain. Or, to use a more gastronomic image: they might have died of indigestion just as well. It's true that this rationale was badly understood by all the humanists, poets, philosophers, and Spanish Erasmists, who at the beginning celebrated our arrival, considering it a liberation, but who are now wondering if they haven't simply exchanged the oppression of the Catholic Kings for that of some bloody popes and Indian chiefs . . .

But you will ask me, Jerónimo de Aguilar, born in Ecija, dead of buboes when the Great Tenochtitlán fell, and who now accompanies, like a distant star, my friend and comrade Gonzalo Guerrero, native of Palos, in the conquest of Spain: What was our main weapon?

And while we'd have to mention an army of two thousand Maya which sailed from the Bay of the Bad Fight in Yucatan, joined by squadrons of Carib sailors recruited and trained by Guerrero in Cuba, Borinquén, Caicos, and Great Abaco, we would immediately have to add another reason.

Disembarked in Cádiz, amid the most absolute astonishment, we gave the same answer (you've already guessed) as that of the Indians in Mexico: surprise.

Except that in Mexico, the Spaniards—that is, the white, bearded, and blond gods—were expected. Here, on the other hand, no one expected anyone. The surprise was total, because all the gods were already in Spain. The fact is they'd been forgotten. The Indians managed to reanimate the Spanish gods, and the greatest surprise, which I share with you today, readers of this manuscript which we two shipwrecked Spaniards abandoned for eight years on the Yucatan coast have stitched together, is that you are reading these memoirs in the Spanish language of Cortés, which Marina, La Malinche, had to learn, and not in the Maya language that Marina had to forget or in the Mexican language which I had to learn to communicate in secret with the great but apathetic king Moctezuma.

The reason is obvious. The Spanish language had already learned to speak in Phoenician, Greek, Latin, Arabic, and Hebrew; it was ready now to receive Mayan and Aztec contributions, to enrich itself with them, to enrich them, give them flexibility, imagination, communicability, and writing, turning them into living languages, not the languages of empires but the languages of people and their encounters, infections, dreams, and nightmares as well.

Perhaps Hernán Cortés himself suspected it, and for that reason dissimulated his feelings the day he discovered Guerrero and me living among the Maya, dark, hair cropped short, an oar on my shoulder, wearing one ancient sandal with the other tied around my waist, an old, ruinous shirt, and a loincloth in even worse condition; Guerrero with his tattooed face and pierced ears . . . Perhaps, as if he'd guessed our destiny, the Spanish captain left Guerrero among the Indians so that one day he'd attempt his enterprise, a copy of his own, and conquer Spain with the same spirit Cortés conquered Mexico, which was that of bringing another civilization to one he considered admirable but stained here and there with excesses: sacrifice and fire, oppression and repression, humanity sacrificed to the power of the strong under the pretext of the gods . . . Once Hernán Cortés himself had been sacrificed to the game of political ambition, necessarily reduced to impotence so that no conquistador would ever dream of placing himself above the power of the Crown, and humiliated by the mediocre, suffocated by the bureaucracy, rewarded with money and titles when his ambition had been exterminated, did Hernán Cortés have the brilliant intuition that if he pardoned Gonzalo Guerrero, Gonzalo would return with a Mayan and Carib armada to get revenge for him in his native land?

I don't know. Because Hernán Cortés, for all his malicious intelligence, always lacked that magic imagination which, on the one hand, was the weakness of the Indian world, but, on the other, might someday be its strength: its contribution to the future, its resurrection . . .

I say this because while accompanying Gonzalo Guerrero with my soul from the Bahamas to Cádiz, I myself became a star so I could make the voyage. My ancient light (all luminous stars, I now know, are dead stars) is only that of my questions.

What would have happened if what did happen didn't?

What would have happened if what did not happen did?

I speak and ask questions from death because I suspect that my friend, the other shipwrecked Spaniard Gonzalo Guerrero, was too busy fighting and conquering. He doesn't have time to tell stories. More to the point: he refuses to tell stories. He has to act, decide, order, punish . . . On the other hand, from death, I have all the time in the world to tell stories. Even (especially) stories about the deeds of my friend Guerrero in this affair of the conquest of Spain.

I fear for him and for the action he has undertaken with such success. I wonder if an event that isn't narrated takes place in reality. Because what isn't invented is only chronicled. Moreover, a catastrophe (all wars are catastrophes) is disputed only if it's told. The telling outlasts the war. The telling disputes the order of things. Silence only confirms that order.

Which is why, in telling, I necessarily wonder where the order is, the moral, the law in all this.

I don't know. Nor does my brother Guerrero, because I've infected him with a painful dream. He goes to bed in his new headquarters, the Alcazar in Seville, and his nights are unquiet because the painful gaze of the last Aztec king, Guatemuz, pierces them like a ghost. A cloud of blood covers his eyes. Whenever he feels his vision blur, he lowers his eyelids. One is made of gold, the other silver.

When he wakes up, weeping over the fate of the Aztec nation, he realizes that instead of tears, down one cheek ran gold and down the other silver, cutting a furrow in them as a knife would, leaving a permanent wound in them which, may it please God, death has healed.

This, I realize, is a doubtful thing. On the other hand, my only certitude, you see, is that language and words triumphed on the two shores. I know because the form of this tale is like a countdown, which has been associated too often with mortal explosions, overcoming a rival in the ring, or apocalyptic events. I'd like to use it today, beginning with ten and ending with zero, to indicate instead a perpetual rebeginning of stories perpetually unfinished, but only on condition that they are presided over, as in the Mayan story of the gods of Heaven and Earth, by language.

That is perhaps the true star that crosses the sea and links the two shores. The Spaniards—I must clarify this point while I still have time—did not understand it at first.

The Two Shores

When I reached Seville mounted on my verbal star, they confused its fleetingness and its light with that of a terrible bird, the combination of all the birds of prey that fly in the deepest obscurity, but less frightening in their flight than in their *landing*, their ability to drag themselves along the earth with the mercurial destruction of a poison: a vulture in the skies, a serpent on the ground, this mythological being that flew over Seville and dragged itself over Estremadura, blinded the saints, and seduced the demons of Spain, frightening all with its newness, was, like the Spanish horses in Mexico, invincible.

Transformed into a monster, this beast was, nevertheless, only a word. And the word unfolds, made of scales in the air, made of feathers on earth, like a single question: How long before the present arrives?

Twin sister of God, twin sister of man: over the lake of Mexico, along the river of Seville, the eyelids of the sun and the moon open at the same time. Our faces are streaked by fire, but at the same time our tongues are furrowed by memory and desire. The words live on the two shores. And they do not heal.

London–Mexico, Winter 1991–1992
June 1, 1992

Sons of the Conquistador

TO JOSÉ EMILIO PACHECO

And if we think about it carefully,
we see that he was unlucky in all his ventures after we
conquered New Spain. They say it's because
curses were put on him.

—BERNAL DÍAZ DEL CASTILLO,
True History of the Conquest of New Spain

MARTÍN 2

My father, Hernán Cortés, conqueror of Mexico, had twelve children. From the youngest to the oldest, there are three girls he had with his last wife, the Spaniard Juana de Zúñiga: María, Catalina, and Juana—a bouquet of pretty little ladies who were born late and didn't have to bear the burden of the harm done to their father, only his glorious memory. Also by the Zúñiga woman he had my brother Martín Cortés: we have the same name. Not only that, the same destiny. There were also two stillborn children, Luis and Catalina.

My father conquered a lot of flesh, as much flesh as land. From the conquered king Moctezuma he stole his favorite daughter, Ixcaxóchitl—"Cotton Flower"—and by her had a daughter, Leonor Cortés. With a nameless Aztec princess he had another daughter, this one born deformed, the so-called María. With an anonymous woman, he had a son named Amadorcico, whom, he told us, he loved, then forgot about, leaving him dead or abandoned in Mexico. A worse fate befell another son, Luis Altamirano, whom he had by Elvira (or perhaps Antonia) Hermosillo in 1529. Our prodigal, astute, conquered father disinherited him in his last will and testament. But no one suffered greater misfortune than his first daughter, Catalina Pizarro, born in Cuba in 1514. Her mother's name was Leonor Pizarro.

Our father pampered her, but the widow Zúñiga persecuted her, deprived her of her property, and condemned her to live out her life—against her will—locked away in a convent.

I am the first Martín, the bastard son of my father and Doña Marina, my Indian mother, the so-called Malinche, the interpreter without whom Cortés wouldn't have conquered anything. My father abandoned us when Mexico fell and my mother was no longer of any use to him in conquests and actually hampered his ability to rule. I grew up far away from my father, my mother having been given to the soldier Juan Xaramillo. I watched her die of smallpox in 1527. My father legitimated me in 1529. I am the firstborn but not the heir. I should be Martín the First but I'm merely Martín the Second.

MARTÍN 1

Three Catalinas, two Marías, two Leonors, two Luises, and two Martíns: our father didn't have much imagination when it came to baptizing his children, and that sometimes leads to tremendous confusion. The other Martín, my elder brother, the son of the Indian woman, delights in the tale of the difficulties we've had. I prefer to recall the good times, and there was none better than my return to Mexico, the land conquered by my father for His Majesty the King. But let's proceed step by step. I was born in Cuernavaca in 1532. I'm the product of the eventful trip my father made to Spain in 1528—his first since the conquest—which he undertook in order to be married and to reclaim the rights the colonial administration wanted to deny him by means of a trial instigated by certain envious parties. Spain, let me state this before going any further, is the land of envy. The Indies, and I can vouch for this in no uncertain terms, emulate and surpass the mother country in this category. Well then: it was in Béjar that Hernán Cortés entered into matrimony for the second time, now with my mother, Juana de Zúñiga. The King confirmed the rights and privileges owed to my father: titles, lands, and vassals. But when my parents and my grandmother returned to Mexico in March 1530, they were all held in Texcoco during my father's trial. He was not able to enter Mexico City until January of the following year and took up residence in Cuernavaca, where, as I say, I was born. From then on, my father wore himself out in lawsuits and equally fruitless expeditions until, when I was eight, he returned with me to Spain, this time to fight not against Indians but against officials and lawyers.

At my father's side, I left Mexico for Spain in 1540. We went to reclaim our property, our rights. The intrigues, the lawsuits, and the bitterness cost my father his life: to have fought so hard and with such good fortune in order to win for the King dominion nine times larger than Spain and then to end up wandering from inn to inn, owing money to tailors and servants, being the object of jokes and dirty tricks in the court! I was at his side when he died. A Franciscan and I. Neither of us could save him from the horrible wasting away brought on by dysentery. The stench of my father's shit could not, however, wipe out the fresh scent of an orange tree that grew to the height of his window and which, during those months, bloomed splendidly.

He spoke some incomprehensible words before dying in Castilleja de la Cuesta, near Seville. He wasn't allowed to die in peace in his Seville house because hordes of creditors and rogues buzzed around it like horseflies. Be that as it may, a great gentleman and better friend than the King himself, the Duke of Medina Sidonia, arranged a splendid funeral in the monastery of San Francisco in Seville: he filled the church with black hangings, burning wax tapers, flags and banners emblazoned with the coat of arms of the marquis, my father, yes sir, Marquis of the Valley of Oaxaca, Captain-General of New Spain, and Conqueror of Mexico, titles the envious could never strip him of. Titles which should have been mine since by my father's will I was declared his successor and heir to his estate. Of course I abstained from promulgating the codicils in which my father ordered me to free the slaves on our Mexican lands and restore those lands to the conquered Indian communities. An old man's attack of conscience, I told myself. If I did it, I'd be left with nothing. Did I beg his forgiveness? Of course. I'm not an evil person, even though I refused to carry out his dying wish. But seeing the fate of the contents of our Seville house was enough to make me feel no scruple whatsoever. Copper pots, kitchenware, trunks, torn tablecloths, sheets and mattresses, even old weapons that had fought their last battle long ago: all of it sold off at infamously low prices by the gates of the Seville cathedral when my father died. Was the final fruit of the conquest of Mexico to be an auction of mattresses and old saucepans? I decided to go back to Mexico and reclaim my inheritance. But first I opened the coffin in which our father, Hernán Cortés, was lying in order to see him for the last time. I was horrified, and my scream scratched its way through my teeth for a long time. Covering my dead father's face was a dusty mask of jade and feathers.

MARTÍN 2

I'm not going to weep for my father. But as I am a good Christian—and I am—I must feel compassion for his fate. Just look at what happened to him after the fall of the Great Tenochtitlán and the conquest of the Aztec empire. Instead of staying in the capital to consolidate his power, he took it upon himself to embark on a mad, spectacular, noisy adventure in which he got lost and ruined himself in the jungles of Honduras. What worm did this man, our father, have within him that he could not rest with the fortune and glory he'd worked so hard to achieve but always had to be looking for more adventure and more action, even if it cost him both his fortune and his glory? It's as if he felt that without action he would have gone back to being the humble son of the Medellín miller he was originally; as if action owed him an homage identical to itself—more action. He could not stand still to contemplate his accomplishments; he had to risk everything in order to deserve everything. Perhaps, aside from his little Christian God (which is ours too, let there be no doubt about that), he had within him a great big pagan god— savage, secular, and pitiless—who asked him to be everything, thanks to action.

To be everything: even to be nothing. There were two men inside him: one blessed by fortune, love, and glory, the other ruined by vanity, display, and mercy. What a strange thing to say about my dear old dad. Vanity and mercy united: one part of him needed recognition, wealth, and caprice as a way of life; the other demanded for us, his new Mexican people, compassion and rights. That he came to identify himself with us, with our land, may well be true. What is certain, something I learned from my mother, is that Hernán Cortés fought with the Franciscans, who demanded that the temples be pulled down, while my father asked that those houses of idols be left standing for memory's sake.

And my brother Martín already told you that he intended in his testament to free the Indians and return their lands to them. Stillborn words. How many stillborn words. But you see, despite all of them, I recognize my father's virtues. But being my mother's son and speaking today with all the truth and clarity I possess—besides, when will I have another chance to do so?—I must confess that I was overjoyed by his failures. The contrast between the honors accorded him and the powers denied him tickled my fancy. He abandoned my mother and me when we got in the way of his political and matrimonial plans, so how could we not secretly take pleasure in his disasters? If he hadn't abandoned the government of Mexico City to go off and conquer new lands in Honduras, his enemies would not have been able to strip him of authority and take over his property. Even if my father's friends threw his enemies into cages, when he returned from Honduras he found that judges had arrived from Spain to try him and deprive him of his power to govern.

My Indian soul trembles in wonder. While my father was in Honduras, he tortured and hanged the last Aztec king, Cuauhtémoc, because he wouldn't reveal the hiding place of Moctezuma's treasure, and in Mexico City, my father's friends were tortured to reveal the whereabouts of Cortés's treasure and then hanged. When he returned to Mexico, my father was accused of all these things: of illicitly enriching himself, of protecting Indians, of poisoning his rivals with lethal cheeses, of not fearing God, of who knows what else . . .

I'm going to talk about the only thing that really fascinates and perturbs me: my daddy's sexual life, its violence, its seduction, and the promiscuity of the flesh. He had myriad women according to the accusation, some in Mexico, others in Castile, and he had carnal knowledge of all of them, even if some were related to one another. He would send the husbands out of the city in order to deal freely with their wives. He had sexual relations with more than forty Indian women. He was also accused of murdering his legal wife, Catalina Xuárez, called La Marcaida. Jerónimo de Aguilar, the translator who had been shipwrecked on the Yucatan coast and rescued by my father, accused him of crimes, infinite corruption, and a rebellious desire to take possession of this land and rule over it himself. Six old, illiterate maids accused him of carnal abuses. Between the traitorous translator and the gossipy chambermaids, I interpose myself: I, Martín Cortés, the bastard, son of the loyal interpreter Doña Marina, also illiterate, but possessed by the demon of language. I interpolate myself because both sides, Aguilar and the old hags, agree that my birth is what drove the sterile Catalina Xuárez mad with jealousy. My father married her in Cuba and brought her to Mexico when the empire fell: the only woman my father had who never gave him any children. Sick, always infirm, always reclining on a sofa, useless and complaining: it was my fault this woman fought one night with my father—according to the maids—about Indian slaves. La Marcaida claimed all of them for herself, excluding my mother and me. My father answered that whatever was rightfully hers, including Indian labor, was hers and he wanted nothing of it, but that what was his, including my mother and me, was his.

Sobbing and ashamed, she went to her bedroom. The next day the maids found her there, dead, with bruises on her neck, the bed stained with urine. Cortés's friends rebutted the maids: the woman died of menstrual flow. This Marcaida was always sick during her periods. Her sisters, Leonor and Francisca, bled to death because of the abnormal abundance of their menstrual flow.

My vision begins to cloud over with blood. Rivers of blood. Menstrual blood, the blood of war, the blood of sacrifice on altars, drowning us all. Except my mother, La Malinche. Her menstruation stopped, the war was over, the sacrificial dagger stopped short in midair, the blood dried, and in La Malinche's womb I was conceived in a pause between blood and death, as if in a fertile desert. I am the son of dead seed, that's all I am. I prefer, nevertheless, drowning in blood to drowning in papers, intrigues, lawsuits; drowning in blood to drowning in things, things we struggle to possess until we dry out, without them and without our souls. My brother would admit that, at least. Would the other Martín admit that great deeds fell to our father while to us, his sons, there fell only lawsuits? Heirs to deserts and shacks.

MARTÍN 1

Hernán Cortés always loved elegance, display, and beautiful things. And he would do anything to get them. Bernal Díaz writes how in Cuba before the expedition to Mexico got under way, my father began to dress himself up, using a plumed helmet, medals, gold chains, and velvet clothes embellished with gold ribbons. But of course he had nothing with which to pay for that luxury; at that time he was deeply in debt and poor because he spent whatever he had on himself and on finery for his wife. I admire my father for that; he's a likable sort, fully capable of admitting he gathered supplies for his Mexican armada by scouring the coast of Cuba like a gentle pirate, robbing or appropriating chickens and cassava bread, arms and money from the inhabitants of the fertile island, who were shocked by the audacity of the man from Estremadura, my father. The son of millers and soldiers who fought in the war against the Moors, my father inherited from them their toughness if not their resignation. He created his own destiny for himself and created it, prodigal as he was, twice over: one ascending, the other descending. Both astonishing.

From him, I inherited my taste for things. The King deprived my father of power in the Mexican lands he conquered. My father requested the governorship of Mexico from His Majesty; the King refused because he thought no conquistador deserved it. King Carlos's grandfather, Ferdinand the Catholic, did the same thing, denying Columbus the governorship of the Indies he'd discovered. At the same time, the King covered my father with honors and titles, which from the time I was a boy I learned to enjoy. Captain-General of New Spain, Marquis of the Valley of Oaxaca. The King assigned to my father twenty-three thousand vassals and twenty-two towns, from Texcoco to Tehuantepec, from Coyoacán to Cuernavaca—Tacubaya, Toluca, Jalapa, and Tepoztlán . . . To gain title to all that and to silence his enemies, my father returned to Spain in 1528.

No captain from the Indies ever returned in such glory, all paid for out of his own pocket and not the King's. From the port of Palos, where he landed, my father made his way to the court, at that moment in Toledo, with a retinue of eighty people brought from Mexico. Besides the Spaniards who accepted the open invitation to join the troop of soldiers of the conquest, there were Indian nobles, circus players, dwarfs, albinos, and many servants as well as hummingbirds, parrots, quetzals, buzzards, turkeys, desert plants, wildcats, jewels, and illustrated codices, which it took my father two ships to bring to Spain. He then hired mules and wagons to travel north from Andalusia to Castile, passing through his hometown of Medellín, where he knelt at the tomb of his father, my grandfather, in whose honor I was named. He kissed the hand of Catalina Pizarro, his widowed mother: mother to one conquistador and aunt of another, Don Francisco Pizarro, also from Estremadura.

The difference between them was that my father knew how to read, while Pizarro didn't. Cortés and Pizarro met this time on the road, when one was already everything while the other was still no one—although in the end bad luck makes all of us equal. Everyone noticed the insane glint in the eye of the other Estremeño as he watched my father scattering gifts to get favors, giving ladies tiaras with green feathers, all covered with silver filigree, gold, and pearls, ordering a supply of liquid amber and balsam so the women he met in courts and royal towns could perfume themselves. In that style, he made his way to the court in Toledo, amid banquets and parties, preceded by a fame and display that impressed everyone. When he reached the court, he entered Mass late and walked in front of the most illustrious gentlemen in Spain to sit down next to the King Don Carlos, amid whispers of envy and disapproval.

Nothing stopped my father! He squandered everything except five extremely fine emeralds he got from Moctezuma and which he always carefully kept for himself, as proof, in my opinion, of the great deeds he'd accomplished. One emerald was carved into a rose, another into a trumpet, the third into a fish with golden eyes, while the fourth was like a little bell with a rich pearl for a clapper and all edged in gold, with the inscription "Blessed is he who raised you." The fifth emerald was a little cup resting on a gold base and attached to four little chains that are fastened to a pearl the size of a button.

My father always bragged about those emeralds, so much so that when the Queen found out about them, she demanded to see them and then wanted to keep them, saying that the Emperor, Don Carlos, would pay one hundred thousand ducats for them. But my father prized them so highly he denied them even to the Empress, using the excuse that he'd promised them to my mother, Juana de Zúñiga, to whom he'd recently been married . . . And that's how it was: he brought her back to Mexico, and if he set out from Cuba to conquer Mexico in ostentatious display and if he returned from the conquest of Mexico to Spain in ostentatious display, now he once again returned to the vanquished land in maximum luxury. Until his enemies, the usual jealous suspects, stopped him at Texcoco outside Mexico City, besieging him in hunger while the suit initiated against him in his absence was resolved. They denied my father bread. They denied bread to my grandmother, Doña Catalina Pizarro, whom my father brought to Mexico so she might see what her son had won for Spain and the King. My grandmother, Doña Catalina, newly widowed, was seduced by her son's words: "Leave Medellín, where you've been a tough, religious, but impoverished woman and come to Mexico to be a great lady." Well, gentlemen, my grandmother died of hunger in Texcoco, of hunger, Catalina Pizarro, my grandmother, died of hunger . . . Of hunger, believe it or not, of hunger! Why in this family is there no pause between happiness and disaster, between triumph and defeat? Why?

MARTÍN 2

My brother speaks of riches, jewels, servants, finery, titles, powers, and lands, but also of hunger . . . I talk about papers. Each thing you've mentioned, Martín my brother, surrendered its hardness and turned into paper, mountains of paper, labyrinths of paper, paper vomited out by lawsuits and eternal trials, as if each thing conquered by our father had one single postponed destiny: the accumulation of briefs in the courts of the two Spains, the old and the new. Victim of an eternally deferred trial in which material things ended up showing they carried within their souls a paper double, flammable and drownable. Things erased by the fire and water of erased paper.

Take a look, Brother: the lawsuit of Hernán Cortés against some parties named Matienzo and Delgadillo over the lands and gardens between the Chapultepec and Tacuba causeways. Another lawsuit, one month later, against the same parties over a dispute about tributes and services from Indians in Huejotzingo. Letters listing grievances against the Crown. Lists of eighty, a hundred, a thousand repetitive questions. Expenditures for scribes, scriveners, messengers. More than two hundred royal documents relevant to our father, denying his grievances, putting off his claims, paying him in chilly gall for the blazing gold of the conquest. A world of shyster lawyers, of laws obeyed but never carried out, of ink-stained hands, pyramids of legal briefs, quills plucked to write a thousand legacies— more feathers in the inkwells than geese in the ponds! The unending residency trial against your father and mine in Mexico over everything already mentioned: corruption, abuse, carnal promiscuity, rebellion, and murder.

And as you well know, the trial involving our father was never resolved. It was consigned to two thousand folios and sent from Mexico to the Council of the Indies in Seville. Thousands of pages, hundreds of documents. The ink itself grows impatient. The pen scratches. The mountain of parchments is interred in the archives, the dead destiny of history. Don't fool yourself, tell the truth with me, Brother Martín: two thousand folios of legal prose were buried forever in Seville because the point was to keep the case unresolved, like a sword of Damocles over the heads of my father and his children. You are moved, my imbecilic brother, by the fatal hand of fame and paternal luxury, but you lack the cunning that always accompanied the fates of my father, his glory and his ruin. Was he great in both? I still don't know. The true history, not the dusty archives, will tell it all one day. The living history of memory and desire, Brother, which always takes place right now, not yesterday, not tomorrow. But what better example can I give than I myself, letting myself be dragged into your mad adventure by you, whom I know so well even though I don't know whether to scorn or fear you. A shame, Brother. Why did it occur to me to confide in you?

MARTÍN 1

I'm not as stupid as you think, Martín the Second. Second, second-rate, although that grieves you. I wound you to wound myself and to show that I too know how to see what's happening quite clearly. Don't think I'm blind when it comes to destiny, an Oedipus from the Indies. I love and respect our father. He died in my arms, not in yours. I understand what you're saying. Hernán Cortés had two destinies. How could he not flee from that eternal lawsuit, from that sedentary courtroom, to throw himself into one insane adventure after another? The same way he left behind the Estremadura of his boyhood to discover the New World for himself, the same way he abandoned Cuba and its placid life to set about the conquest of Mexico. He did the same thing leaving behind the world of intrigues and paper wars that followed the conquest to rush off to Honduras first and then to the exploration of the most sterile territory in the world, that long coast on the Southern Sea, where he did not find, as perhaps he dreamed he would, either the kingdom of the Seven Cities of Gold or the loves of the Amazon queen Calafia. All he found were sand and sea. How could he not feel himself humiliated when on his return from the Californias he found that the sinister and cruel Nuño de Guzmán would not allow him to pass through the lands of Xalisco?

With a rare display of sarcasm, our father, before he died, told me that perhaps there were two things worthwhile on that expedition. The first was discovering a new sea, a deep, mysterious gulf with water so crystal clear that from the beach it looked as if those in the water were swimming in air, except that there were myriad silver, blue, green, black, and yellow fish swiftly playing around the knees of the soldiers and sailors delighted to find that pleasant paradise. Was it an island? A peninsula? Did it really lead to the lands of Queen Calafia, Cíbola, and El Dorado? It didn't matter, he said—for an instant it didn't really matter. The meeting of desert and sea, the immense cactuses and the transparent water, the sun as round as an orange . . .

That was his other pleasure. He remembered that when

he reached Yucatan, he was astonished to see an orange tree whose seeds had been brought there by the two disloyal castaways, Aguilar and Guerrero. Now my own father, humiliated by the satrap of Xalisco, the murderer Nuño de Guzmán, had to get back on his ship at the Barra de Navidad and sail to the bay of Acapulco, where he disembarked to continue to Mexico City. He had an idea. He asked the ship's chief petty officer for some orange seeds and put a handful in his pouch. Then, on the Acapulco coast, he found a well-shaded spot and, opposite the sea, dug deep and planted those seeds.

"It will take you five years to bear fruit," my father spoke to the orange seeds, "but the good thing is that you grow well in a cool climate, like ours, where the cold lets you sleep away the whole winter. Let's see if here, too, in this aromatic and burned-out land, you can bear fruit. I think the most important thing, Orange Tree, is always to dig deep to protect yourself."

Now, the perfume of the orange flowers was filtering through the window of his dying hour. It was the only gift of his broken, humiliated death . . .

MARTÍN 2

Just a moment now. How your vanity pains me. You see everything as a loss of dignity, a humiliation, a besmirching of nobility. Shitass criollo! Admit our father was not as astute as people say. What an incredible rash of naïveté in such a wise man! Admit what I'm saying is true, Brother Martín. Only once did his astuteness marry another astuteness. Then they were divorced, and one astuteness was left without a mate, while the other married naïveté. Very foxy, but very dumb at the same time. Why don't you admit it? Are you afraid the flame you think you're going to light with your filial piety will go out? Are you afraid your father will bequeath you not triumph but failure? Are you fleeing the damned and frivolous side of his fate because you're afraid it will be yours? Don't you prefer my frankness? Don't you know that his imperial return to Spain with his own court and a flood of wealth confirmed the King's suspicion that this soldier wanted to be king of Mexico? His exaggerated gifts to women infuriated their husbands. His insolence in passing without permission ahead of the grandees at Mass to sit next to the King, his impudence when he didn't give or even sell the emeralds to the Queen: don't you think all that chilled the King and the court, predisposing them against our father, getting their backs up? Did he keep those famous emeralds for your mother? Well, he would have been better off throwing them to the hogs. Don't look at me like that.

MARTÍN 1

I'm leaving you, Brother. Once again, I relegate you to the third person, not even to the second in which, without your deserving it, I've been addressing you until now. You are not going to strip me of the desperate frankness of my speaking badly of my mother. Did you mention papers? Possessions, things, inheritance? I can accept the fact that the King, our master, granted Indians and towns to my father only to take them away bit by bit later on, taking away an Acapulco here, a Tehuantepec there . . . But that my mother would try to take things away from her own children . . . I've been frank. I recognize that I violated my father's will in order to avoid the squandering of Indians and lands in the name of some senile, disorderly humanism. I didn't know then that my own mother, Juana de Zúñiga—imperious and arrogant as she was, devoured by envy and by my father's absences in Spain (seeking what was his by right and finding only his death), humiliated first by his abandonment and later by his demise, only too aware of his carnal weaknesses, isolated for years with six children in an Indian village like Cuernavaca, irritated by the facility with which her husband contracted debts to finance insane expeditions, maintain his houses, procure women, pay his lawyers, and meet the exorbitant sums he owed Sevillian bankers and Italian moneylenders (who wouldn't lend money to the man who conquered Moctezuma, he of the Golden Chair?!), and insulted by my father's will (in which he returned the two thousand ducats he received as her dowry but gave her nothing else)—would become when our father died a pitiless crow pecking at her own children.

With affection and attention, my father always overindulged the bastard daughter he had with Leonor Pizarro, the fruit of his early loves in Cuba, named simply Catalina Pizarro. Doña Juana, my mother, vented her rage especially against her, using sinister lawyers to trick her, forcing her to sign papers in which she ceded her property to my mother, and then, with the help of the hypocritical Medina Sidonia, who flattered my father so much in Seville, confining her by force to the Dominican convent of Madre de Dios, near Sanlúcar, where the poor, defenseless thing lived the rest of her days, in anguish and confusion.

All of that should have told me what my own destiny would be: when my mother, Hernán Cortés's widow, refused to allow the executors of my father's will into our house in Cuernavaca, having the lawyers received by her servants, refusing to allow the inventory and even less the ceding of what was mine to me. She sued me for board;

for the dowries of her two daughters, my sisters Catalina and Juana, married by then to men of rank in Spain; for the lands, ever more scattered and reduced, that were part of the Marquis's estate. She sued me for food, for dowries, for benefits from my father's estates I had supposedly appropriated without right, for a life pension which, according to her, I was supposed to pay to a brother of hers who was a monk. She alleged that I was ten years in arrears in payments to my sisters Juana and María, two thorns from my father's bouquet of Mexican daughters.

But my mother stripped my unfortunate sister Catalina, Hernán Cortés's eldest daughter, of her properties in Cuernavaca, and, as I've said, had her locked up forever in a convent. So much for maternal love, so much for filial piety. She never trusted my generosity, which I never withdrew. She did not understand that I had to concentrate all the wealth of our family in my hands to make a strong impression on my return to Mexico after the death of my father and reestablish our fortune on a foundation of political power. Her greed and ambition transformed her into a statue. Forever on her knees, pretending to pray to God, my mother of stone lives on her knees in the House of Pilate in Seville, covered by a veil of dissimulation, peering at the world with avid, bulging eyes, her lips pursed, her jaw protruding. The old hypocrite prays with her hands joined, wearing no jewels. But even now it's possible to hear, sounding like a reproach, the beating of the wings of a falcon, which was the only thing my father committed to her care when he died: "Madam: I implore you to take care that my falcon Alvarado be cured. You know how much I love him, and for that reason I commend him to you." When will that falcon swoop onto the praying head of my mother? He will smash against her, poor thing. The good lady had a head made of stone. Things and papers, hard materials, inflammable paper erased by the waters of the Ocean sea: how sad . . . You are right, Martín, son of La Malinche. The world is made of stone: papers, water, and flames can do nothing to fight against it.

MARTÍN 2

I'm making an effort to ingratiate myself with you, Brother Martín. I accept that, for different but ultimately shared reasons, we have something to do together. We'd be better off doing it with a good will, I think, like good pals. It doesn't matter if you treat me formally and relegate me to the third person. Look: to please you, I'll personally tell the manner in which you returned to Mexico at the age of thirty, in the year 1562. Your return took place amid the joy of all the sons of the conquistadors: by then there was a second generation of us, and in you they saw the justification of their Mexican wealth, if they had it, and the justice of demanding it if they didn't.

They all gathered in the main square of Mexico City to receive the criollo son of the conquistador. They all contributed out of their own pockets: Mexico City was rich —there wasn't a poor Spaniard in it. There was such an abundance of silver that even the beggars got rich because the least amount of money anyone ever gave was four silver *reales*. We all know that in Mexico fortunes are made quickly; but in the years just after the conquest, if you were a poor Spaniard all you had to do was become a beggar and in a short time you could found an entailed estate, even if that annoys the children and grandchildren, ennobled now, of those beggars.

This is a country, as you well know, where money grows on trees: after all, the most common form of money among the Indians is cacao, which grows on a bush the size of an orange tree and whose fruit is the size of an almond. A hundred of them are worth a *real*. All anyone has to do is sit back on a mat in the marketplace and sell cacao, and he can end up, like that gentleman Alonso de Villaseca, with an estate worth a million pesos. That should give you an idea of how monstrous a celebration the arrival of my brother Martín Cortés was when he came from Spain and entered the main square of Mexico City: it was crowded with more than three hundred horsemen on very fine horses and saddles, wearing silk livery and cloth of gold. Then they put on mock jousts and duels in honor of the conquistador's son. Later, two thousand more horsemen wearing black capes to make a greater effect entered the plaza, and at windows appeared the ladies (as well as some who weren't) wearing jewels and tiaras.

The viceroy himself, Luis de Velasco, came out of the palace to receive my brother with an embrace. But if the viceroy was looking at a square which had only been loaned to him, my brother could look at his own property: the center of Moctezuma's capital, where our father took the palaces of Axayacatl to build the Old Houses for himself and his people and, on top of Moctezuma's palace, the New Houses, that is, the palace from which the viceroy emerged to greet you, Brother Martín. I saw it all from the construction site of the cathedral of Mexico, which had just been begun. I was there, amid scaffolding and screens, no different from the bricklayers and carriers crowded together, they so far from the luxury surrounding you, they without silver, without entailed estates, without even the cacao beans, their faces scratched by smallpox, snot running out of their noses because they still weren't accustomed to those vile European colds.

And I, Brother, watching you, surrounded by glory,

make your entrance into the city conquered by our father. I, Brother, standing on what was left of the vast Aztec wall of skulls, on top of which the cathedral was beginning to rise. I stopped looking at the horsemen and their mounts. I looked at the grimy people around me, wearing only cotton smocks, barefoot, their foreheads wound with ropes and their backs loaded with sacks: I thought to myself, My God, how many Christians will someday come to this cathedral to pray and never imagine that on the base of each column of this Catholic temple is inscribed an insignia of the Aztec gods? But, with your permission, the past was forgotten and the Crown restored a part of our father's estate to my brother, a reduced portion, but still the greatest fortune in Mexico.

MARTÍN 1

That's what I like to remember! Just imagine that in the great Mexico City the art of toasting was unknown. It fell to me to introduce that Spanish custom at dinners and soirees. No one in Mexico knew what it was! I made toasts fashionable, and there were no gatherings of hidalgos, descendants of conquistadors, or mere viceregal officers where there weren't toasts, amid joy, drunkenness, and disorder. Let's see who can drink the most, who can be the wittiest, and who would refuse to carry through to the end! The toast became the center of every party, and if someone refused to accept a challenge, we would snatch off his cap and cut it to shreds before everyone. Then a hundred of us, wearing masks, would ride out on horseback and go from window to window talking to the women and entering the houses of gentlemen and rich merchants to speak with ladies, until those good men became enraged at our behavior and locked their doors and windows. But they did not take our ingenuity into account: we reached the balconies of the ladies with long blowguns, whose darts carried flowers. Nor did they take the audacity of the ladies into account: defying paternal and marital orders, they would peek between the shutters to look at us gallants. My life in the capital of New Spain at that time was pure pleasure: joy, wit, honor, and a thousand seductions.

Who did not see in me my father reborn and now enjoying the benefits of the well-earned fruit of the conquest? Who didn't admire me? Who didn't envy me? Who among the handsome and elegant in this capital of novelties—male or female—did not gather seductively around me? I already know what you are going to say. You. Martín Cortés, the second-rate, the mestizo, the son of the shadows. Without you, I could do nothing in this land. I needed you, son of La Malinche, to carry out my destiny in Mexico. What a disgrace, my disgraced brother: to need you, the least seductive of men!

MARTÍN 2

There was no one more seductive, of course, than Alonso de Ávila, whose richness of attire could not be found even in the courts of Europe. To his luxury he added the natural wealth of a land of gold and silver, and to those Mexican metals, he added the contrast of the whitest skin ever seen on a man, here or there: only the whitest women were as white as Alonso de Ávila, who perhaps looked even whiter in a dark-skinned land. And what he allowed others to see were his dazzling hands, which moved and led and, sometimes, even touched, with an airy lightness that made air itself seem heavy. My, how light this Alonso de Ávila was, forced to walk on mere earth only because of the richness and gravity of his damask and jaguar-skin suits, his gold chains, and his tawny mantle decorated with a reliquary—all of it lightened, let me assure you, by the feathers in his cap and the volutes of his mustache, the wings of his face.

Martín and Alonso became friends; together they organized and enjoyed the toasts and masquerades; they admired each other, like young, rich hidalgos who are surprised to find themselves occasionally (as I surprised them more than once from the shadows) admiring each other more than they admired the women they courted. They competed to conquer a beautiful lady only in order to imagine her in the arms of the other; they screwed, the bastards, so each one could imagine himself in the place of the other. That's how close Alonso de Ávila and Martín Cortés were.

What's so strange about that in this realm of luxury and parties, disorder and feasting, mirrors and more mirrors, perfumes, and mutual admiration? What's so strange about Martín and Alonso, Alonso and Martín, the son and heir of the conquistador, Hernán Cortés's prodigal son, embracing the nephew of another headstrong captain of the conquest, Ávila the King's commissioner? He was the rogue who dared put his hand (Mother herself saw it and told me) on Moctezuma's gold vestments, the son of Gil González, commissioner and land dealer, who stripped the real conquistadors of their lands, confidence man and fraud, who wisely hid his wealth only so his sons, Alonso and Gil, could show it off and spend it. The two joined in a whirlwind of pleasure. My brother Martín and this Alonso de Ávila brought their pleasure to its greatest heights in a singular party. The pleasure of telling about it I leave to my brother Martín.

Sons of the Conquistador

MARTÍN 1

By God in heaven: I didn't invent the parties and uproar of the Mexican colony; by His Holy Mother, I reached a capital already enamored of luxury and parties, where wild bulls were run in Chapultepec and excursions on horseback echoed through the forests: jousts, rings, mock duels. The viceroy, Don Luis de Velasco, said that even if the King were to deprive the criollos of their towns and estates the viceroy would see to it they were consoled by having bells rung in the streets. So, when the viceroy died, there was great sadness. Everyone, young and old, wore mourning, and the troops about to sail for the Philippines dressed for the funeral with black flags and emblems of grief, their drums muted, dragging their pikes. A gray, weak, and boring Interim Council took over the government while a new viceroy was being named, but Alonso and I, royal heirs to New Spain, because we were sons of conquistadors, respectful of the dead viceroy and the viceroy to come— though not of the mediocre Council—decided to keep alive joy, luxury, and the rights of heirs in these lands conquered by our fathers.

The viceroy died; he wasn't the first and wouldn't be the last. The viceroys changed; we, the heirs of the conquest, remained. The viceroy died, but I had twin sons and felt that was sufficient reason for shedding the mourning I wore for the viceroy and showing the Council who the real owners of New Spain were. My brother wants me to tell it: I'll give him that pleasure. On our own, we took over the main square; half the houses in it were ours in any case. I had a raised wooden walkway constructed from my house to the cathedral to open a path for the procession, so I could carry my sons to the Door of Pardon and announce to the world that now there were grandsons of

Hernán Cortés to maintain our dynasty. I announced it with noise, of course. Artillery, tourneys on foot on the walkway, and feasts to which all were invited, Spaniards and Indians. Roasted bulls, chickens, and game, pipes of red wine for the Spaniards. For the Indians, an enclosure of rabbits, hares, and deer, following tradition, along with myriad birds. When the enclosure was broken open, they all came out running and flying, to be shot with arrows and given to the humble people, who were delighted and thankful. Jousts, fireworks, piñatas . . . A week of feasting, surrounded by the people, with toasts, masquerades, and, at the end, a grand dinner and soiree as a culmination of the celebration, given by my true brother Alonso de Ávila at his house.

What a beautiful surprise we gave to all—to our relatives and friends but also to the rancorous Council: the enviable contrast of one table made up of insignificant lawyers and ink-pissing officials and the other, opulent one made up of hidalgos who, if we piss anything at all, it's pure gold! Laughing childishly, I followed the suggestions of my trickster friend Ávila. We dramatized, to the astonishment and praise of the guests, the interview between my father, Hernán Cortés, and the emperor Moctezuma, when my father was the first—the very first, are you all listening? —white man to see the grandeur of the Great Tenochtitlán.

I of course played the part of my father. Alonso de Ávila dressed up as Moctezuma, placing around my neck a chain of flowers and jewels, telling me in a loud voice: "Not only do I venerate and respect you but I obey you. I am your vassal." (In my ear he whispered, "I love you like a brother.") Everyone applauded the pageant with pleasure, but I felt how the joy settled into another kind of delight when Alonso de Ávila, catching me unawares, placed a crown of laurel on my head and, smiling, awaited the exclamation of the guests: "Oh, how well the crown suits your lordship!"

MARTÍN 2

I wasn't invited to those celebrations. But I watched them from a distance. Actually from close up, from very close up, I was keeping an eye on things. I mixed in with the crowd, at the barbecue pits, the pulque stands, next to the people making wicker chairs, tortillas, carrying pots of drinking water; next to the ditches and dumps and eating stands, I listened to the new, secret language being forged between Nahuatl and Spanish, the secret curses, the secret sighs of this man who just yesterday was a priest and is now an old pockmarked ruin, or that man who was as much the son of an Aztec prince as my brother and I are sons of the Spanish conquistador, but now he was carrying loads of firewood from house to house, and my brother had his twins baptized in the cathedral, but the sons and grandsons of Cuauhtémoc were entering the same cathedral on their knees, their heads bent forward, their scapularies like chains pulled by the invisible hand of the three gods of Christianity, Father, Son, and Holy Spirit, the dad, the kid, and the succubus: Which one do you like best, new little Mexican boy, Indian and Castilian like me, the daddy, the brat, or the ghost?

I saw them there in the festivities with which my brother celebrated his progeny, saw them inventing for themselves a color, a language, a god—three instead of a thousand. Which language? Will you call him the son or the *escuincle*, a boy or a *chaval*, a turkey or a *guajalote*, Cuauhnáhuac or Cuernavaca, where my brother was born, agave or *maguey*, black beans or *frijoles*, kidney beans or *ejotes*? Which God:

mirror of smoke or Holy Spirit, plumed serpent or crucified Christ, god that demands my death or God that gives me His, sacrificing father or sacrificed Father, obsidian knife or cross? Which Mother of God: Tonantzín or Guadalupe? Which language? If it happens to be Spanish, much of it comes from Arabic: Guadalupe herself, Guadalquivir, Guadarrama, *alberca, azotea, acequia, alcoba, almohada, alcázar, alcachofa, limón, naranja, ojalá*? Which language? If it happens to be Nahuatl: Seri, Pima, Totonaca, Zapoteca, Maya, Huichol?

At night, I stroll around among the fires from the torches lit to celebrate the criollo descendants of my whoremongering and insatiable father, wondering about my own blood, my progenitors and my progeny as well. Which will it be? I look at the dark skin, the glassy eyes, the averted eyes, the laden backs, the callused hands, the split feet, the pregnant wombs, the worn-out teats of my Indian and mestizo brothers and sisters, and I imagine them—barely forty years ago!—occupying their proper places, hoarding fortunes, doing what they pleased, commanding sacrifices, demanding tribute, receiving the solar gold on their heads and shooting it forth from their haughty stares, overcoming the sun itself, overcoming gold itself!

Exactly the same as my brother Martín and his pal Ávila, and the damned twins baptized today in the name of the God who conquered my mother with one single, outrageous announcement: Stop dying for me; look, I died for you. Son-of-a-bitch Jesus, king of faggots, you conquered my mother's people with the perverse pleasure of your phallic nails, your sour semen, the lances that penetrate you, and the humors you distill. How to reconquer you? What name shall I give to our next time: reconquest, counterconquest, anticonquest, retroconquest, cuauhtémoconquest, preconquest, shitconquest? What will I do with it,

with whom will I make it, in whose name, for whom? My
mother, Malinche, without whom my father wouldn't have
conquered anything? Or my father himself, stripped of his
conquest, humiliated, dragged to court, worn out in banal
trials and perverse paper wars, accused a thousand times,
and only punished in an eternally postponed decision?
Sword of Damocles, Cuauhtémoc's flint knife, the stiletto
of the Hapsburgs, it all hangs over our heads and my
brother Martín knows it. He amuses himself, sharing
Alonso de Ávila's arrogance, he doesn't realize how the
Council sees him. As the owner of the city. He doesn't
realize the Council can do nothing against him: a junta of
mediocre men, cowards immersed in an unresolved col-
legiality, lacking authority. They see that a conspiracy is
forming, that danger approaches, but they fear Martín, my
brother, they fear him . . . And he doesn't know it. Nor
does he know that they restored our father's property to
him to keep him quiet and lead him out of the temptations
of political power. I tell him and he almost hangs me,
calling me envious, the son of a whore; he has his money
with no conditions, like a free man. He shouted that at
me, and I say, in my perpetually opaque, perpetually obsequious voice, high-pitched with melancholy: "Well then,
prove it. Do what they fear most."

THE TWO MARTÍNS

What has my brother come to say to me? That there is
no higher authority in New Spain than I myself? That I
only want to enjoy my wealth and show it off to others as
I do, in toasts and masquerades, soirees and baptisms,
processions and entertainments? Has he come to remind
me that I am the firstborn by right of inheritance, the heir

of the entailed estate of a humiliated father who depends on me to do what he wished to do but couldn't? I, greater than my father? I, superior to Hernán Cortés, Conqueror of Mexico? I, capable of doing what my father did not do? Rebel? Rebel and take over the land? Revolt? Revolt against the King?

My brother says he's gone to the tomb of his Indian mother, a flooded grave near Ixtapalapa, moist but surrounded by nervous flowers and floating plots of land. He's gone to that tomb and told his mother, Malinche, that thanks to her my father conquered this land. He comes to me to ask if I'm less than his Indian mother. He offends me. He riles me up. He shits on me, as he says himself. He starts talking a language I don't recognize. But he uses it well, with malice and temptation. Because if he talks to his mother, I can't talk to mine, Doña Juana de Zúñiga, walled up in her Cuernavaca palace, surrounded by ravines, constables, and watchdogs. She denies me access to my inheritance—well, to a part of it.

My brother, on the other hand, speaks directly to his mother and tells me he says this to her: Dear Mother Malinche, what more would I want than to be king of this land. But look at me, dark and with averted eyes, what the hell do you want me to be? On the other hand, my brother is as beautiful as the sun, an all-powerful marquis, coddled by fortune, and yet he will not dare, will not dare. He's afraid of taking over the land. The land. Yesterday I brought him (my brother the mestizo brought me) to the highest point on Chapultepec, and there I showed him (he showed me) the beauty of this Valley of Mexico.

It was morning, and the cool air announced a hot day. We both knew that the dawn would smell of roses pearled with dew and ripe fruit, open to pour the secret juices of the papaya, the cherimoya, and the guanabana. The beauty of this valley is that it makes mirages tangible. Distances change thanks to the trickery of mountains and plains. Faraway things seem close, and what's close seems faraway. The lakes dry up and evaporate, but they still mirror the trees newly born next to them, laurels, *pirús*, and weeping willows. The century plants reclaim their ancestral dominance over the dust. And the bluish mountains, the volcanoes crowned with white whirlwinds, the hillsides covered with thick forests, the liquid air, the breath of the sun like an oven, the punctual afternoon shower: all that, we two brothers contemplated one morning.

And then one afternoon, he says to me that what counts is power over this land, not over things, not over the inventory that gave my father sleepless nights and that now threatens, Brother, to overwhelm you: the houses, the furniture, the jewels, the vassals, the towns . . . Be careful: back in Seville you saw the auction of our father's house, and you feared the conquest of Mexico would end in a junk-shop sale of pots and old mattresses. Be careful. Take the land; forget the things. Do what your father didn't do. Look at the earth and remember. Hernán Cortés wasn't the only one to see it for the first time. Many men—soldiers, captains, a few criminals, a few other hidalgos, the majority honorable people from towns in Estremadura and Castile—came over with him. You aren't alone. Our father was never alone. He triumphed because he kept his ear to the ground and listened to what the land had to say. Don't be like Moctezuma, who waited to hear the voice of the gods; the gods never spoke to him because they'd already run away. Be like our father. Listen to what the land says.

These arguments were useless in the face of the physical enchantment of this Valley of Mexico. In it, there was room for all climates at the same time: summer and spring, autumn and winter all linked together, as if eternity had decided to meet itself in that transparent air. The shock of that purity engulfed us. And we trembled together, listening to the noise of the city to come, the incessant arguing, the growl of a million tigers, the plaintive howl of hungry wolves, the terror of serpents that revealed a skeleton of metal when they changed their skin. The valley fills with multicolored lights, as bright as the liquid silver of a sword pointing between the eyes of the world, red as a breath exhaled from hell, but all of them overcome by an evil-smelling mist, a foam of gas, as if the valley were a flatulent belly, pitilessly opened by a knife to carry out a premature autopsy. We, the two Martíns, plunge our hands into that open stomach, we smear ourselves with blood up to our elbows, we remove the guts and viscera of Mexico City, and we don't know how to separate the jewels from the mud, the emeralds from the gallstones, the rubies from the intestinal chancres.

Then, from the bottom of the lagoon, unexpectedly, there surges up a chorus of voices, which at first we two brothers can't manage to understand . . . One sings in Nahuatl, another in Castilian, but they end up blending together: one sings the unfolding of the flower-like Quetzal mantles, another the swaying of the Sevillian poplars in the breeze; one begs that the flowers not die, that they last in someone's hands; another, that the wounded, love-struck crane not die . . . The voices fuse to sing together in the fleeting passage of life; they wonder if we've come in vain, we pass through the earth: we touch the flowers, we touch the fruit, but a loud, disconsolate scream remembers, adding another voice to the group: Within the garden I shall die, within the rose garden shall I be slain, words that fuse with the responsory of the Indian land, No one, no one, no one, in truth, lives in the land: we've only come to dream, and the words flow far from the valley, into a distant sea where the silent rivers of life come to a halt; We, says the Nahuatl voice, shall have to go to the place of mystery . . . And then, as if borne along by a wind that scatters the pestilential smoke and puts out the cruel lights and silences the strident noises, the singing ends without ending:

> My flowers will never end,
> My songs will never end.
> I raise them up,
> I am only a singer . . .

MARTÍN 1

He wants me to forget my existence, my honors and pleasures. He doesn't realize that those things are enough for me. I have no plan to govern this land. Let the others govern it; the more mediocre they are, the more they will envy me. What's wrong with that? He thinks I don't know how to read his arguments. Anyone who lives here understands them. He wants to avenge his mother. He seduces me by convincing me I should avenge my father. Our revenge does not unite us. It goes beyond that. He reminds me that our father ended loving Mexico more than he loved Spain, that he considered Mexico to be his land and wanted to return here to die. Spain, time, papers, and official perversity denied him that wish. Perhaps, my brother alleges, the reason is that the presence of our father in Mexico was feared. The long court trial was in reality an exile. Hernán Cortés wanted to save the Indian temples; the Franciscans stopped him. He wanted to end the system that made the Indians into bound vassals; the commissioners prevented that from happening. In our father's humanism, the King saw the thing he most feared: the unrestricted government of the conquistadors. Their caprice. Their insolence. For the good of all, the King had to impose his will on the conquistadors—they weren't to think their deeds gave them the right to govern.

Didn't Gonzalo Pizarro take up arms against the King in Peru? Didn't the traitor Lope de Aguirre go deep into the Amazon to found a new kingdom against the King of Spain? Better to corner the conquistadors, surround them, strip them, leave them to die drowned in ink and papers or stabbing each other to death; let Pedro de Mendoza die of hunger and syphilis on the banks of the Río de la Plata; let Francisco Pizarro die assassinated by the supporters of Diego de Almagro, his rival; let Pedro de Alvarado die crushed by a horse; and let our father Hernán Cortés die of rage and despair. Does my brother, the son of the Indian woman, want me to add my name to theirs? Like hell: my resentment is not his, and he does not share my secret. I know my father wanted to free both the land and the vassals. I violated my father's testament. Let others sing his glory and his humanism—Father Motolinia for example: "Who loved and defended the Indians in this new world as Cortés did?" I base my pride on my modesty. I did not carry out my father's will in his testament, which was to free this land. How could I possibly reclaim that same freedom now? Especially if it's going to cost me my toasts, my masquerades, my baptisms, my envies, and my fortune.

MARTÍN 2

My poor brother. Blinded. Deluded. Proud. He has an immense power in this land, but he doesn't know how to use it. He is a mirror held up to the deeds of our father.

A presentable mirror. On the other hand, I . . . He: annual rents paid him: fifty thousand pesos. Educated, refined. I see him. I see myself. I am his distorted mirror. There is no gentleman more powerful than he in the colony. All the honors and income owed my father, denied my father, were given to him. Unlike my father, he represented no political danger. Arable land, estates, tributes, tithes, first fruits: everything was given him as if to say: Keep quiet. We are giving you all the honors, all the wealth. But we deny you power, just as we did your father.

I tell him: "Take power, too." He doesn't want to: he accepts things as they are, and that's his nature. But the idea of rebellion to win Mexican independence is not an idea born of my rancor (as he sees it) or his vanity (as I see it). These things happen despite us. Behind our backs. They have their own laws. Mexico is no longer Tenochtitlán. But it is not Spain, either. Mexico is a new country, a different country, which cannot be governed from a distance and at one remove, just like that. We are the Crown's stepsons. My father knew it, but he as yet did not have a Mexican homeland, although he did want it. He wanted it; I want it. We, his sons, not only have a new country. *We are* the new country. I hear its voices and tell my brother, "Don't make a sound, keep quiet, speak softly, rape with dissimulation; Mexico is a country wounded at birth, nursed on the milk of rancor, brought up with the whisper of the shadow. Talk to it tenderly, coddle it, support it, and make it yours in secret. Don't tell anyone about your love for Mexico. Public light offends the sons of the shadow. Go on dying discreetly, find supporters, promise everything to everyone, then give out just a little and no more (since no one here ever expects anything; they're happy with a little, which to them seems a lot). Take advantage of political opportunity."

The viceroy died. There were three justices in expectation of a new viceroy. They went on taking care of the affairs of the day, almost through inertia. The permanent subject of the administration was still just one: to define the powers of the Crown and those of the conquistadors. The sons of the conquest presented their briefs to the Council. The Council put them off—weakly. But the descendants saw in it an insolent affront and responded with insolence of their own: "Let's hope that what they say about those who want everything—that they lose everything— doesn't happen to the King." The arrogant Alonso de Ávila said that, and everyone attributed the idea to my brother. Two sides formed, and all because of some gloves. A certain Don Diego de Córdoba was given twenty thousand ducats by the criollos under the pretext that he buy them Spanish gloves not made here. It was a pretext for this Don Diego to negotiate the rights of the criollos in court, without any appearance of bribery.

Since Don Diego got nowhere and kept the ducats, and no gloves reached the hands of the hidalgos, two sides formed. One approached my brother to ask him to lead the revolt and take advantage of the weak Council. The other group went directly to the impotent Council to denounce my brother, Ávila, and their friends. The Council, fearful of my brother's power, vacillated. My brother, fearful of royal power, also vacillated.

Offstage, those who did not hesitate acted. In my brother's name, his supporters seized the symbolic opportunity offered by a memorable date: August 13, 1565, the anniversary of the capture of Mexico City–Tenochtitlán by Hernán Cortés. It was the so-called Festival of the Banner. The conspirators decided to take advantage of the revelry, the crowds of people who would be present, and the tradition of mock duels and skirmishes to put a boat with cannon on wheels and pretend to attack a rolling tower, which would also be filled with artillery and soldiers. The acting governor would pass between them with his banner. Just then, armed men would pour out of both, seizing the Council and its banner and proclaiming Don Martín Cortés King and Master of Mexico.

Oh . . . What I feared most took place: you lost the initiative, Brother.

They were one step ahead of you.

MARTÍN 1

All of that went on behind my back, I swear it. Buying gloves for rich hidalgos! Who could think up something like that . . . It is true that they came to see me, to compromise me, to sing me the eternal litany of criollo woes —that no one ever took them into account, that they were badly governed by inept people sent from Spain, that the judges and governors got in the way of their business, that they did not have the right to govern the country as their fathers, the conquistadors, did, without consulting anyone. I let them talk. I didn't discourage them. But I did warn them: "Do you really have people behind you?" "Many," they answered, and they named them. One was a certain Baltasar de Aguilar, a captain in the army. "Well, let's hope that it all doesn't fall apart"—I warned them—"and we lose our lives and estates. As far as I'm concerned," I said (and I repeat it here and now as proof of my sincerity, which has never been denied), "if you don't go forward, I'll keep quiet. But if you make some headway, I'll step forward and denounce you to the King. I'll say, 'Majesty, my father gave you this land. Now I give it back to you.'"

But before anything like this could happen, this Baltasar

de Aguilar person, named captain by the plotters, stole the march on all of us and went to the Council to tell everything he knew about the uprising, about how they were going to make me king and about how he was supposed to be captain of all the plotters. I knew nothing. I was at the time deeply involved with a lady, and because of her influence, I favored members of her family, who were convinced both that I had Moctezuma's treasure hidden and that it would ultimately turn up in her skirts. Now you tell me if I had any time to think about becoming king, when my lady love's relatives, not seeing any signs of the treasure, grew impatient, locked her up, started spreading libelous papers about me all over town, and walked in front of me on the street without tipping their hats.

I recovered from those insults by celebrating the birth of another son of mine and by trying to repeat the festivities of the previous year: triumphal arches, artificial forests, music, lots of pomp and circumstance. There was a jolly masquerade and then a grand dinner given by my dear friend Alonso de Ávila. Now, he was master of the town of Cuautitlán, which specialized in making little clay pitchers. He had some made up marked like this: a U with a crown above and a tiny yardstick below to express the idea: YOU SHALL RULE. The soiree was interrupted by a squad of armed men led by a man I'd never seen before—large-headed, powerful, badly dressed, whose thin hair, like that of a mandrake root, grew above a scraped face, as if he'd washed it with pumice stone. The contrast between his vulgar clothing and the identical outfits which for that gala evening Alonso and I were wearing could not have been greater. It was a summer night in July of 1565: we were both wearing long damask robes with black tunics—and our swords. Which is what the man with the stone face, as square as a die painted orange by a miserly rather than a just nature, demanded of us: "Your lordships will please give me your swords. You are under arrest by His Majesty's order." "Why?" we asked in one voice, Alonso and I. "You will be informed in due course." "By whom?" we asked, once again at the same time. "By Dr. Muñoz Carrillo, a newly appointed judge, which is to say, me myself," said this apparition made of a flesh that was much too solid for him to be a ghost. Then he picked up the Cuautitlán pitcher and smashed it violently against the floor. We were clay, he stone.

MARTÍN 2

They accused him of such banal things. That he fancied himself a Don Juan. That he had Moctezuma's treasure hidden somewhere. Utter crap. The real accusation was about seizing control of the land. That is, rebelling against the King. And to my eternal sorrow, that accusation included me. They dragged me out of the shadows. That night, the streets and entryways to the plaza were patrolled by men on horseback and foot soldiers. Everyone was in an uproar, and my brother deeply distressed. They put him in a very closely guarded room in the government house, completely surrounded by troops. But the room did have a window that faced the small square on the side of the cathedral under construction, where a platform was immediately built. He was disarmed, but they left him his elegant damask summer suit; they never laid a hand on him. Me the Indian, on the other hand, they threw onto a burro, stripped me, tied me down, and then tossed me into the same jail where they held my brother, just to see if my rancor would grow, to see if his pity would insult me.

On the way, tied naked to the burro, facedown, ass to

Carlos Fuentes

the breeze, I had to put up with the jokes of every beggar in the city: Since when does one burro carry another, which one was the real burro? and the embarrassment of having my tiny little John Thomas compared with the burro's huge phallus: Hey boy, don't you *long* for that thing down there? or, Do you really think little things mean a lot? or, Are you going or coming, getting in or getting out, taking or giving, screwing or screaming? And there I am, face-down with the blood pounding in my temples and eyes, my testicles cold, emptied, and shrunken from fear.

I look at the city's garbage and realize that I've always tried to look up—at the palaces being built, the balconies from which my brother and his friends used their blowguns filled with flowers, the niches of the saints (this stone city slowly sinking into the mud; the water went when the gods departed). Now my position forced me to look into the gutters flooded with garbage, the mud streets marked with animal tracks and cart wheel ruts, footprints in the dust, the dog prints indistinguishable from the human prints. I try to look up, although it pains my neck, at the cathedral under construction. A force that doesn't touch me makes me bend my neck again. Every single thing I took for granted, I realize now, has been taken away from me. I look at Mexico's soil, and I realize it changes cease-lessly, that the seasons change it, that sorrow changes it, that weeping changes it, footsteps, fainting, the disintegra-tion of this porous, sunken ground that can't decide be-tween water and dust, between heaven and hell.

The burro stops and a small, misshapen woman wrapped in a black rebozo comes over to me, caresses my hand, slaps me. Then from her sunken, toothless mouth, from her dwarfish cheeks, from her wet tongue that can't hold back her saliva decently, come the words I expected, the words that have hung over my life like that sword of

88

Damocles that hangs over the heads of all Hernán Cortés's descendants in their perennially postponed trials. The little misshapen woman violently raises my head by yanking on my hair and says to me what I expected to hear: "You're a son of a bitch. You're my brother. You're the fucking son of *la chingada*."

MARTÍN 1

They've thrown my brother, the other Martín, into the same jail I'm in. How little imagination our father had. Always the same names. Martín, Leonor, Catalina, María, Amadorcico. What ever became of him? What ever became of the humpbacked María? I look toward the platform that's been set up in the plaza, next to the scaffolding that will one day be that cathedral, and I tell my poor brother, the son of the Indian woman, to get up and come see the dawn, as we did one day from Chapultepec. But the other Martín's ribs ache. They brought him in naked and beaten, filthy and stinking. No matter. It's in situations like this when more than ever we've got to be good Christians, which I swear I am. "Look," I told my brother, "it's going to rain at daybreak; what a strange thing." "Sometimes it does happen," he painfully answers me. "The fact is"—he added—"that you never get up early." I laughed. "But I do go to bed late. I would hear the raindrops; my hearing is very sharp." "Well then, try to tell the difference between the rain and the drum that announces death," said my ailing brother.

I leaned out the window. The little plaza had filled up with rabble, held back by horsemen. The Ávila brothers, Alonso and Gil, marched in between two ranks of armed men. My brother Alonso was wearing the finest stockings and a satin doublet, a damask robe lined with jaguar skin, a cap decorated with gold ornaments and feathers, and a gold chain around his neck. I could just make out a rosary made of tiny, white orangewood beads in his hand. A nun had sent it to him for days of affliction, and he, laughing, told me he'd never touch it. Next to the brothers were the Dominican friars. I took no notice of his brother Gil. He must have been coming into the city from some town when they arrested him because he was dressed plainly, in greenish cloth, and was wearing boots.

The Ávila brothers climbed onto the platform. First Gil lay down with his head stretched forward, but I could only keep my eyes on Alonso, my friend, my comrade, seeing him there, holding his cap in his hand, the rain soaking the hair he always took such pains to curl, he was so careful about his hairdo to make himself look handsome, seeing him and hearing the clumsy chopping of the executioner until he'd finally managed to cut off Gil's head in bad style, amid the shouts and sobs of the people.

Alonso stared at his decapitated brother and heaved such a huge sigh that even in our prison I could hear it. Still staring, he went down on his knees, raised his white hand, and twisted his mustache, a habit of his, until the monk Domingo de Salazar, who later became bishop of the Philippines, helped him to die with dignity. He told Alonso it was not time to fix his mustache but to arrange his affairs with God. A voice intoned the Miserere; the monk said to the crowd, "Sirs, I commend these gentlemen, who say they are dying unjustly, to God." Alonso made a sign to the monk, who bent down over the kneeling man and heard something in secret. They blindfolded Alonso. The executioner took three swings, as if he were cutting the head off a lamb, and I bit my hand, asking myself: Alonso, what things did we forget, did we forget to say to each other, Brother? Are we departing without doing something we should have done, be closer, talk to each other, love each other more? Were you unfaithful to our friendship in the hour of your death? Did you die without me, my adored Alonso? Are you condemning me to live without you? Condemning me to live desiring you, regretting everything that wasn't?

MARTÍN 2

I know my city well. Something is changing it. I hear the haste. I see the ugliness. I don't need anyone to tell me that the execution scaffold outside our window was put up overnight: something is changing the form, the face of Mexico City. It isn't only the heads of the Ávila brothers that have been displayed on pikes in the great plaza. They've been placed such that my brother and I can't avoid seeing them. Judge Muñoz Carrillo, always with his freshly washed face, does not have to visit us to say that these lodgings are only temporary, because he has ordered a jail to be built within two weeks so that all those who conspired against the King—and there are many—will be able to fit inside it. As soon as it's ready, we'll be brought there, to a jail, he tells us, where not even a bird will be able to fly over without his seeing it. He looks us up and down and warns us that those found guilty are sentenced at midnight so they have no time to send word to anyone, not even themselves. At dawn, the proper authority will simply appear at our door with two burros for us to ride and two crucifixes for us to carry in our hands. We will all hear the bells of the Town Hall. The executioner and the crier will accompany us to the place of execution.

The crier will shout out: "This is the justice His Majesty

and the Royal Council, acting in his name, order meted out to these men as traitors to the royal Crown." Etcetera. That's what I say to the judge: "Etcetera." It's one of those Latin expressions my mother taught me. Newly converted to Christianity, she was excited by the idea that the language of religion should be different from the language spoken by the people. Since she would have liked to be, or go on being, a translator, that seduced her and she began to dot her everyday speech with the occasional hallelujah, oremus, dominoes woesbiscuits, requestete in patchy, paternostro, and especially etcetera, which, according to what she told me, means "everything else, the lot, the whole boring thing. In a word: the law." But on hearing me, the judge took it the wrong way and gave me a huge slap in the face. Then my brother Martín did something unexpected: he punched the insolent Council officer back. He defended me. My brother stuck his neck out for me. I looked at him with a love that saved me, if not him, from all the differences that separated us, some serious and some silly. At that moment, I would have died with him. Begging your pardon now, and if it's not too much of a bother, I'll repeat myself to make things clear. I wouldn't die for him. But I would have died with him.

MARTÍN 1

I can't explain why they neither sentenced nor executed us. The entire city is a jail and a torture chamber. It's easy to see, to know, to smell, and, besides, we're told. Opposite us, the platform where we, like the Ávila brothers, would have our heads cut off was already finished. Why don't they get it over with? Is this the judge's torture for my having slapped him? Well, the Quesada brothers paraded past us, crucifixes in hand, still stunned by the rapidity of their sentence, convinced right down to the last minute they weren't to die; Cristóbal de Oñate was drawn and quartered; Baltasar de Sotelo was found innocent of any wrongdoing in the Mexico conspiracy, but he was executed in any case for having served in Peru during Gonzalo Pizarro's uprising against the King—a victim of guilt by suspected association; right before our eyes passed Bernardino de Bocanegra mounted on a mule, preceded by the crucifix and the crier, followed by his mother, his wife and family, the women all barefoot and hatless, their hair as tangled as Mary Magdalene's, dragging their mantles in the dust, weeping, begging that the gentleman be granted a pardon. That was the only time the dreaded Muñoz Carrillo showed compassion: he commuted Bernardino de Bocanegra's sentence to destitution of all worldly possessions, twenty years in the King's galleys, and, after that, perpetual exile from the kingdoms and territories of His Majesty Don Felipe II.

Thus my brother and I had no idea what to expect. Would we lose our heads, be exiled, or row for the rest of our lives? The wily Muñoz Carrillo dropped no hints, but had bells rung at our door as if it were already dawn and our turn to go to our final rendezvous. He had crucifixes paraded under our noses and tied burros under our windows. Why didn't anything happen? We saw the heads of those already executed displayed on pikes and then disappear from the plaza and the government buildings. The town councillors protested. The heads on display were a sign of treason. But the city had not been disloyal. The orgy of executions, however, went on.

Each time a head fell, that hypocrite Judge Muñoz would intone these words: "He was merciful to himself, he went to enjoy the presence of God because he died a good Christian and was rewarded with many Masses and prayers." I told my brother Martín, the son of Malinche: "The judge is doing all this to show that His Majesty is being well served and will, in his turn, grant the judge many favors." More astute than I, my brother saw a sign of Muñoz Carrillo's waning power in all this. Then he added, "But you're right. He's trying to get on the good side of the King. He's a miserable lackey. The motherfucker." I'd never heard that word and supposed it was one of the many La Malinche had taught my half brother. Even so, I liked the expression: *Hijo de la chingada*.

It gave me great pleasure to apply it to the man who'd informed on us, Baltasar de Aguilar, when the new viceroy finally reached Mexico. Don Gastón de Peralta, Marquis of Falces, found himself in a city silently rebelling against Judge Muñoz Carrillo. The first thing he did was to decide that my brother and I should be immediately sent to Spain because the Council of Mexico was not impartial and could not try our case properly. And that was the intent of the King himself, Don Felipe II, with regard to the sons of a man who had given such glory to Spain.

The moment that pimp Baltasar de Aguilar, the informer, learned the viceroy was proceeding benevolently with us, he withdrew his accusations in order to appease all sides. I think it was then, only then, that the divine flame of justice began to blaze within me. I requested the opportunity to meet the motherfucker (I'm talking like my brother now) face-to-face, and Muñoz Carrillo decided to be present. Contrite, Baltasar de Aguilar knelt before me and begged forgiveness. I told him there was no way to forgive the death of Alonso de Ávila, my most beloved brother, which was his fault. Aguilar was beside himself, but not the judge, who had only a few days left of power. "Why didn't Alonso de Ávila defend himself?" the judge asked me. I didn't know what to say. The boorish Muñoz Carrillo dragged his callused hands across his face and in a cavernous voice, in whose depths neither laughter nor resentment could be detected, told us: "Among his possessions were found a multitude of love letters from the most highly placed women in this city." "Then he died in order not to compromise them," I said, full of admiration. "No. He died because in his little notes Don Alonso bragged about his conspiracy, described it in detail, and promised the ladies infinite riches and privileges when he and you, Don Martín, would share the governing of Mexico."

The sentence was just. I was a perfect fool.

MARTÍN 2

I think that out of all these errors we were saved only by the innate sense of justice of the viceroy, Don Gastón de Peralta, who determined that in the case of this conspiracy to seize the land and tear possession of Mexico away from the King of Spain he would proceed according to the following criteria. The first to denounce the conspiracy would receive benefits. When he heard that, Aguilar shouted for joy. But the second to denounce the conspiracy would only be pardoned. Aguilar's face became serious. And the third to denounce the conspiracy would be executed. The miserable Aguilar went down on his knees, imploring: "And what about those of us who simply repented and backed down?"

I mean that there is some justice in all this after all. That bastard Baltasar de Aguilar was sentenced to ten years in the galleys for perjury, with the loss of all his property and the towns he possessed, as well as perpetual exile from all the Indies of the Ocean Sea and Terra Firma. Returned to Spain in a schooner, Judge Muñoz Carrillo suffered a fit of apoplexy when he read a letter in which King Felipe removed him from office, becoming even squarer than he was already by nature: "I ordered you to New Spain to govern, not to destroy." He lost the ability to speak, and to cure him the doctors pried open his mouth with sticks so he could swallow their concoctions. He died, this man with the sandpapered face and strands of mandrake hair on his head. Everyone knows that these homunculi are born at the base of the gallows. Our particular homunculus, Judge Muñoz, had to be gutted and salted so he wouldn't be buried at sea. Just before dying, he managed to say: "I want to be buried at El Ferrol." But storms broke out, and the sailors mutinied. Carrying a dead body on a ship brings bad luck. They threw him overboard, tightly bound and wrapped in filthy mats covered with pitch.

My brother Don Martín, the man who could have been king of Mexico, was sent back to Spain. Why? His enemies rejoiced, thinking that there things would go worse for him and the King would bring the full rigor of justice down on him for his crimes. His friends were also happy, seeing in the decision a way of protecting Martín and deferring sentence. I, on the other hand, fully aware of my failure, told him, "Brother, stay in Mexico, take a chance, but hurry the sentence. Don't you realize that if you go back to Spain the same thing will happen to you as happened to our father? Your trial will never end. It will go on eternally. Cut the thread holding the sword over our heads. If you go back to Spain you will be deprived of all power, just like our father. That's the secret of bureaucrats in Spain and everywhere else: to prolong matters until everyone forgets about them." But my brother answered me simply: "Neither I nor they want to see me here anymore. Neither they nor I want what awaits me here. Fighting and perhaps martyrdom. I don't want it."

MARTÍN 1

Carlos V gathered a great armada in 1545 to strike against the eunuch Aga Azán, who governed Algeria. Twelve thousand sailors, twenty-four thousand soldiers, sixty-five galleys, and five hundred other ships gathered in the Balearic Islands. The Emperor led the armada. With only eleven ships and five hundred men, my father had conquered Moctezuma's empire. Now they didn't even give him command of a galley. But he took the galley. I was thirteen years old. My father enlisted as a volunteer and took me by the hand to take possession of the galley *Hope*. No one knew more about war than he, not even the Emperor. He warned them about bad weather. He warned them about the excessive size of the expeditionary force. All they had to do was wait for good weather and launch a surprise attack with a reduced force. No one paid him any attention. The expedition failed amid the storm and the confusion. My father always traveled with his five emeralds. Fearing to lose them in the Algiers disaster, he wrapped them in a handkerchief. He lost them swimming for his life. Now I would like to sink in the Mare Nostrum until I find them: one carved like a rose, another like a trumpet, another like a fish with golden eyes, another like a little bell, another like a little cup resting on a gold base.

But were those his real treasures? I remembered then the death of my father, the scent of the flowering orange tree entering through the window in Andalusia, and I tried to imagine that in his purse, from when he disembarked one day in Acapulco and there planted an orange tree, my father had carried those well-kept seeds, and they were not lost, they did not go to the bottom of the sea, they allowed the twin fruits of America and Europe to grow, flourish, and, one day, to meet without rivalry.

Very forgotten things reappear at moments that cause pain. I curse until the fourth generation all those who caused us pain.

MARTÍN 2

Mother: Only with you did our father triumph. Only at your side did he have a rising fortune. Only with you did he experience the seamless destiny of power, fame, compassion, and wealth. I bless you, my mother. I thank you for my dark skin, my liquid eyes, my hair like my father's horse's mane, my bare pubis, my short height; my singsong voice, my obstinate silence, my diminutives and my curses, my dream longer than life, my suspended memory, my satisfaction disguised as resignation, my desire to believe, my longing after paternity, my face lost amid the dark-skinned human tide, subjugated as I am: I am the majority.

MARTÍN 1

I don't want to be a martyr. I prefer this farce to an interminable court case that wears down both my judges and me. I'm leaving Mexico, as they asked me. They want to keep me quiet. Fine. I'm leaving and placing my property under the care of my older brother, the son of the Indian woman. In Spain, they pursue the case against me and I'm sentenced to exile, fines, and loss of property. That happens in 1567. The punishments are reversed in 1574, except for the fines. I'm forty-four years old. My properties are restored to me, but they force me to make a loan of fifty thousand ducats to the Crown for the war effort. A worthy cause. My Mexican power is dismembered when the Crown annexes my Tehuantepec and my Oaxaca. Lord and Master! Not me, although I will leave something to my descendants. More money, ultimately, than power. That's how it will always be. No dictator will last long in Mexico. The country doesn't want tyrants. It's too fond of tyrannizing itself, day after day, rancor after rancor, injustice after injustice, envy after envy, submission after submission, from the lowest to the highest. I will never return to Mexico. I will die in Spain on August 13, 1589, at the age of sixty-seven, the anniversary of the taking of Tenochtitlán by my father and of the failed conspiracy for the independence of the colony. I leave my property to my children, but in dying I sink into the sea off Algiers seeking my father's five lost emeralds. They are the same ones Moctezuma gave him. They are the same ones that, to his grief, my proud and blinded father did not want to give, or even to sell, to the Queen of Spain.

MARTÍN 2

I was tortured in Mexico and exiled to Spain. I died at the end of the century. How old was I? Seventy, eighty? I lost count. The truth is I was always just eight years old. I nestled in the arms of my mother, the Indian Marina, La Malinche. In each other's arms, every night, that's the only way we saved ourselves from terror. We heard the gallop of horses. That's the terror, that's the strange new thing. Horses gallop and birds fly, flies buzz. We hug each other, my mother and I, shivering with fear. We know we shouldn't be afraid of the horses my father brought to Mexico. We should fear the incessant upheaval of the world over our heads. I remember my mother's worn, sick skin. I would have wanted to see, as did my brother Martín, who embraced him in death, my old father: his skin. Now I see my own, I'm so old, and I remember the morning my brother and I spent staring at the Valley of Mexico. My skin is a field. My wrinkles and my veins are plowed fields, accidents on the land. My bones are rocks. The lines on my palm are skin, field, and paper. Written land, suffering land as sensitive as a skin, inflammable as a codex. My mother and I embrace at night to defend ourselves, poor us, from the dream of the land. In nightmares, we've seen the spectacle of death. My father's escorted by death. He's dying. How many died before he did? With how many is he dying? How many in fact survive us? I tell all this and I am astonished by the world, and at times I wish I hadn't been in it. We lose our illusions about what we wanted so much. I'm sick of the spectacle of death. I don't understand how a nation is born.

El Escorial, July 1992

The Two Numantias

TO PLÁCIDO ARANGO

Oh walls of this city!
If you can speak, then say . . .
—CERVANTES,
The Siege of Numantia

THEY, the Spaniards, are a coarse, savage, and barbarous people whom we Romans lead, whether they like it or not, toward civilization. Thanks to the Greeks and Phoenicians, there is some development in the peninsula's coastal areas. But just penetrate this surly, arid land the slightest bit and there's nothing: no roads, no aqueducts, no theaters, and no cities worthy of the name. They have no idea what wine, salt, oil, and vinegar are. Which is why our soldiers have such a hard time of it in the Iberian campaigns. They're forced to eat barley and rabbit boiled in salt water, so dysentery has become endemic among our troops. Our satiric poets laugh, but so do our ordinary foot soldiers. We're fertilizing Spanish soil with Roman shit. And one more thing: the Spaniards never bathe.

But they are brave. We found that out during the hundred years (a hundred and four to be precise) of our constant war against Spain: from the moment Hamilcar Barca crossed from Africa to Cádiz and challenged us by sacking Spain and turning it into a base for Carthage's campaign against Rome, until the fall of the hardheaded and suicidal city of Numantia to the cohorts of our hero Publius Cornelius Scipio Aemilianus.

They live on an island. Or almost. Surrounded by water on all sides except the narrow but thick neck of the Pyrenees, the Spaniards are insular beings. Or peninsular, to be precise. To them the world matters nothing. Their land, everything. And to the world they matter nothing. It's possible we Romans might have left them in peace: let them choke to death on their barley and boiled rabbits. But Carthage intervened and transformed Spain into a gamble and a danger. The road to Rome from Africa runs through Spain. In Spain, Africa defeats Rome. And after conquering Rome, there will be nothing more to conquer. That was the threat, and Carthage placed its bet on Spain.

They always viewed themselves as the end of the world, the tail end of the continent. That's how they wanted to be seen, and that's how they were seen. The farthest point, the limit, the corner, the hole, the ass end of the known world. What a shame Carthage chose Spain to defy Rome. Rome had to come to Spain to defend itself and to defend Spain.

Hannibal, son and successor to Hamilcar, marched on Saguntum, surrounded the city, and laid siege to it. The Saguntines gathered all their possessions in the forum and burned them. Then they left the city to fight instead of dying of hunger. They were decimated by Hannibal. From the city walls, the women watched their men die in unequal combat. Some of them threw themselves from the rooftop terraces, others hanged themselves, still others killed themselves along with their children. Hannibal entered a ghost town.

That's the way they are. That's how Carthage's war in

Spain began and also how it ended: Saguntum was the prophetic mirror of the siege of Numantia.

YOU people don't know how to tell history from legend. Rome feels it's civilized. I, Polybius of Megalopolis, Greek of ancient lineage, tell you you are mistaken. Rome is an immature nation, as coarse and barbaric as the Celtiberians. Less so than they, but in no way comparable to the refined Greeks. And yet, something that has abandoned us Greeks has taken its place in the heart of Rome: Fortune, what we Greeks call *Tyché*. In matters of history, *Tyché* leads all the affairs of the world in a single direction. All the historian has to do is provide an order for the events determined by Fortune. My great good fortune (my personal luck) consists in having been a witness to the moment in which Rome became Fortune's protagonist. Until then, the world lived under the sign of dispersion. Beginning with Rome, the world becomes an organic totality. The affairs of Africa are linked to those of Greece and Asia. All these facts lead to the same end: the world united by Rome. That is history's very reason for being. All of you are the witnesses of my good fortune. In fifty-three years (which is how old Scipio was when he reached Numantia), Rome has subjugated almost all of the inhabited world. Fortune gave Rome dominion over the world. If I respect the goddess *Tyché*, I would have to say: this occurred because Rome deserved it. You will remember this history. I leave the rest to antiquarians.

WE Romans began and finished the war against Carthage in Spain and then against the Hispanic resistance once Carthage was swept from the peninsula. We, the young Roman republic, wanted to infuse into our undertakings a tradition of both military power and civilization.

Luckily, we could count on heroes from the same family, the Scipios. Two brothers, Publius Cornelius Scipio and Gnaeus Cornelius Scipio Calvus, were the first to whom the Senate and People of Rome assigned the mission of subjugating the Hispanic tribes and incorporating their territories into the Roman republic, wiping out proud Carthaginian ambition forever. The two Scipios brought the war against Carthage to Spain. They arrived with sixty ships, four hundred cavalrymen, and ten thousand infantrymen. The Carthaginians sent Hasdrubal with thirty masked elephants. The Scipios killed many elephants, which were blinded by masks that were supposed to save them from the vision of fear. But death killed the two Scipios.

The two of them were taking their ease, as is usual in wars when winter comes. A tacit truce is established, and the adversaries take refuge in mountain passes. Sometimes the power of the storms is so great that the wind smashes the very eagles against the flanks of the mountains, and their feathers fall like a dark rain on the snow. A real warrior, however, is not disheartened by the whims of the seasons. He's devoured by the worm of war. Publius Cornelius, nervous and stiff with cold, decided to catch Hasdrubal the Carthaginian by surprise. But Hasdrubal, even more nervous, had already come out searching for Publius Cornelius: Hasdrubal surrounded his force and killed him.

THE other Scipio, his brother, Gnaeus Cornelius, knew nothing of what had happened. Moved by an obscure fraternal instinct, he marched out to reconnoiter the frozen countryside. He was guided by a dread apprehension. The Carthaginians attacked him, forcing him to take refuge in a tower, which they immediately set on fire. There that valiant man died, amid the flames and the frost. Thus we

confirm that in winter truces, there can only be rest if one
of the adversaries abstains from fighting, because it is certain that the other will always be lying in ambush. Who
can understand the fatality of these mortal games?

The collapse of the winter truce was an evil omen. Five
Roman commanders followed one after another in Spain.
Marcellus came with a thousand cavalry and ten thousand
foot soldiers. He failed resoundingly, to such a degree that
his defeats gave virtually all of Spain—except for a tiny
corner in the Pyrenees—to Carthage. That's how we discovered that in Spain a perverse Archimedes' Principle
obtains: give me a tiny corner, however dark, however
small it may be, from which to fight, and from there I'll
move the world . . .

No one wanted to follow Marcellus's path to disgrace.
In Rome the alarm spread. What cowardice, what deca-
dence is this? Once again, it was a Scipio who stepped
forward: Noble family, we shall never cease to praise you
and to tell of the fame and fortune you've given us!

The young Cornelius Scipio, as he lamented the death
in Spain of his father and his uncle, who had mocked
Carthage, swore to avenge them. The Senate, holding fast
to the law (justice is a shield, but sometimes a refuge for
cowards), pointed out that the young Scipio, at the age of
twenty-four, did not have the right to command troops.
Whereupon, the youth challenged the old men. If the old
men prefer it that way, he said, let them take command.
No one did so. The youth departed with five hundred
horse and ten thousand foot. Spain, tired of African dom-
ination, awaited him with joy. Cornelius Scipio took advantage of their temperament, adding his own, which was
highly dramatic. He says providence is inspiring his actions.
He mounts his horse, sits bolt upright, speaks in the name
of the gods, and stirs up the troops with his youthful pres-

ence. He fascinates with his graceful body that barely tolerates the heavy bronze muscles of his breastplate and with the golden down of his legs that seems to blend with the body of his blossom-colored horse. Then he takes up his position opposite New Carthage, on the Mediterranean coast, with siege machines, stones, darts, catapults, and javelins. Ten thousand Carthaginians defend the gates of the city. Cornelius takes advantage of low tide for a surprise attack from the rear and takes the city using only twelve ladders, while out in front the trumpets bellow as if New Carthage had already fallen.

And New Carthage does fall. In a day. Just four days after Cornelius Scipio reaches Spain. He captures provisions, entire arsenals, ivory, gold, and silver (which the Spaniards disdain and the Carthaginians adore). Money, wheat, and docks with thirty-three warships. Prisoners. Hostages.

The young Scipio frees the prisoners in order to reconcile the two peoples. He wears a saintly expression. He does it very well. He does everything well, but this inspired expression is the one that works best. He dominates our splendid rhetoric, the double source of our politics and our literature. From the walls of New Carthage, he exclaims, "Do not forget the Scipios!"

He consecrates himself. He consecrates, by prolonging it, the glory of the family line. And by doing that he consecrates Rome, her law, her arms, her Senate, and her people. He is the worthy son of the sacrificed Publius Cornelius. Who could reproach him for his triumph? Outside the walls of Carmona, the young general acts as if he were in an amphitheater. He wears his best expression of inspiration. He says he's waiting for a divine sign to attack. As if Jupiter himself were directing, a flock of blackbirds passes at that instant, spins into a circle, and screeches.

Cornelius imitates the birds, running around in circles, making noises. The whole army imitates him, amid astonishment and laughter. The passion of victory inspires them.

But from the rear, a great number of Africans advance. Discourses and inspirations are just not enough. The birds, like all actors, have moved on to the next town. Cornelius dismounts, hands his horse over to a boy, takes a shield from a soldier, runs alone into the open space between the two armies, and exclaims, "Romans, save your general in danger!"

Moved by a thirst for glory, or fear or shame, we rush to rescue our commander from a danger he himself invented. Eight hundred of us die at Carmona—along with fifteen thousand Carthaginians. Victory would have been unimaginable if our general, acting on his own, hadn't exposed himself unnecessarily to death . . .

Cornelius Scipio is a favored man; he has youth and beauty, inspiration and courage, a theatrical gift, rhetorical power, and the ear of the gods. But every hero has his Achilles' heel. Linked by the neck of the Pyrenees to the continent, Spain, as we've noted, would be an island without those mountains. But that throat is vulnerable, as was that of our hero Cornelius Scipio in his next battle, against the Ilurgians, our allies, who went over to the Carthaginians. Cornelius conquered their town in four hours but was wounded in the neck, the only exposed place between his trunk and head: helmet, breastplate, shield, and short sword transformed our commander into a metal beast. But he had an Achilles' neck.

Wounded by their leader's wound, our men forgot to sack the town and instead, without being ordered to do so, slit the throats of all its inhabitants. The blood of Ilurgia flowed out of the slashed throats of its men, women, and children.

When Cornelius fell ill, Marcius took his place. He was weak and could not control our men. Deprived of the fascination our young hero provided, they drifted into an indiscipline which they would never dare to exhibit, which they perhaps repressed, when Cornelius Scipio stood before them. The hero would not have wanted to do what he then had to do, namely, to abandon his sickbed to restore order among the unruly troops. First came whipping. Then they were skewered to the ground through the neck and decapitated. All that made Cornelius ill. He lived just one moment beyond the glory allotted him. He knew it and withdrew. Cornelius Scipio dominated the rhythm of time. He measured his own, and four years later, at Zama, he defeated Hannibal and Carthage forever and was granted the glorious title of Scipio Africanus. That was the grandfather of the Scipio who besieged and destroyed Numantia.

The hero Cornelius Scipio and the weak Marcius were replaced by the young Cato. He wanted to emulate the hero and began with a dramatic gesture. He ordered the fleet back to Rome and announced to the soldiers that they should fear the absence of ships more than they feared the enemy: there was no way to return to Italy.

The audacity of Cato the Younger, who inspired his troops more with fear than with hope, succeeded in having all the cities along the Ebro River pull down their walls rather than be sold into slavery. Even so, the triumphs of Cornelius Scipio and Cato were demolished by the blind infamy of Galba in his so-called Lusitanian War. The trick of this commander of ours, lacking all honor, was to befriend the Iberian peoples, propose peace treaties, tell them he understood the reasons for their rebellion—the result of the poverty in which they lived—and promise them fertile lands if they would yield. After they did so, he would assemble them in an open place where he could divide them into groups and then kill every single one of them.

A rebel named Viriatus escaped from one of those contemptible ambushes. During eight years of fighting, he kept us in check. He set up his headquarters in a freshly planted olive grove called the Mount of Venus. He defeated our commanders, beginning with Vitellius. Accustomed to the elegance and beauty of the Scipios, no one recognized their successor in that old, fat man. Because they did not recognize him, the Spaniards killed him. Plautius, who followed Vitellius, fled Spain in complete disorder. Right in the middle of summer, he declared, "It's winter," and ran away to hide. But since the seasons were not subject to his commands, Viriatus paid him no attention and occupied the entire country.

At first, his guerrilla tactics, now familiar to all, disconcerted our generals. Used to formal warfare, face-to-face, cohorts lined up, and limiting feinting movements to the logical pattern of flanks, vanguard, and rearguard, we were, at the outset, slow to understand the style of the guerrilla fighter. He would attack by day or night, whether it was hot or cold, whether it was raining or whether the earth was dying of thirst. Sun and darkness were equally useful to him. His troops were lightly armed, his horses swift while ours were slow and weighed down by heavy armor. He was invincible, so we offered Viriatus a generous peace. Fabius Maximus Servilianus declared him our friend, promising land and peace to his followers. But Caepius, the next commander in chief, decided those agreements were unworthy of Rome and Rome's greatness. He started the war again, and one night managed to introduce our spies into Viriatus's camp. The Spanish leader slept fully armed, always ready for combat. The murderers plunged a dagger into the only unprotected spot on his body: his neck. When he was found the next morning, his people thought their chief was still sleeping. But this time Viriatus was only a fully armed corpse.

That's how we conquered rebellious Spain: we killed her leaders and prepared to conquer the last focus of resistance: the tenacious, stubborn, and, for all that, terrible capital of Celtiberia, the proud city of Numantia.

HE knows very well what's going on in Spain. But above all, he knows what's going on in Rome. I don't know if you've taken the trouble to count the number of troops sent over the course of a century to fight in Spain. Between infantry and cavalry, beginning with the command of the two Scipios and ending with that of Fabius Maximus Servilianus, it comes to ninety-three thousand soldiers. A thousand per year. Few ever came back. He knows that. He feels that. He feels and knows Rome's disquiet over the interminable Spanish war: a whole century, enough is enough . . . But the troops keep pouring in. The terrible thing is that now they're fighting a single city, and that one city is eating up as many thousands of soldiers as the entire peninsula once did.

He knows the name of that city.

The reason for the new war was a repeated conflict. Segueda, a Celtiberian city, persuaded a number of smaller towns to rebuild within its urban perimeter, making it larger. The Roman Senate denied the Spaniards the right to found new cities. The Spaniards pointed out that they were not founding anything new, they were simply fortifying something already extant. The arrogant Senate answered that Spanish cities could do nothing—not even what had been agreed to by treaty—if Rome didn't like it.

The Spaniards stubbornly colonized new lands. Quintus Fulvius Nobilior took up positions outside Segueda with thirty thousand men to stop the new settlements. Since the Spaniards hadn't yet finished building their fortifications, they took refuge in Numantia.

Nobilior made camp there, about three miles from the city. The African king Masinissa curried favor with Rome by sending ten elephants and three hundred wild horses to the gates of Numantia. The Celtiberians watched them advance heavily toward the city and panicked when they saw how the feet of the pachyderms flattened everything in their path. But when the invincible herd reached Numantia's walls, a huge stone fell on the head of one of the elephants. The animal went wild, that is, it stopped distinguishing between friend and foe. Spinning around like an obese dervish, the beast became faster in its madness. It shook its tentlike ears and then spread them wide, as if they weren't ears at all but bat wings, as if it wanted to hear its own painful despair better.

The other nine elephants, alarmed by the high-pitched whine of their wounded comrade, all raised their trunks at the same time and let them fall like whips on the Roman infantry. Then they proceeded to trample our fallen soldiers. We were ants under those feet with their old nails —broken, yellow nails like the deepest vein in a mountain and the deepest throb of a jungle. With their trunks twisted and flailing they made our men fly through the air. All of us were their enemies. They turned the field around Numantia into the ancestral territory of their fear and their freedom. He knew then that the two things could be one and the same. He was informed of the disaster with the elephants, and he decided to separate fear from freedom forever. The discipline of law would be the arbiter between the two.

The Romans fled in disorder, pursued by the stampeding pachyderms. The city of Numantia became confident. Nobilior withdrew to the winter quarters of happy memory. Then fell the worst snowstorms in the history of Tarraconian Spain. The trees froze, and the snow drifted down from the mountaintops to the lowest corral, killing the animals. The soldiers couldn't go out to cut down trees for firewood: both soldiers and trees were frozen. Locked in, shivering with cold, the soldiers of Rome finally asked for peace.

Marcus Claudius Marcellus, leader of a great family, reached Numantia with eight thousand foot soldiers and five hundred cavalrymen and found there what the Senate did not want: a readiness to make peace. The elephant incident and the cold had convinced both sides that man had even worse enemies than other men. No, said the Senate, replacing Marcellus with the ruthless Lucius Licinius Lucullus, man must be a wolf to man, his mad elephant, his merciless winter, his bat with sharpened fangs thirsty for the blood that throbs in the throat of humanity.

Lucullus brought him, the young Cornelius Scipio Aemilianus, grandson of the man who conquered Hannibal, to the war against Numantia. Ambitious, nervous, quick-tempered, fearful, Lucullus was the worst commander for the conquest of Iberia. The young Scipio understood that the opportunity had been lost. Numantia wanted peace. Rome wanted peace. The Roman legions were dying of dysentery and cold. The gold Lucullus sought did not exist: there was none in Spain, and the Celtiberians did not value it in any case. Lucullus's cruelty and deception hurt Rome's reputation. He breaks all treaties. He promises a truce and executes whole towns. He disobeys the Senate, a rather easy thing to do given the uncertainty and wavering of that august body, more and more influenced by, on the one hand, an arrogant idea of Rome's dignity, and, on the other, by the growing impatience and grief of the Roman people: when will the Spanish bloodletting end?

Cornelius Scipio Aemilianus seizes the opportunity to reconnoiter the land surrounding Numantia. Quintus Pompeius Aulus, who succeeded the dishonored Lucullus, attempts to change the course of the Douro River, along which come and go Numantia's supplies and men. But the Numantines charge out in numbers no one could have imagined, attack the Roman sappers, and end up cornering the Roman army in its own encampment. Cold, diarrhea, and shame eventually run Pompey out of Spain. His successor, Popillius Laenas, does no better: he reaches a Roman fort surrounded by Numantines who dare to threaten the new commander with death if he doesn't agree to peace. The next commander, Hostilius Mancinus, grants it on terms of equality. Rome becomes indignant. The commander is summoned to a court-martial. But it's the Numantines who capture the Roman general and return him to Rome as a joke. They send him back completely naked. Rome refuses to receive her own general. Put into a boat, he's condemned to drift without lowering his anchor until he disappears in the water. The humiliated commander in turn refuses ever to put on clothes again. He will die as he was born. Damned be Rome, bleeding to death in Spain . . .

The naked Mancinus is followed by Aemilius Lepidus, captured amid the Senate's vacillations: one day he attacks; the next he sues for peace; the next it's We've had enough of this disaster, the people will no longer put up with it; and a day later, Forward until we die.

"Ignoramuses!" Lepidus responds to the senators. They don't even know where Numantia is.

Rome grows tired of Spain. Lepidus is surrounded in

Palencia by the Celtiberians. He's out of food. His animals die of hunger. The tribunes and the centurions use night as an opportunity to escape, leaving the wounded and sick behind. The abandoned soldiers hang on to the tails of the fleeing horses, begging, "Don't abandon us!" At night, running around in circles, the Romans fall to the ground in each other's arms wherever they happen to be. "Don't abandon us!" But Rome is no longer listening. The noise of its war machine deafens all of them; the painful clamor of the people cannot be heard, nor can the screams of the soldiers abandoned while their leaders run away.

Five thousand with Marcellus. Twenty thousand with Lucullus. Thirty thousand with Caecilius Metellus. Thirty-five thousand with Pompeius. Thousands and thousands more with Popillius Laenas, with Mancinus, with Aemilius Lepidus: the casualties of the Spanish campaign fill the cemeteries of Rome. Ships sail away filled with life and return with the only certain fruit of Spain: death. It's Charon's armada. Mothers shriek from the rooftops; sisters march through the streets, rending their garments. The senators are insulted wherever they appear. Rome is weary of Spain: Spain threatens life, order, the very future of Rome.

And Spain is Numantia.

He, Publius Cornelius Scipio Aemilianus is chosen to subdue Numantia.

YOU are a man with weaknesses and insecurities. You look at yourself in mirrors and do not see what others say they see in you. You are going to die this very year, but your mirrors reflect a young man eighteen years of age, perfectly combed and curled, plucked and perfumed, who every day caresses his neck in order not to find, not even on waking up, the smallest bristle there. You have set yourself the task of being perfect twenty-four hours of each and every day. But your body is nothing but a metaphor for your spirit. From the time you were a child, you have been troubled, even to the point of nightmares, by the separation of soul and body. You live with that division without resolving it totally, you put yourself to sleep in order to believe that both are one and the same thing; but all you have to do is stare into a mirror, knowing that it reflects a lie, in order to know that it isn't true. That reflection is another. And that other is also divided, if not between body and mind then between past and present, appearance and reality. You will soon be sixty-seven. In the mirror you see a boy of eighteen.

You know your own insecurities. What? Could there be any security greater than that of being the grandson of Scipio Africanus, the victorious hero of the Second Punic War, the conqueror of Hannibal? You are his grandson, but only by adoption, and the mirror confirms that. You are someone else. You inherited nothing. In other words, you cannot be sure that through heredity your gifts will come to you naturally, biologically. Your grandfather Scipio Africanus says that to you every day from heaven: You will have to conquer the inheritance of our lineage on your own. The name *Scipio* is still not yours by right. You will have to earn it. You will have to emulate our virtues, be worthy of them. And to be worthy of the Scipios means as well to be worthy of Rome. In any case, simply by being a citizen of the capital of the world you would already have that obligation.

You see your image as an eighteen-year-old in the mirror your fifty-seven-year-old hand is holding, and you admit that everything, not only the stain of adoption, conspires against your obligation to be great. You're apathetic. You learn with difficulty. It's true that your adoptive family has subjected you to the rigors of the best patrician education, which is Greek. You have studied rhetoric, sculpture, and painting. You have learned to hunt, ride, and take care of your dogs. But your inclinations are not toward the disciplines but toward the pleasures. On horseback, in a forest, chasing a wild pig, with the dogs bringing up the rear, you are a happy boy. You add the pleasure of the other bodies to your own. That of the captured animal, whose cadaver you revive by embracing it. The cold nose, the warm spittle, the melancholy eye of a hound are your body reflected in another body that never thinks of the soul. Does a dog have a memory? Does a dog pass sleepless nights thinking about the divorce of its body from its soul? You pat the neck of your lead dog. It throbs in peace with itself. It is a single thing. You are two. You touch your neck. It has no bristles that would make it ugly, either at dawn or at nightfall. What you do have is a fear of uncertainty. Where does your soul begin, where does your body end? In the tremor of your body, the union of your mind and your guts? You exile the life of your flesh to south of your neck. But your head is left empty, divorced.

Son of consuls and censors, your true father, Lucius Aemilius Paulus, divorced your mother, Papiria, two months after your birth, as if you were the cause of the divorce. Abandoned, you and your brother, you were both adopted—by different families. How lucky you were to enter the clan of the Scipios, to inherit the fame of the conquerors of Hannibal and Perseus. Secretly unlucky, as your inheritance divided your soul from your body even more. Will you someday learn to whom you owe your spirit, to whom your flesh? You will deliver flesh to play, hunting, galloping, indiscriminate sexual love, the company of dogs that do not suffer as you do . . .

A Greek prisoner is delivered to your house, Polybius

of Megalopolis, once leader of the Achaean League, the last effort for the independence of his nation. Your family chose him as a slave because they wanted to read his books. That's how Polybius earned the protection of the Scipios. At first you avoided his company. He spent his time in the library, you in the stables. The tension between the two of you began to grow. He was fifteen years older than you but still young and goaded by the memory of his military experience in Greece. You laughed at him: bookworm, effeminate, owner of his head only, not his body. You didn't need him. In those days you wanted to break a wild black stallion which had come from Africa along with other presents from Prince Jugurtha, nephew of Masinissa, ally of Rome and your family since the wars against Hannibal. What happened was foreseeable. The horse threw you. Polybius mounted and broke him. On the librarian's bare chest you saw the scars left by Roman lances. Polybius's chest was the map of his homeland.

"I will teach you to speak and comport yourself so you will be worthy of your ancestors."

That is what this man, to whom you owe everything, said to you. In him, matter and thought, Greece and Rome, were united. He was not your lover, only your teacher, your mentor, your father. He calmed your anguish about the divided world, which had been the legacy of your childhood and the succubus of your nights. The sentiment your animal strength was already expressing, the power of your body, he reconciled, harmonized, infused with thought and reason: To honor Rome. To serve her. To obtain for your nation glory, fame, and military triumph.

But Rome had no books, only sentiments. Her literature did not exist; it was only rhetoric. The urns of triumph had to be filled, like the cask of the body, with the wine of thought and with poetry. Polybius taught you to think and speak like a Greek in order to act like a Roman. Hand in hand with him, you visited the Garden of Epicurus, Zeno's stoa, Aristotle's Lyceum, and Plato's Academy. In the garden you learned to think and speak pleasure; in the lyceum you learned to moderate pleasure; in the stoa you discovered you were imperfect, although perfectible through virtue; and in the academy you learned to question everything. For example, though Polybius thought the logic of history was the unity of the world through Rome, thanks to the support that Fortune gave your country, he would instantly doubt his own assertion. History, he would say, has not only logic but meaning, and meaning consists in teaching us to withstand integrally the vicissitudes of Fortune by reminding us of the disasters of others. You will recall that lesson for your own campaigns. Your pride in what you are learning and in the person teaching it to you leads you one day to ask Polybius: "What shall we name our school?"

He answers that it will not be a school but a circle: the Scipionic Circle. You two will do important things, especially the translation of Greek thought into Latin terminology and the attempt to achieve poetry through public speech. Oratory would be the Roman school of virtue and action, which would be inseparable. Polybius and you spoke as well of the events of the day. The growth of the city of Rome. The arrival of slaves from conquered provinces to till the soil and the subsequent migration of peasants to the city, which congested it. The growth of luxury and financial manipulations. From Greece came knowledge but also the urge to live luxuriously. Many young men, Polybius would say, thought that being like Greeks was a matter of dissipating their energies in love affairs with other young men, courtesans, or in music and banqueting. A single example will suffice to show to what level of degradation

Roman youth had fallen: it cost more to pay for the favors of a male prostitute than it did to buy a parcel of farmland, and if the daily wage of a peasant was thirty drachmas, a pot of pickled fish cost three hundred.

They talked about scandals, couples separating, illicit affairs, but also about the continuity of the family as an institution and their admiration for the matron Cornelia, daughter of your grandfather Scipio Africanus and mother of the Gracchi, your cousins. "May we see your jewels, madam?" "My jewels are my sons, sir." Weren't they both a bit strange, these impatient, rebellious young brothers? Didn't they talk about equality? Can there be equality if there is no immortality? Is it only death that makes us equal? No, immortality itself can be selective: only select spirits rise to the celestial domain. Does that idea disgust you? Don't you think at least that fame confers immortality and that, therefore, fame is always rather badly distributed? Do you accept fame but demand equality as well? Polybius suggests an intermediate route to you: Serve your nation well, use language, the gods' gift to men, well, and you will have served both fraternity and glory.

They talk about the happy movement away from the Etruscan architectonic grotesquerie to the simplicity of the Hellenistic line. Various new basilicas have been built to speed the flow of the growing legal matters of the republic. On the other hand, there is a complete absence of theaters, a problem often brought up by the young author Terence, a member of your circle. Terence talks about his fear of playing his dramas to vulgar and noisy audiences. Polybius smiles and insists that fame is the thing worst distributed in the world. He amiably accuses you of being too modest. You and he and the young Terence know that you wrote some of the most famous works by the young playwright, who died at the age of thirty-six—*The Women of Andros*, for example, and *The Brothers*, comedies of manners whose permissive morality and urbane wit could offend more rigorous souls. Is that why you preferred that Terence sign them? Who in these cases is the debtor, who the creditor? You can dream that your dramatic ideas—a school to educate husbands; a rogue who fools his master but saves him from himself—will have long life and fortune . . .

But Polybius tells you that only a boy like the one the Greek found when he came, a captive, to Rome could combine the frivolity of drawing-room comedy and bedroom farce natural to his world with the formal and rhetorical perfection he knew how to distill from Greek teachings. Could a man like you—sensual first, intellectual thereafter—become a great man in war? The world will know you as a military leader. But the world separates you, divides you from yourself. Did you want to be only one thing? A privileged young man first, a glorious warrior immediately after, but one single thing, the one the consequence of the other?

All these questions arose from the company in the courtyard of your wealthy mansion in Rome: the circle of Scipio Aemilianus, where the cult of language would be a major factor in the creation of a Latin literary tradition. Properly speaking, there was no Roman literature until you surrounded yourself with people like Terence and Polybius, Lucilius the satirist and Panaetius, the Greek stoic. Until then, literature had been a minor affair, the work of slaves and freedmen. With you and your circle it became a concern for statesmen, warriors, aristocrats . . .

What shall we call our school?

The only answer Polybius of Megalopolis gives is some seeds he hands to you, requesting that the two of you should plant them in the center of the patio. "What are they?"

"Seeds from a distant tree, Oriental, strange, named from an Arab word, *narandj*. A friend brought them to me from Syria." "What is this tree like?" "It can be tall, with wide, perennial, shiny leaves." "Does it have flowers?" "Few are as fragrant." "And fruit?" "Delicious fruit: its skin is attractive, wrinkled, but as smooth as oil. Its flesh is sweet and juicy." "So we can name this patio of our conversations, this circle, not this school: the Orange Tree?" "Wait, young Scipio, this tree will not bear fruit for six years."

Time enough for you to become quaestor, a volunteer for Spain (where no one wanted to go with the unfortunate General Lucullus), and finally, at the age of thirty-nine, conqueror and destroyer of Rome's nemesis, the once proud Carthage, as if you were reliving the destiny of your grandfather Scipio Africanus, conqueror of Hannibal at Zama fifty-six years earlier. You subjugated the city, razed it, and burned it. They say you wept when you saw Hannibal's former capital city, now reduced to a center of commerce devoid of political power, disappear from the map.

What could be more natural than that the victory over Numantia be entrusted to you, the most virtuous and wise, the most valiant of Romans?

I reach Spain knowing a few things. This is what I've learned: the Spaniards are brave but savage. They don't bathe, they don't know how to eat, they sleep standing, like horses. But for that reason they know how to put up a stiff resistance. We've got to break down that resistance. No half measures. To their hardest resistance I've got to oppose something that's even harder.

I know they're brave, but only individually. They don't know how to organize themselves as we do. I must fear their individual courage and disregard them as a collective danger. I must be on guard against the organization of their disorganization, the genius of their anarchy. They call it guerrilla warfare. They use it to give impetus to their individual courage and imagination. Attacks that don't entail risk carried out day or night, in the heat or the cold, in sunlight or rain. They are chameleons, masters of imitation; they take on the color of the earth and the season. They move swiftly, without armor or saddles. I must hem them in where they can't move. I must besiege them to take away their mobility and turn their will to be heroic into a will to resist within a circumscribed space. Let's just see if it's true that all they need is a tiny corner where they can take a stand to reconquer everything.

I know all their tricks. They've been using them against us for a century. What tricks do I have that they don't know?

I must surprise the Spaniards. But I must not offend the Romans. We've wasted one hundred thousand men in a hundred years of war against Spain. We've wasted the tears of a hundred thousand Roman mothers and sisters. I will not bring any more men to Spain. I've boasted about leaving Rome without a single foot soldier or cavalryman. Everyone remembers the triumphant departures of twenty generals, from Marcellus to Lepidus. But they also remember their humiliating homecomings. I will depart modestly in order to return triumphantly.

I accept volunteers from our cities who come out of friendship. In effect, I'm creating a squadron of friends so they will accompany me. They are friends of great distinction. First among them, my teacher Polybius: he has become the most excellent of historians, living proof of how Rome embraces and assimilates the other nations with shores on Mare Nostrum. How she gives them the opportunity we also want to extend to Spain and its stubborn fanatics of independence. For that reason, Polybius commands the cohort made up of my friends. But there are also other friends of rank gathered around the orange tree in my patio in Rome. Accompanying us are the chroniclers Rutilius Rufus and Sempronius Aselion: so there will be no version of any event whatsoever that dies of squalid objectivity. Chronicles from now on will require the prophecy of memory, the affective quality of fiction, and the style of representation that are the soul of history. To that end, the poet Lucilius is with us, because poetry is the light that reveals the relationship existing among all things and connecting them. Rhetoric creates history, but literature saves it from oblivion. And sometimes, literature makes history eternal.

From our encampment, I look over the stadia that separate us from Numantia. My friends don't have to tell me that, before a single javelin is thrown against the capital of the Celtiberians, I must hurl a thousand darts of discipline against the army of Rome in Spain. My first battle has to be against my own army.

First I expel the prostitutes, pimps, homosexuals, and fortune-tellers: there were more omen readers and purveyors of vice than there were soldiers. That army of murky pleasures was ejected from the Roman encampment to the mute shock of the troops, who needed them to raise their morale. Now I will give them a different morale, one that comes from victory. We've had enough of standing face-to-face with the Numantines, each side fooling the other, with no decisive moves made by them or us.

I order my soldiers to sell their carriages and horses, putting them on notice: "You are going nowhere except forward. And Numantia is only a few steps from here. If you die, you won't need carts, only the benevolence of the vultures. If you triumph, I myself will carry you in a sedan chair."

I had twenty thousand razors and tweezers confiscated from the troops. I started wearing a two- or three-day beard to give an example of roughness, and in doing so I renounced one of my most sensual habits, one I'd practiced since the age of twenty: keeping my neck clean-shaven. Here we would all let our beards grow until Numantia fell. I banned mirrors.

I threw out the masseurs, who went their way giggling nervously, on the lookout for new bodies. I informed the soldiers that they would no longer need massages to reduce their obesity because from now on we would be eating only roast meat and that no one would be allowed to have more tableware than a copper pot and a plate.

I forbade the use of beds, and I myself set an example by sleeping on common straw.

I arranged things so that each man would bathe himself without the help of whores, masseurs, or orderlies. Only mules, who have no hands, need other hands to wash them.

I ordered daily exercise beginning at dawn for each and every soldier. I urged them on with switches. I used them to discipline those who were Roman citizens. Those who weren't I ordered to be beaten with rods. But they would all be whipped, whether they deserved it or not, as part of my plan to harden these troops that I had found flaccid, milky, and sleepy.

The daily marches were carried out in perfect formation, and what was previously carried by mules was now carried by the men.

But nothing disciplined them as well or prepared them as well for the long siege to come than my decision to fortify new encampments every day and then have them destroyed the next. First there were expressions of astonishment, instantly followed by disillusion. Then came incipient apathy, which was held in check by the exhausting repetition of the same useless work. All of that told me I'd achieved what I wanted: to temper them against the repeated failure that awaited us before we won our victory.

I organized a geometry of the useless, a physiology of the absurd. Every morning, my men (they were beginning to earn my affection) would dig deep trenches only to fill them up again in the afternoon. They would then immediately march back to our encampment, dragging their feet and grumbling to themselves, first against me and then against their own uselessness. A good soldier should see his first enemy in himself.

Every day they raised high palisades out on the plains: they defended us against nothing and offended no one. We all knew that. The waste was exemplary. The gratuitous acts were perfect in their consummate disinterest. In war, it's essential to be ready at all times. A soldier is like unclaimed property.

All the neighboring territories from which Numantia received provisions I sacked, destroyed, and then occupied. The brave young men of another Iberian city named Lutia rushed to the aid of their brothers in Numantia. Their courage contrasted with the apathy endemic among our troops. I captured four hundred young men from Lutia, and I ordered the hands of each and every one cut off.

I built seven forts around the city. These I did not order destroyed the next day. When my troops realized that, they cheered me. My acts of discipline had not been, ultimately, gratuitous. The fact is that nothing is gratuitous if it is backed by power. I then gratified the melancholy of my supporters. Their efforts were no longer useless. They never had been. What seemed capricious had merely been an exercise in how to adapt to the possibility of failure. We cannot act unless we have the horizon of failure in mind. Nothing can guarantee constant success to anyone. Actually, failure is the rule, success the exception that confirms it . . . It's a sad nation that thinks it deserves the felicity of success. I learned Polybius's lesson.

I divided the army into seven parts and put a commander in charge of each division. I warned all of them not to abandon their position without prior orders. I would punish withdrawal with death.

The first objective of the forts was to keep anyone from ever leaving Numantia. All exits would be marked by day with a red flag on the tip of a lance. At night, fires would be used. That way everyone would be aware of the danger and we would all close ranks to keep even a single Numantine from leaving.

The first time I was inside Numantia, during the campaign of the unfortunate Lucullus, I noted that its inhabitants used the Douro River to bring in provisions and men. The Numantines were skillful at swimming underwater without being seen and knew how to use light skiffs propelled by sails filled with strong winds.

It was impossible to build a bridge between the two shores. The Douro was too wide, too swift. I gave up on the bridge. Instead, I ordered two towers built on opposite sides of the river. And from each tower I ordered large tree trunks tied over the river, connected to the structures by thick but loose ropes. I covered those trunks with knife blades and lance heads, turning them into wooden hedgehogs. They were untouchable: any hand would avoid contact with that prickly, razor-sharp device. The spiny trunks were in constant movement because of the force of the current. It was impossible to go over, under, or around them.

Let no one be able to leave or enter, no one, let no one know what goes on inside or outside Numantia. (Not even me?)

I finished off my plan by surrounding the city with ditches and dirt walls. That boundary wrapped tightly around the perimeter of the city, which measured twenty-four stadia.

It was then I got the idea that decided Numantia's fate. Around the city walls, I left open a free space that duplicated the area of the city and its perimeter. In turn, I enclosed that second field with walls eight feet wide and ten feet tall.

That way I established a possible battlefield in which the two armies, if in fact they met, would fight a war itself surrounded this time by the second series of towers and trenches. That is, there were now two Numantias: the walled city of the Celtiberians and the second city, the barren space that duplicated the city, surrounded by my own fortifications.

It was only then that I set up the siege machinery, the catapults, the ranks of archers and slingers, the mountains of darts, and javelins on the parapets.

Then the nephew of King Masinissa, Jugurtha, joined us, bringing that obsessive African contribution: ten elephants. I thanked him for the gesture, but I was afraid of a repetition of the disaster that befell Hasdrubal in his battle against my grandfather, the first Scipio. I invented other places, also hypothetical ones, to which he could take his pachyderms to put some fear into the Spanish people, who were potentially rebellious. For Jugurtha and his elephants, I invented thickets, slag heaps, fields enclosed by wire, all in the land of Arecans, Carpethians, and Pelendons. I think he's still looking for them. They say elephants never forget, but first they have to remember something. Lost in Spain, Jugurtha's nine elephants must still be wandering around, gigantic nomads in search of invisible fortresses and fields of mirage. So that I wouldn't seem discourteous, I kept one elephant for myself, to hold in reserve opposite Numantia.

(Perhaps it was because of that fantastic joke that Jugurtha went back to Africa in a fury and rebelled against Rome, trying to liberate his native Numidia from "Roman political corruption." But that's another story.)

For the moment, from the top of the parapet, surrounded by archers and slingers, with the elephants at my back and the Roman army deployed around the seven towers that surrounded Numantia, I felt satisfied. With me were Polybius the historian, the chroniclers, Lucilius the poet, the engineers and sappers, five hundred friends. I myself was dressed not as a Roman warrior and patrician but as an ordinary Iberian commander, with a woolen cloak—the *sagum,* a simple black cape—over my shoulders to express my grief about Rome's previous disasters at Numantia. I also ordered the troops to wear black mantles. May our ignominy end here. We shall purge the mourning of our defeats.

Quickly, in the final moment of the preparations, all these signs came together in me, offering me a double vision of the world. What had I done here? Only in the minute before the start of the siege, in the meridian of my mind, did I realize what it was. Before my eyes sprawled Numantia, the unconquered city. Around Numantia, I had constructed a purely spatial double of Numantia, the reproduction of its perimeter, a new space that corresponded precisely to that of its model. Now I was seeing, in the duplicated area, the empty phantom of the city devoid of time. In this divided Numantia, which was the city's soul, which its body?

My old anguish took control of me. Was the empty space the invisible spirit of Numantia? Was the verifiable city its material body? Or was it just the other way around? The real city a mirage, and only real, corporeal, the space invented to make room for another, identical city?

At that climactic moment, overwhelmed by my own thoughts, I tried to tear off my black tunic and offer my own naked body in sacrifice to Rome and Numantia, to the lost battles of the past and to the virtual battles, lost or won, of the future . . .

I closed my eyes to stop the duplication of Numantia, my creation, from becoming a permanent, insufferable, mortal division between the body and the soul of Cornelius Scipio Aemilianus, the abandoned son and the adopted son, the man of action and the aesthete, apathetic during his youth and energetic in maturity: Scipio, I, the materialist who loved concrete things, and Scipio, also myself, who was the patron of the most spiritual intellectual circle in the republic . . . The lover of war. The husband of the word.

Why wasn't I one single thing, happy or unhappy, but indivisible: cherished son, epicurean, and warrior; or stepson, stoic, and aesthete?

The knives hung in the river were cutting me cruelly, finely, while I realized that I'd come here not to besiege Numantia but to besiege myself; not to conquer Numantia but to duplicate it. I reproduced my own self; I lay siege to myself.

I cleared away the suffocation in my lungs, the blindness in my eyes, the choking in my throat, and the whir of prophetic birds smashing against my eardrums, as the eagles smashed against the mountains during the winter campaign of my grandfather Scipio. I also smelled the stench of all the corpses from all the wars. I imagined in that moment the destiny of Numantia and asked why I was being forced, at the end of this chapter in our history, to do all these things. I knew all the tricks of the Iberians; they knew all the tactics of the Romans. Neither side could surprise the other. Political gambits had been used up. I was left with no other arms than discipline—first—and death—second.

I already knew all that. I merely wanted to disguise destiny with beauty. Beauty would be the final surprise of an exhausted politics and an exhausted war. I arranged everything (now I realized it) so that above the blood and stone, above the soul and the body, would ultimately float an aura of beauty, despite death. The wood bristling with knives. The army dressed in mourning. Red flags by day. White fires by night. The dark feathers of dead eagles studding the snow. And Numantia duplicated. Numantia represented. Numantia become an epic poem, acting itself out thanks to the spaces and things that I one day put at the disposal of history.

How to transform representation into history and history into representation?

I see my own answer. Numantia empty represents Numantia inhabited. And vice versa. My two halves, body and soul, don't know if they should separate forever or unite in a warm embrace of reconciliation. In anguish I seek a symbol which would allow me to join my two halves. The gust of time carries the exact moment far from me. I've had to fight against the fatal, exhausted history that preceded me. I've tried to turn my experience into destiny. The gods will not forgive me that. I've wanted to usurp their functions just as I usurp Numantia's duplicated image.

I give the order to attack. I, Cornelius Scipio Aemilianus, also duplicated, representing myself thanks to the spaces and things I've placed at the disposal of history: I give the order to attack—that, at least, is implacable, undivided. Thus I disguise my own divided self.

THEY thought that if they left Numantia, if they came out to fight, they would never return. The women would be raped by the Romans, the children enslaved, and the houses destroyed by foreign hands. Hadn't this same general burned great Carthage to the ground? Better to resist. Better to die. Let the siege triumph. They themselves will give the triumph to Scipio. Without them, without their resistance, the siege would be a stage: a charade against nothing. Thanks to them, Scipio Aemilianus will find his own destiny. He will be the conqueror of Numantia. They are the allies of Fortune: they direct it with their tears, their hunger, their death. They, the men of Numantia.

YOU know how this story ended, and I, Polybius, who was there, am telling it now, because I never wrote it down, out of respect for the suffering of my friend General Cornelius Scipio Aemilianus. I wrote the history of the Punic Wars and of Roman expansion in the Mediterranean. But I abstained from narrating what I saw in Numantia in the company of my disciple and friend, the young Scipio. I led posterity to believe I'd lost my papers. I am only giving an account of the young Scipio to exalt his virtues and our friendship: he was generous, honest, disciplined, and worthy of his ancestors.

I told nothing about Numantia because the truth is that once the city had been besieged and as the Numantines became more and more isolated because of the severity of the siege imposed by Scipio, we would only find out what happened within the walls when it was all over. However, I did take it upon myself to attempt to imagine what was happening in order to tell it, as fiction, to my friend, but also my disciple, General Scipio. If I hadn't, I think he would have gone insane.

No one left Numantia anymore, except one brave man who one day dared to step onto that territory created by Scipio. A double, forbidden space is what it was, for the battle that never took place. On a foggy night, this Retrogenes, the bravest of the Numantines, crossed the prohibited space accompanied by twelve men and a folding ladder. They killed our guards and went off to ask for help from the other Iberian cities. None gave any. They were all afraid of Scipio. The eight hundred hands chopped off in Lutia were still not dust. The stumps of four hundred boys had still not healed. Retrogenes, punctilious in matters of honor, returned to give the news of his failure to Numantia. Of course he did not cross the imaginary perimeter of the city again. He was the only Numantine to die in the space of the invisible battle.

Later, a Numantine ambassador emerged to ask for peace.

"We have done nothing wrong," he said to Scipio. "We are only fighting for the freedom of our homeland."

Scipio demanded unconditional surrender: the Numantines would have to give up their city.

"That's not peace; it's humiliation," responded the ambassador. "We will not give you the right to enter our city so you can destroy us and take our women."

I say to the general: "The granaries must be empty. There is no bread, no flocks, not even food for animals. What will they eat?"

The siege of Numantia lasts eight months.

The first Numantines give up. They emerge from behind the walls like ghosts. For the first time, the only elephant Jugurtha left behind lifts his trunk and bellows horribly. But the dogs also bark, the horses whinny, and the ducks quack. They recognize other animals. Animals with long hair hanging to their waist, with skin eaten up by sickness. Many on all fours. Scipio refuses to fight with animals. He points to the sky: two eagles are locked in combat, turning martial circles. A fetid stench. Long fingernails clotted with excrement. Scipio chooses fifty Numantines to bring to his triumph in Rome. He sells the rest. He reduces the city to rubble.

"Great calamities," I tell him, "are the foundation for great glory."

"Shit," he says.

WE, the women of Numantia, always knew our men were willing to die for us and our children. But we did not know exactly how willing we were to die for them. The siege lasted eight months. Soon our grain, meat, and wine were all used up. We began licking boiled leather, then eating it. From there, we went on to the bodies of those who'd died a natural death. We vomited: the sick flesh made us nauseous. We are afraid: when will we begin to eat the weakest among us? An old man gives us a lesson. He commits suicide in the main square so we can eat him without having to kill him. But his flesh is tough, stringy, useless. The children need milk. That's the only thing we don't lack: our breasts are prodigal. But if we women don't eat, soon there will be no milk for the children. At night we listen to the creaking of our own bones, which are beginning to crumble from within, as if their burial ground were our own flesh. There are no mirrors in Numantia. But we see our faces in those of the others. They are corroded faces, devoured by cold and scurvy. As if time moved forward by devouring us, consuming bit by bit our gums, our teeth, our eyebrows, and our eyelids. Everything is falling away from us. What do we have left? A strange tree in the center of the plaza. A long time ago, a repentant traveler, Genoese to be precise, passed by here and made a big show of planting some seeds in the center of the main square. He said time was slow and that distances in the world we were living in were great. It was necessary to plant and to wait for the tree to grow and give its fruit in five years. He told us not to worry about the cold. The best thing that could happen to this tree was for it to go through a cold spell from time to time. It was a tree that slept during the winter. The cold doesn't hurt it. It flowers and bears fruit in spring. Its annual growth ends in autumn and it goes back to sleep during the winter. What is its fruit like? Identical to the sun: the color of the sun, round as the sun . . . The memory of those words did not console us. This was the last winter before the tree, after five others had died, was to bear fruit. Would we last until spring? We had no way of knowing. Time, we women say, has become visible in Numantia. Its ravages are visible in our mangy skin, our calluses, and the mushrooms of our sexes. We uselessly scratch our anuses to find out if there remains a crust of excrement to eat. Snot, the sand in our eyes. Everything is useful. The earth does not abandon us. We are planted in it. Our eyes tell us our granaries are exhausted. Our noses have stopped smelling bread; they've forgotten it. Our hands no longer touch grass, our ears no longer hear the noise of cattle. And the tree planted by the Genoese will only bear its round, golden fruit next summer. But the soles of our feet tell us that the earth has not abandoned us. The world has, but the earth hasn't. We Numantine women make a distinction between the world and the earth. We are eating the men who kill themselves for our sake, so we can eat them. The men who remain alive howl with grief: for the death of their brothers, for the horror of our hunger. We speak to them. When we do, we remember we have not lost language. Earth and language. They sustain us. The bodies we devour together with our children are earth and language transformed. The men don't understand that. They are ready to die for us and our children, but they think we are all dying and that nothing will be left alive. We disagree. We see the world disappear but not the earth, not language. We, men and women, weep for the extinction of our city. But we celebrate the enduring life of a clay pot, a metal cup, a funeral mask. The metallic head of a sheep, a stone bull: these are the only cattle left to us. Empty urns, barrels of dust: this is the bread and wine we leave behind. We women weep for the extinction of the city. We accept that the world dies. But we also hope that time will triumph over death thanks to wind, light, and the enduring seasons. We will not see the fruit of this tree. But the light, the seasons, and the wind will. The world dies. The earth undergoes transformations. Why? Because we say it does. Because we have not lost language. We bequeath it to the light, the wind, and the seasons. The world revealed us. The earth hid us. We return to the earth. We are disappearing from the world. We are returning to the earth. From there we shall come forth to haunt.

SHE saw the last men leave Numantia: mute, bearded, filthy. She saw the last horrified women, the last emaciated children. They gave up because they lost language. They forgot how to speak; they gave up. She, with her dead child in her arms, approached the sterile tree buried in the depth of winter. They awaited the promise of the fruit in vain. Damned tree, sterile fruit. She spreads her legs and screams with her child in her arms. She lets the fertile blood of her vagina, the fruit of her womb, the moist and red mass of her menstruation fall onto the sterile scrub.

YOU ask yourself if everything in the universe has an exact double. It's possible. But now you know that even if it is true, it's dangerous. As a young man, you walked through the stoa and the garden, the Academy and the Lyceum. But you always knew that through a crack in all those doors and windows in the Greek *paideia* our minds escape us when we are most certain we possess them. Your military life was as true and direct as an arrow. Your spiritual life proved to be tortuous and unforeseeable. Is there a god that synchronizes the two? Are the connections between the body and the mind only apparent—an illusion created by the gods to console us? Is reality only the sum total of physical events—I ride a horse, I attack a city, I love a woman? Are mental events only and always consequences of those material acts? Do we fool ourselves by thinking that it's the other way around only because, occasionally, the mental state precedes the physical event for an instant, when in reality the physical event has already taken place?

Polybius sees you suffer because you can't resolve this dilemma. He suggests to you that centuries will pass without anyone's resolving it. Men will torment themselves trying to separate, conciliate, or suppress the two extremes of their cruel split: this is my body, this is my spirit. Are we pure physical event? Are we pure mental event? Are both one and the same thing? At Numantia, Scipio presented himself as an integral man, at peace with himself. A Roman *cives*. But something betrayed him. A game, a perversity, a character trait, an imagination: he duplicated Numantia in order, perhaps, to avoid duplicating himself.

To be the complete, decisive, efficient general he showed himself to be.

You realize that Polybius is imagining what's happening within the besieged city in order, perversely, to tell it to you. Perversely, but also charitably. The writer's version, it goes without saying, is the one that passed into history. He was very clever. He established once and for all, at the very dawn of Roman historiography, that texts should never be quoted verbatim but interpreted. History is invention. Facts are imagined. Without fiction, neither you, Scipio, nor you, other readers, would ever know what took place inside Numantia. Unsatisfied imagination is dangerous and terrible. It leads directly to evil. We only hurt others when we're incapable of imagining them. Which is why you wept one day before a Carthage in flames. Polybius tried to save you by giving you the imagination of your victory. Believe it. That is what happened. You've just read it. Your victims were flesh and blood. You didn't fight against doubles, the phantoms of Numantia.

You failed.

In the same way you duplicated the city, you duplicated yourself.

You lived five years more, but you were never the poet you wanted to be nor the warrior you were. Did something diminish you? Did you lose forever the unity of your body and your spirit before the two Numantias? In one of them, a desolate space, an invisible time, nothing happened. On the other hand, within the city, there took place sacrifice, madness, and death. Ultimately, the second space was useful only to be crossed by the mute, savage survivors of Numantia. The procession of conquered defenders, transformed into animals. It must be terrible to see an abstention of yours converted into degradation and death. Thus, Cornelius Scipio Aemilianus, your presence before Numantia was in fact an absence. You never fought. You did nothing. And when Numantia fell, your saw the atrocious presence of what was an absence.

You quite properly used yourself up, conqueror of Carthage and Numantia. Quite properly, you never again lived in peace.

I wonder, as I remember the heroic enterprise of Numantia, what the perimeter I invented for the city without Numantia, its double facing it, might have been. A barnyard, a meadow, a farm—all or any of them peaceful and ordinary? Why do we choose one place and give it a name in history? I withdraw, conquered by my triumph. I can't bear its weight. I look for new avenues for my energy. In the campaigns against Carthage and Numantia, I met many simple soldiers who held rather precarious title to the land they occupied. They weren't large landowners; but the radical agrarian reform promoted by my cousins, the turbulent Gracchi, stripped bare both the owners of latifundia and small settlers without title to their land. I became their defender. I made lots of enemies, more invisible than the ghost of Numantia. But my external activity, once again, did not calm my own internal disorder.

I spend hours at a time sitting on my throne facing the orange tree in my courtyard in Rome. It's about to bear fruit, and I want to be the first to see it flower. I shall make the orange tree my interlocutor during these afternoon hours. I've given up shaving; I can only think if I caress my neck, which is covered with bristles. The problem of duality obsesses me. I invent a theory of geometric duality. If it is true that any two lines define a point at their intersection and that any two points determine a line, it follows that when all points touch an ellipse they exhaust themselves. Their unity concentrates and immediately requires the protection of a double to shield and prolong that unity. From this it follows that all unity, once attained, requires a duality in order to prolong itself, to maintain itself.

I think I've resolved the problem of Numantia, and, as the afternoon declines and I feel cold, I wrap myself in my black Spanish cape, the one I used facing the besieged city. I go into my bedroom. I shut the curtains, but no sooner do I lie down in my bed than the noise of mice distracts me. How do I fight them? That is not my problem. Let me not be distracted or annoyed by mice hunts. What I wonder is if everything in the universe has an exact double. It's possible. But now I know that even if that's true, it is also dangerous. Twins staring each other in the eye would annihilate themselves without raising a finger. The unleashing of two identical powers would destroy both. That is the basic law of physics. In Numantia, I gave the inevitable doubles, generated by the geometric encounter between my forces and those of Numantia, the opportunity to see each other for only a moment in history. The cleverness of my strategy consisted in making the first Numantia believe that when she looked outside her walls she would see a second Numantia. The first Numantia was ready to lose her life in the clash with the second Numantia. But since that second city did not exist, she waited in vain and killed herself. My strategy consisted in transforming Numantia into her own enemy.

I tell myself that my time was that of a slow haste. There is, perhaps, no better rule for a field commander. I acted in the instant when my strength, by embodying Numantia's double, destroyed her but not me. I found the exact point

on the earth where a force, disguised as Nothingness, destroyed its opposing force, which was the real double of
an absence traced by my military genius. Thus the two
propositions combined, geometry and physics, in a purely
bellicose action. The *geometric* intersection demanded a
double to maintain unity. But the gravity of *physics* rejects
the presence of two identical forces staring each other in
the eye. I fooled geometry, which is a mental thing, and
physics, which is a material affair. I proved that in any
circumstance in human life NOTHINGNESS IS WHAT
IS POSSIBLE.

I was quite properly received in triumph on my return.
But then there was light. Now the afternoon reaches my
bedroom only with difficulty. Glory, glory to the conqueror
of Carthage and Numantia. Glory twice over. I hear the
noise. Is it the mice? Is it the footsteps of those who received
me in triumph? I hear footsteps. I caress my neck. I remember that as a boy I argued with Polybius and the other
friends of the Scipionic circle about the nature of immortality. How curious: that debate arose because the Gracchi
spoke about equality. Then we asked each other: Can there
be equality if there is no immortality? Does only death
make us equal? "No," argued Polybius, "immortality itself
can be selective. Only select spirits ascend to the heavens
and know God. Does that idea disgust you? Don't you
think at least that fame confers immortality? Do you accept
fame but also demand equality? Serve your country well,
Scipio Aemilianus. Use language well, the gift of the gods
to men. You were born to honor Rome, to guarantee her
power through arms and her moral strength through
language."

Equality, immortality. I hear the footsteps. The curtain
is violently pulled open. I caress the bristles on my neck.

A single, long bristle, cold and hard, enters through my neck, and I think of Spain as I die.

YOU are dreamed. Dead, you have reached the celestial mansion, and there you see yourself again at the age of eighteen, when Polybius arrived with slavery and books at the house of your adoptive family and began to make you worthy of it. You dream of yourself when you were young. You want that to be your image for immortality: an eighteen-year-old boy who is going to attempt to be the perfect combination of statesman and philosopher. God receives you and praises you. He says that your name, first a mere inheritance, is going to be yours by your own right. You will burn and raze Carthage. You will besiege and conquer Numantia.

"Two destructions," you say to God. "Is that to be my monument: death?"

God doesn't answer you, but He does offer you the renewed vision of Numantia. What really took place in the besieged city? Numantia was isolated. Almost no one survived. You again see the survivors leave. Not only did they look like animals, they were animals. They never spoke again. Who knows what they did with their women and children. They no longer want to remember anything. From then on, they communicated only with vultures and wild beasts. They were animals. They never spoke again.

You hear these words that speak to you of the end of language and you quickly return to life. Your face shines, you know at the age of eighteen, young, what you did not know old at the age of fifty-seven, when you died. You ask yourself what shall be the monument to your glory, Cornelius Scipio Aemilianus. Carthage? Numantia? Two names buried in fire and hunger? Two monuments to death? You see once again the ruin of Numantia: storms whip it, the sun burns it, the winter freezes it. Time, the climate, add to its ruin; the elements destroy as they pass, ruining the ruin. And yet, what is it that shines in the heart of Numantia? You can barely make it out. A clay pot, a bronze mask, a stone bull, plant, tree, orange tree . . . Orange tree? Another identical to yours in the center of the city you destroyed? Is it an illusion, have you imagined your own orange tree in the ash-covered center of Numantia?

You open your eyes to see yourself dreamed.

No, you have only said an ancient, unknown, Arabic word: *orange tree*. The survivors left through the walls of Numantia and could no longer speak. By saving themselves, they died. They were animals without language. That was their defeat, their death. And you, Scipio Aemilianus, you don't know, now that you've died, what you already knew when you were a boy filled with hopes about the future of your life. Weren't you going to be the one to reconcile and harmonize the power of your body by giving reasons to the sentiment that translated your animal power: to honor Rome? And how did you intend to do it if not through language? Isn't this your most profound reason for living, young Scipio, old Scipio, dead Scipio? Use language well, the gift of the gods and of men. Reach poetry through public speech. Turn your life into an epic poem. Sing to Numantia, restore it to life with language. That which destroys the material thing constructs the work of art: light, wind, seasons, the passing of time. Save stone from stone and make it into words, Scipio, so that the very thing that eats away the stone—storm, time, sun—confers life—poetry, language, time.

You are dying, but you know at last that you will always be the master of language, which is the foundation of life and death on earth. Burn the earth there, the residence of language and death. For you, on the other hand, the world has died.

HE dreamed himself being dreamed. Cicero dreamed him, the greatest creator in the Latin language, seventy-five years after the mysterious death of Cornelius Scipio Aemilianus, who won for himself the title of his grandfather, Africanus, and added to his dynasty a new title, Numantinus. Cicero honored him by dreaming him. By dreaming himself the day of his death, but also by seeing himself as a boy who dreams about heaven and eternal life. Such was the verbal monument Cicero erected to the man who best incarnated the qualities of the statesman and the philosopher in ancient Rome. Posterity's monument to the ancient hero was to show him from the divine realm the composition of the universe: God made him see stars never seen from earth. Scipio recognized the five concentric spheres that, united, maintain the universe: Saturn, a hungry star; luminous Jupiter; red and terrible Mars; accommodating Venus and Mercury; Moon of reflections. Heaven embracing it all, in the center the Sun like a great orange in flames, and under everything a minuscule sphere and within it an even smaller empire, its scars invisible from on high, its wars and conquests whimpering with a voice of dust, its frontiers wiped out by waves of blood . . .

"What is that noise, so strong and so sweet, that fills my ears?"

Fame. It isn't fame the hero hears from heaven. The universe is very large. There are distant regions of the earth itself where no one has heard the name of Scipio. The floods and conflagrations of the earth—natural, human—set about doing away with any personal glory. Who cares what those yet to be born say about us? Did the millions who preceded us say anything about us? Do you think that noise is fame, glory, war?

"If it isn't," asked the young Scipio, "is it the noise of reincarnation? Can we return to earth one day, transformed? Is Pythagoras right when he asserts that the soul is a fallen divinity, imprisoned in our bodies and condemned to repeat endlessly, circularly, a cycle of reincarnations?"

What ambition men have! God laughed on high. If they have neither glory nor fame, if they don't have immortality, then they want to go through reincarnation. Why aren't they content with living in heaven? Why don't they listen to the celestial music? You have lost the ability to listen. Do you think that the vast movements of the heavens can be accomplished in silence? Men's hearing has atrophied. Too concerned about what is said about them, they've stopped listening to the movement of the heavens. Look up, Scipio Aemilianus: learn now to look and to listen far off and outside yourself so you can finally reach yourself. Abandon glory, fame, and military triumph. Look up. You are rather better than the best you thought you were. YOU ARE GOD. You have what I have. Alert liveliness, sensation and memory, foresight as well, language and the divine power to govern and direct your body, which is your servant, in the same way God directs the universe. Dominate your weak body with the strength of your immortal soul.

And he, Cornelius Scipio Aemilianus, listened then to the music of the spheres.

WE saw the fall of Carthage and the destruction of Numantia. They were glorious visions. But they only postponed our own defeat.

The Two Numantias

• • •

YOU will remember this story. The rest I leave to antiquarians.

Valdemorillo–Formentor, Summer 1992

NOTES

1. Genealogy: The brothers Publius Cornelius Scipio and Gnaeus Cornelius Scipio fought against Hannibal in Spain and perished in the year 212 B.C. With his wife Pomponia, Publius Cornelius had a son, Publius Scipio, called Africanus because he defeated the Carthaginians during the Second Punic War (the battle of Zama, 202 B.C.). With his wife Emilia, Scipio Africanus had four children: Cornelia, Publius Scipio Nasica (consul in 162 B.C.), Lucius Scipio (praetor in 174 B.C.), and Publius Scipio, whose poor health kept him from taking up a political career. However, Publius Scipio adopted the younger son of Lucius Aemilius Paulus and his wife, Papiria, who were divorced shortly after the birth of the child, our protagonist, which took place in 185 or 184 B.C. He entered the Scipio family under the name Publius Cornelius Scipio Aemilianus. His older brother, Quintus Fabius Maximus Aemilianus, was adopted by another family. Scipio Aemilianus captured and destroyed Carthage in 146 B.C. and conquered Numantia in 133 B.C. These two triumphs won him the titles "Africanus" and "Numantinus." Thus there are two Scipio Africanuses: the Elder, the adoptive grandfather, and the Younger. Cornelia, the sister of Scipio's adoptive father, was the mother of the Gracchi, leaders of the social reform movement of the year 133 B.C., which was opposed by their cousin Scipio Aemilianus, who died in 129 B.C. under mysterious circumstances. Rumor had it that he was assassinated by the followers of the Gracchi. Scipio Aemilianus was married to Sempronia, his cousin, the daughter of Cornelia and sister to the Gracchi. Did they have any children?

2. Bibliography: My principal sources regarding the life of Scipio Aemilianus and the siege of Numantia are: Appian, *Iberica*, book six of his *History of Rome*; Polybius, *Histories*; Cicero, "Scipio's Dream," in his *Republic*; and, of course, Miguel de Cervantes's play *The Siege of Numantia*.

THE SCIPIOS

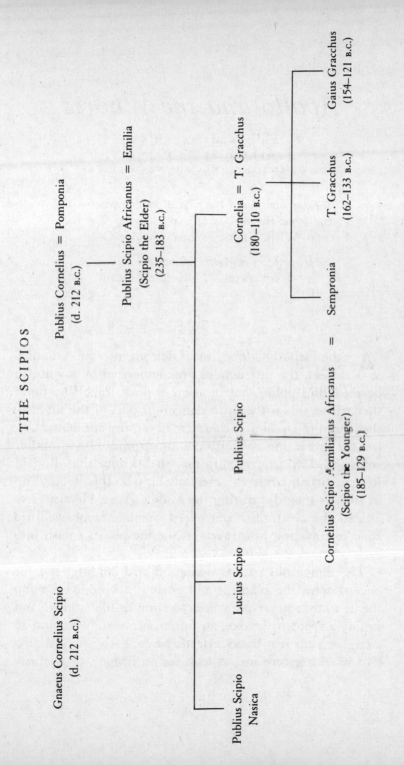

Apollo and the Whores

TO CARLOS PAYÁN AND
FEDERICO REYES HEROLES,
COMPANIONS ON AN INNOCENT TRIP

But one man loved the pilgrim soul in you,
And loved the sorrows of your changing face . . .
—W. B. YEATS, "When You Are Old"

Et le temps m'engloutit minute par minute . . .
—BAUDELAIRE, "Le Goût du Néant"

17:45

As the Delta DC-9 begins its descent into the Acapulco airport, the instructions are announced by a voice so peaceful and polite that it seems hypocritical. Why don't they tell us this is the most dangerous part of the flight—the landing? Up above, there are never any accidents. Unless the increasing congestion ends up multiplying midair collisions. I'm from California, so I know that Ronald Reagan cut off aid to the mentally ill, who then wound up in jails, as they did during the Middle Ages. He also devastated the air traffic controllers' union. Maybe we'll go back to traveling in caravels, while the planes smash into each other in the skies.

The dangerous part is taking off and landing. But for once, I wish the plane would go into a nosedive, giving the lie to that sugar-pie voice caressing us like a glove and urging us not to smoke, to fasten our seat belts, and to straighten our seat backs. All the while, I long for a drama that would restore me, at least for an instant, to celebrity

148

status and shout in every headline in every paper: FAMOUS HOLLYWOOD STAR DIES IN FATAL CRASH OVER ACAPULCO BAY.

Instead, the bay itself, as if it were sorry for me, unable even to laugh at me, flashes its afternoon postcard image up to the plane. The bad thing is that this glory of scattered gold, this cocktail of orange, lemon, and grape is identical to the immutable sunset waiting for me at the Universal set, always prepared to be a sunset, the background to a duel, a serenade, or a final kiss. I prefer a catnap, even if I know the recurring dream I've been having these past few months will return. In it, someone places a mask over my immobile face and a feminine voice whispers into my ear: This is the face of your ideal beauty.

18:30

All planes smell alike. Plastic, disinfectant, metal, stagnant air, reheated food, recycled microbes. Air in a tube. There must be an invisible factory worth millions dedicated to making airplane air, canning it, and selling it to all airlines. But now I'm the first at the locked door of the immobile machine, waiting to escape like an animal from a laboratory squirrel cage with all my baggage in one hand—an airline bag with the few shirts, underwear, sandals, and shaving kit I need, a comfortable airline bag I always carry with me, with two outside pockets where I can carelessly stick a copy of the *Los Angeles Times*, my plane tickets, my passport, and Yeats's poems. The *Times* announces, to the relief of the entire world, the defeat of Bush the wimp in the presidential election; the tickets, roundtrip in first class, LAX-ACA-LAX; the passport, a name, Vincente Valera, born in Dublin, Irish Republic, on September 11, 1937, naturalized U.S. citizen at the age of seven, black hair, bushy brows, five feet ten inches tall, one hundred and fifty pounds, no scars. In case of death, notify Cindy Valera, 1321 Pico Boulevard, Los Angeles, CA. And the underlined poem says:

> *. . . and dream of the soft look*
> *Your eyes had once, and of their shadows deep*

The door opens, and I am the first to receive the blast of blazing air, the contrast with the cold but stagnant air of the plane. The afflicted air of the cabin, an air that seems bereaved. A furnace blast in the face is Acapulco's greeting as I walk down the gangway, an air that burns but is alive, that smells of mangrove, of rotten bananas, of melted tar. Everything the interior of the plane denies, isolates, renders aseptic. But this radical change of temperature, as I instinctively grab the metal handrail on the gangway in order not to trip, brings me another memory I'd like to avoid. My burning hand when I received the Oscar for best actor of the year. My burning hand and the frozen little doll, as if I were being handed a statuette made of ice that would never melt.

Ever since that Oscar presentation, my hand has been afraid of the cold; it seeks heat, touch, a moist, burning, hiding place. So it's only natural I'm here this afternoon, in the tropics, eager for contact with everything that burns.

19:40

As I register in the hotel, I order a boat so I can go out fishing the next morning. The receptionist asks me if I will be sailing it alone, and I answer that I will. "At what time?" "I don't know, sometime after 6:00 a.m. would be fine, the important thing is that I want a ketch or if you don't have that then a small sloop or a yawl." The receptionist is a dark-skinned little man with almost Oriental features. He looks as if he were dusted with coffee, but his high cheekbones shine, and in his slanty eyes there is a touch of doubt about his own mask. Should he be obsequious to the point of being vile or abjectly mocking? His mustache, as fine as the feet of a fly, gives him away. But his white, starched guayabera shirt hides a torso I judge to be strong, muscular, used to swimming. Maybe he's an ex-Quebrada cliff diver. You don't usually associate a man tied to a reception desk with adventures on the high seas. A hidden part of his nature overwhelms him. "Yes," he says mellifluously, "there is a ketch, but its name is *The Two Americas*."

"So what?"

"Well, many North Americans get annoyed."

"It doesn't matter to me what the boat's name is."

"It bothers them to know there is more than one America."

"Just so it doesn't sink." I *tried* to be friendly, smiled.

"You aren't the only Americans, see? All of us on this continent are Americans."

"Okay, just give me my key. You're right."

"The United States of America. That's a joke. You aren't the only states, and you aren't the only Americans."

"If you'd just give me the key, please."

" 'The United States of America' isn't a name; it's a description, a false description . . . a joke."

"The key," I said, grabbing him violently by the shoulders.

"There are two Americas, yours and ours," he stammered. "Would you like us to carry up your bags?"

I picked up my airline bag and smiled.

"Excuse me. I hope you won't tell on me." That was the last thing he said.

"I can't contain myself," I heard him say, like a refrain hanging in the heat of the reception area, as I walked away with the key in one hand and my bag in the other.

20:00

I'm up to my neck in a lighted pool more decked out with gardenias than a funeral parlor. I was tempted to call the desk: Get these gardenias out of the pool. But the idea of having to deal with the little man in the guayabera made me forget about it. Besides, what the hell, the maid who turned down my bed (scattering gardenia petals all over it, of course) stood staring at the illuminated pool and the flowers for quite a while. She hugged the towels against her pink apron, and her stare was so melancholy, so self-absorbed that it would have been a personal betrayal to ask them to take away what certainly delighted her.

"Don't you have flowers in your house?"

She was a limp little Indian girl, a bit lost in the labyrinth of the hotel. She answered me in an Indian language, saying she was sorry. She turned away from me and quickly went to the bathroom to hang the towels. Then I heard how she softly closed the door to the room. By then I was already in the water, my chin leaning on the edge of the pool and the book of poems getting soaked by the little waves my body inevitably made. It upset me to read the continuation of Yeats's poem: "How many loved your moments of glad grace, / And loved your beauty with love false or true." I preferred to look at the nocturnal lights of Acapulco, which so cleverly disguise the double ugliness of this place. The façade of skyscrapers on the beach hides the poverty of the poor neighborhoods. The night hides both, returning everything to the firmament, the stars, and the beginning of the world. Who am I to talk, dreaming every night that someone puts a mask on me and says: This is your ideal beauty. You will never be more handsome than you are tonight. Never again?

20:30

Naked, I got out of the pool and threw myself onto the pink-sheeted bed. I fell asleep, but this time I didn't dream that a woman came over to put a mask on me. My dream, unfortunately, was much more realistic, more biographical. Again and again, I walked up onto a speaker's platform. Like a squirrel in a laboratory cage. A dream can be an endless staircase, nothing more. On the platform, Mister Smiles was waiting for me. Not Faces. Teeth. They smiled at me and congratulated me. They handed me the golden statuette. The Oscar. I don't know what I said. The usual thing. I thanked everyone, from my first girlfriend to my dog. I forgot the pharmacist, the president of my bank, and the guy who sold me a used Porsche without ripping me off. The old German machine is still dominating California freeways, and if I weren't in Acapulco, you'd probably find me searching for impossible answers at 120 m.p.h., heading toward the San Fernando Valley and an accident, physical or sexual. Which is to say, a worthwhile encounter. Instead, I came to Acapulco running away from a dream, and I'm calling the desk to tell them to have a ketch I can sail alone ready for me tomorrow. The receptionist did not exactly inspire my confidence. Did I want fishing tackle? I tell him yes, even if it's not exactly true, just so everything will seem normal. Of course, fishing tackle. Tomorrow at

6:00 a.m. I'm going out fishing. That's why I came. My ketch will be ready at the Yacht Club pier. Its name is *The Two Americas*. Everything should look normal.

22:05

I'm driving a pink jeep along the mountain highway. You can't get lost, the hotel parking lot attendant tells me. There's nothing until you get to the discotheque lights, *you can't miss it*. He doesn't know that the night is much more densely populated than the day, that it's much more visual than the sun, because the night is like a gigantic Cinema-Scope screen on which you can project anything that comes into your mind.

I'm fighting the powerful breathing of the tropics, which at night becomes drunker and crazier as the rest of the world calms down. Apollo and his chariot of light have sunk into the sea. The jeep's motor can't drown out the cicadas, the frogs, the fireflies, or the mosquitoes. I make out other lights on the mountain that aren't electric; they're eyes—emerald, silver, and blood-colored eyes. Foxes, coyotes, solitary animals—like me—who feel the need for a little company—like me.

I accelerate and, thanks to the intermediary aid of my rearview mirror, project onto the screen of my mental night the picture that won me an Oscar, the first prize given by the academy to an American actor in a foreign film. I conquer the darkness with the unforgettable images of Leonello Padovani's last film, in which I had the honor to have the lead. And the extraordinary thing is that the images of the film that I conjure up like something luminous are images of night and fog.

The film is set in northern Italy. Everything happens at

night or on cloudy days. A poor man can't stand his hard-working, good wife any longer. He doesn't know what to do, but he's convinced he should cut his ties with his routine life and expose himself to chance. One winter night, he abandons his wife. But he takes the only thing he really loves in his house, his nine-year-old daughter. He doesn't take clothing or money. Only the girl. But along with her, unintentionally, he brings a past and a habit. The child follows naturally, as if any decision that affects her is neither good nor bad but natural. Especially if it's her father who makes the decision. He wishes she would understand that he's taken her along because he loves her. He doesn't understand that it's possible to love naturally, obediently. For him, love is a matter of will. He confuses the love of the heart with the love of the mind. The girl doesn't. She loves and obeys her father without having to force herself.

For a few days, the two of them wander aimlessly through that landscape of fog and cold, relying on charity but subjected to the father's inability to tell the child why they've run away and why he loves her. What does she think? Will she abandon her father? Or will she go on with him to the end? What is solitude? The absence of company or a shared abandonment? Padovani provides no answers. Each member of the audience has to provide his own.

I felt that for the only time in my life my acting was in the hands of an artist. I felt that the film went along discovering itself at the same time that he, debilitated, suffering, and, ultimately, dying, filmed it. The difference between theater and film is that movies are made in a choppy way, without continuity. Padovani managed to turn that technique into artistic creation. He transformed the obligatory method in filming—the end at the beginning, the beginning at the end—into a means of searching out the picture. Besides, in each pause between scenes, in each take, in each save, and even in each coffee break, he forced me to search out myself. It wasn't just a matter of memorizing lines and saying that tomorrow I've got to do from page such-and-such to this other page. It meant searching myself out as an actor and as a man, and what I discovered is that this is what a character is: someone who *exists* and who *acts* at the same time.

In my hand, I hold the hot hand of the girl who was my audience, free to decide to abandon me or to go on with me.

Then I held the Oscar statuette in my hand, and that was ice cold.

A Short Time Later

I'm dancing by myself surrounded by a thousand persons jamming the floor of this fantastic discotheque, which is floating over Acapulco Bay like one of the hanging gardens of Babylon in one of those extravaganzas that made Cecil B. deMille famous. I never saw anything like it, because European and American discotheques are usually enclosed, surrounded by cement and gasoline. They isolate you completely, but they can also turn into death traps. Here, on the other hand, the discotheque floats over the sea, a glass bubble with a roof of stars that segue into the real Pacific firmament.

I'm not dancing with anyone, and my solitude doesn't matter to anyone. Most of the people here are between seventeen and twenty-five. I'm past fifty-five. I don't have complexes anymore. I dance alone, not actively conscious, my eyes closed, smiling, unhappy that I don't have fifteen-year-olds who would do me the favor of identifying the music I'm hearing and dancing to. However, I'm shamefully satisfied when some song from my own youth— "Michelle" by the Beatles, "Satisfaction" by the Stones, or "Monday Monday" by the Mamas and the Papas—sneaks into the endless rock tape whose energy spreads from the song you can dance to while hugging someone to acid rock, which demands individual, savage frenzy—the return to the tribe, the clan, the oldest and most forgotten blood ties.

An image of Ireland, the land of my fathers, crosses before my black eyes. A valley inundated with dew. A bay, which in reality is a valley flooded by the catastrophes of time. And in the center a white island where the wild ducks gather. A white chestnut forest, white, white, all smothered in its own whiteness.

I close my eyes in order to feel all that, and when I suddenly open them I'm no longer alone. My wife is dancing with me, created by my eyes (my eyes: my desire), staring at my outfit, my Gucci loafers, criticizing me for not wearing socks, and I'm telling her that in Italy no one wears socks in summer with loafers, to which she replies that I look sloppy. What? My beige slacks, my pink shirt that looks (I only realize it now) like an ad for the hotel where I'm staying? And she says to me:

"Everything you know you learned in Italy, right?"

"No, you taught me everything."

I say it trying to be agreeable, knowing it's just an illusion on my part.

"You're right. With me, you had your Hollywood career. A good career at that. You know what I mean: I mean *good*. You had a personality, a secure place, audiences knew who you were. You know what I mean: they *knew who you were*."

"Come on, all I ever made were B films, don't try to

put one over on me or on yourself. I was typed as a hood, a gangster, the guy who always loses the girl."

"Stop complaining. You kissed Susan Hayward, Janet Leigh, Lizabeth Scott . . . You probably even slept with them."

"Cindy, Italy got me out of a rut."

"You know what I mean? Audiences knew who you were. That's what counts in this business."

"What you mean is that I was character-typed."

"Did you really go to bed with Lizabeth Scott?"

"All I ever did was offer them my arm to walk down one of those marble stairways. Universal had its own ideas about what the mansions of rich Americans look like. Marble stairways."

"You always liked blondes."

"Like you."

"No, husky-voiced blondes like Lizabeth Scott."

"I offered them my arm. They might have slipped."

"Husky-voiced, blond, and with thick, black eyebrows, like yours and Lizabeth's."

"They would wear incredibly high heels so they wouldn't look like midgets next to me. Or they'd stay one step above me. Stairs are indispensable to create illusions in movies. Just tricks, sweetheart. Like the kisses. You're kissing Lizabeth Scott, but you're thinking about the rent. And you know it. So don't get jealous."

"Audiences want something they can rely on, stupid. Audiences don't want to see you in realistic dramas with Italian dubbing, unshaven, walking through the mud in the dark with a nine-year-old girl. Audiences want to see you with Susan Hayward, kissing her or slapping her around, whatever, but with Susan Hayward!"

"I won the Oscar, Cindy."

"You mean you lost the Oscar. You never got another

good part. You got too important for gangster parts in B movies. No one ever called you again for a great movie. But you've got your Oscar on the mantel. Keep it. You won't have any other company than that gold-plated statuette. I wasn't born to live with a has-been. I want a man who *will be*."

I suspect that Cindy knew the lines in my pictures better than I did because she would repeat them from memory long after I'd forgotten them. She had a surprising way of slipping them into our real-life conversations. I knew that a script that's been filmed is worth about as much as used toilet paper. You toss it and flush it. And you don't bend over to see what's at the bottom of the toilet bowl. She didn't know that. For her, those despicable, stupid words —"I wasn't born to live with a has-been, I want a man who *will be*"—are part of her ridiculous, messy unconscious. That film was never even made! The script ended up in a drawer, and she, the jerk, knows it by heart and repeats it as if it were something like "Sleep no more, Macbeth has murdered sleep"! Cindy's unconscious is like her periods: a filthy, uncontrollable bleeding (unless, God forbid, she was pregnant, which I never wanted with her). But she's right about something, the bitch. The Oscar can be a curse, a perverse mascot, a bad omen. Just like *Macbeth*, which is supposed to put the evil eye on you. Instead of Oscar, why don't they call it the Macbeth. I joined company with Luise Rainer and Louise Fletcher, both condemned by the Oscar. But my name's not Louis. Louis Loser. My name's Vince Valera.

You're a black Irishman, Cindy told me when I fell in love with her. She was platinum-blond then and identical to everything I've seen today from the heavens. As if I were Apollo and she the firmament lit up and traversed by my light. Cindy, identical to the tropical nightfall. Cindy, identical to the pool filled with flowers. My wife identical to a hillside glittering with lights. My love like a crystal discotheque. My beloved Cindy from the starry sky. She loved me so much she wouldn't let me see her. Your name is Vince Valera. You're a black Irishman, which is to say, a shipwrecked sailor. A descendant of the Spanish sailors washed up on the coast of Ireland after the disaster of the Invincible Armada. A son of squalls and foam, offspring of the wind and the rocks. A Latin from the north, Vince, dark-skinned, with the blackest, thickest eyebrows in the world (they say they're my main feature), your black, shiny hair, and the perfection of your body, Vince, as smooth as an Apollo, with no hair on your chest or legs, shiny as black marble or an ancient gladiator, strong as the breastplate of a Roman legionnaire, muscular as a Spanish guerrilla, but with more hair in your armpits and pubis than any man I've ever known before, we women notice those things, Vince, the hair that creeps down from your armpits and creeps up from your sex, and our hairs mix when we make love, yours black, mine blond, don't be anything but my lover, Vince, don't kiss anyone else, don't screw anyone else, only belong to your Cindy, Cinderella, make me feel I'm in a fairy tale.

Then she said this to me:

"You can only be a hood, a gangster, at most a private eye, you're part of film noir, don't stop being the dark villain, Vince my love, go on being the cursed Apollo of B movies forever . . ."

I couldn't stand her anymore. I opened my eyes and grabbed her by the arms the way I'd grabbed the receptionist in the guayabera, right there in the middle of the dancing and the colored lights I let my violence run wild when I saw how, no matter how tightly I shut my eyes, the lights gave Cindy a fluid face, now green, now red, as if her jealousy and rage were nothing more than descriptions of the play of lights in a discotheque, and I slapped her a few times while the woman screamed and I told her that picture was my salvation! Understand? That picture gave me a past, I don't have any past that isn't my Italian movie! Don't take the only film that's really mine away from me! Don't you understand that only once in my life was I a dream with soft look and shadows deep, and millions of people loved me, loved my moments of glad grace and my beauty, false or true . . . ?

The woman screamed, and the captains wearing blue blazers, white trousers, and white hair separated me from the fat, fiftyish woman wrapped in a sarong, shocked, who swore: "I was dancing alone, I don't have any hang-ups, I came to have fun, it isn't my fault I'm divorced, this man hit me, I just came over to him because I saw he was as lonely as I was!" And when the Acapulco maître d's calmed everyone down and opened bottles of Dom Pérignon and arranged a lambada and the music and lights rapidly changed, I was led firmly out of the place, into the night, to my jeep, and my muttered excuses, first for these poor devils who didn't deserve them, then immediately for myself, excuse me, excuse yourself, any question makes me crazy: don't you see that I know nothing about myself, if someone asks me why I am what I am or do this or that, because I no longer am or do, I get mad, I punch reporters, I break their cameras. They don't know that I have a past and that one single film gave it to me. They insist on giving me a future and blame me because I don't look for it. I have no right to be what I was. In Hollywood that's the worst sin, to have been, to be *a has-been* like Gertrude the Dinosaur or the dodo bird or the Edsel, a figure of fun, a wax figure. All that matters to them is what will be, the promise, the next project, the deals necessary to get the next picture shot.

Where is my Italian picture?

They're right. It's shown in art houses. At best it's a videocassette that sells badly. Classic European film in black and white. Bargain: $5.45. Less than a ticket to a real movie. Cindy's right.

This place is a jewel box, a fucked-up little jewel box filled with fucked-up jewels.

After midnight

Maggie's, next to Condesa beach, is a tiny piece of England outside of England. The British flag, the Union Jack, is used to decorate everything, beginning at the entrance, which announces:

BRITONS!
THIS IS YOUR HOME AWAY FROM HOME!

even including the tablecloths, the napkins, and the beer mugs, although the mugs also have pictures of Charles and Diana painted on them. I'm sitting at the bar, and the bartender explains that there's so much money in Europe that even bank employees can take a charter flight and spend a week in Acapulco.

That much is clear. They have the pallor of Devonshire cream melting on a scone. I remember, when I made a picture in London, that as soon as the first rays of sunlight appeared in May, bank employees would emerge from their banks and roll up their trousers so the sun would toast their skinny, pale calves, which for the preceding months had not known any light. London is a lake of shadows: darkness in the streets, the apartments, the offices, the train stations, the Underground tunnels, the malls . . . The Acapulco sun must seem a miracle to them, a blasphemy, and a temptation. Some of the girls drinking at Maggie's haven't even had time to change out of the dark clothing they wear when they do business in Barclays Bank or Marks & Spencer.

The barman stares at me, not knowing where I come from, and, since he sees I'm dark-skinned, he becomes suspiciously animated.

"How many Mexicans do we have here? One, two . . . counting you, there are five of us."

He says he hopes there will be seven Mexicans in Maggie's Bar, his seven dwarfs he says. He serves me an insipid margarita, then a sour bellini, and confesses (I'm drinking but he's getting drunk) that the erotic dream of his childhood was Walt Disney's *Snow White and the Seven Dwarfs*. Actually, he winks at me, it was more than erotic, it was a sadoerotic fantasy. He says he imagined himself as Snow White—he laughs insinuatingly—waiting for the little dwarfs to abuse her. All those leather belts, those boots, those nails and hammers, how I wanted to ask all those little people, Crucify me, little guys, or let's play Saint Sebastian, wham!

I smiled and said that the good thing about *Snow White* is that we can talk about the movie without revealing our ages because they bring it out again every two or three years. He didn't understand what I said, but he did get annoyed because I said it in English and fouled up his national arithmetic.

I went out for a stroll along the Costera, invaded now by bars, Polynesian restaurants, hamburger joints, Kentucky Frieds, and Tastee-Freeze. In the third world, people must think Colonel Sanders is a hero of the Civil War: his round face, white and bearded, his benevolent spectacles —you see his face more often around here than the Divine Face of Jesus Christ. More Colonel than Savior! I say to myself, a little drunk now because of the bad combo the sadomasochauvinist bartender at Maggie's served me. I stop off for a minute at Carlos 'n' Charlie's. It's decorated with old movie posters, and on one of them I find my name, very tiny, very far down in the order of credits. This for sure is no fairy tale. This ages you for sure, bartender. I'm fifty-five and really in need of a fairy tale. Instead, I get a glass of warm tequila and think about a frozen Oscar.

1:22

The kid sitting next to me in the jeep told me how to get to the garden illuminated by Chinese lanterns and shook hands with me when we got out. Only then did I realize that my small guide looked like me: he had bushy brows, was smooth-faced, and had sharply delineated features despite the fact that he was ten or twelve years old. It's hard to tell how old people are in the tropics: there are twelve-year-old mothers and grandmothers of thirty, old people without a single gray hair and children with no teeth left. In the case of my little companion, what was left of his baby fat had been sliced off long ago by a calendar whose pages were steel knives. In the eyes of that Acapulco baby, time went by with no respect for childhood, old age, or any other age.

In those black eyes, I saw a time that had no consideration for individuality. That's a fear I have at times, when I escape from my own more or less protected singularity, which I've constructed, I think, carefully and patiently, when I face a bereft humanity whose circumstances neither differentiate nor respect anyone. That's why I got so much out of being directed by Leonello Padovani. In my role, I found the proper balance, the exact quality that put me between this Mexican bereavement I fear so much and the American overprotection I despise so much. It was possible to be oneself with others, a myself with the themselves. I learned that then and don't want to lose it. Cindy doesn't understand. She associates success with protection; Latin Americans associate it with unhappiness. In Europe, it was possible to be something else, something like a collective subject in a shared intimacy.

The boy led me to the whorehouse where I'd asked him to bring me. This boy: How many tons of deodorant, refrigerators stuffed with frozen food, cereals with fiber, Jacuzzis, Porsches, and VHS systems would he need to protect himself from the hopeless fate devoid of individual handholds already in his eyes? If I could take him away, living in real life my screen character, take him by the hand to the roads of pure chance, freedom, encounters . . . The way things are, he's going to need much more than the ten dollars I gave him at the entrance to the bordello named the Fairy Tale.

Immediately after

Palapa palms are the Gothic cathedrals of the tropics. Anything can take place beneath the protective umbrella of their dry, dusty leaves: protection from the sun, sanctuary from the night, subverted space. The palapa of the Fairy Tale is a perfect if overflowing circle of humanity (men only) around a dance floor where girls between fifteen and twenty years old are dancing naked, breasts exposed, with sometimes only a bikini bottom covering their sex. Sometimes even less than that: what they call a string bikini in Rio de Janeiro—dental floss. Sometimes nothing. And sometimes, at most, a coquettish silk shawl draped around their hips when they serve drinks to the throng of young men.

Few tourists. Almost all the customers look as though they come from Acapulco. I've been seeing them since I got to the airport. They're almost like old friends. I saw them driving buses and taxis, loading luggage, loitering at the doors to pharmacies or the balconies of clinics devoted to venereal diseases. I saw them in bank offices and hotels. I will have to make Western man's effort at differentiation when faced by third-world masses. Chinese, Africans, Mexicans, Iranians: they're all the same for the gringos, hard to tell one from another. And I tell myself we must be the same for them. But not me. I'm a black Irishman, remember? The Apollo of B films. At the age of fifty-five, I can trick myself out to look forty-five. A real rejuvenator. That's what everyone tells me, and I've ended up believing it. Besides, in movies my youth is preserved forever. I shouldn't belie it, even if it brings me to an early grave.

I laugh, fix up my hair a bit, roll up my sleeves a bit, have a burning desire for a little mustache, even if it were as ridiculous as the one the hotel receptionist has; I try to imitate a look of oily lust so I can mix in, lose myself in the macho clientele shouting clothes, clothes, and ass, ass, and who stretch out their hands to touch the girls dancing to a salsa; but one voice dominates everything, the shouts, the music, the dancing of the naked girls on the dance floor: You can look, you can listen, you can even sniff, but around here you can't touch anything.

I make out a woman sitting under a Count Dracula light opposite the sound equipment, protected by a shield of plastic and Plexiglas. She wears a pearl necklace and a velvet bustier with a white, raised collar, like a cloud or a parachute, behind her neck. She's just like Snow White. She protects herself in front with the plastic shield and covers her back with the stiff, high collar. The fact is she dominates the scene the way she dominates her head, which is covered with hairpins and looks like a porcupine. She must be afraid that not every hair's in place.

"Welcome to a night hotter than last night," she declaims. "You can look, you can listen, you can even sniff, but around here you can't touch anything."

A drunken guffaw, and a potbellied man rushes out onto the dance floor expressly to touch a dancer. Everyone shouts in protest: the rules of the establishment—a gentlemen's agreement—are being broken. All Snow White has to do is speak calmly into the microphone, "Security, security," and a phalanx of bare-chested masked men in wrestling tights disposes of the drunk in two or three quick movements. He's rushed out amid the laughter and wisecracks of the young men present.

Snow White invites a man to step out onto the floor and sit down on a little straw chair. The spotlight falls on me. Snow White shouts, Lights, lights on the guy in pink; The guy in pink they all shout, pushing me onto the floor, the too low chair where I sit down and receive instructions: You just look, listen, and sniff, but please don't touch.

No one may touch the girl, as svelte and sinuous as a cobra, with traits of all races, Chinese, African, and Indian, and perhaps even Danish. Every movement of her undulating dance around me, my chair, my nervous hands, my open arms, my powerless legs (all movements I don't know how to control) invites me to do that which is forbidden: touch her, give a face to this woman, distinguish her from her faces without face: Chinese, African, Indian, all the same among themselves but not her; she brings her hands closer with their long fingers, a diabolic extension of her small, slave-girl body, closer to my face, as if she were using her fingers to draw me new features, my unexpected face, my ideal mask . . .

I take her by the wrist, I bring her mouth to mine, the music stops, silence takes over, no one says anything, no one protests as they did before, the bouncers don't grab me and throw me out on my ear, Snow White approaches slowly, abandoning her little platform, and slowly separates us, softly, almost like a tender mother who discovers the first kiss exchanged by an innocent brother and sister.

(Her getup is grotesque: she's potbellied, and her mini-skirt reveals fat knees and clear-plastic sandals. She has trouble getting the skirt to stay put on her gut; the same with the velvet bustier that squashes her tits flat. Only the white collar, like a cloud, detracts from her being anchored to the earth and creates the illusion that she's floating.)

Just before dawn

I'm sitting next to Snow White. I try to convince her: "They should all come with me." When she shakes her head, I'm afraid her hairpins are going to fly into my face, like the arrows in the face of Saint Sebastian, evoked by the gay bartender at Maggie's. "No, my dancers aren't for sale. If someone told you this was a whorehouse, they put one over on you." "Are you telling me your girls don't screw? What is this, the School of the Sacred Heart of Jesus?" "What do you know about nun schools when you're a heretical gringo?" "I'm Irish: Do they fuck or don't they?" "No, they get cocaine from their lover-boys, very late, when the party's over and the sun's coming up." "How long does the pleasure last them?"

Snow White raises the volume of the music, and the men still there (quite a few) pay the girls to dance on their tables. The bids keep going higher, as if it were a Christie's auction, to see a little more, but what the girls give most is their own supreme position: standing, but bent forward, the ass toward the customer, they reveal the slit between the cheeks but then suddenly shake them again, attracting toward their perfect smoothness the real attention, the real temptation, the promised pleasure.

When they finish dancing, the girls wash up in four transparent shower stalls, strategically placed so the public can watch them comfortably, Snow White explains to me in the most precise terms. Four glass shower stalls, four svelte girls, gorgeous, perfect, soaping themselves up, rinsing themselves off, like Venus from the sea. The foam bubbles up and concentrates in their hair; the water runs between their breasts in two streams, the lather pausing on their nipples before pouring down toward their navel, then, in one rush, gathering, captured and happy, in the pubis. A fat guy, asleep against the glass partition, is missing the best part of the show. Everyone laughs, and Snow White proclaims from her plastic and Plexiglas cage: "NO TO PROSTITUTION, NO TO SEX FOR MONEY. MY MAIDS CAN GET AIDS."

In Los Angeles, I'd just read García Márquez's bestseller. Now I'm thinking about love in the times of AIDS. No matter. I didn't come here to take precautions.

6:47

I told them I wanted nothing from them, that I was just offering them a little pleasure sail. Get a little sun, Snow White told them, let a little light into the place where the sun doesn't shine, assholes. No one said anything about money. I only asked that there be seven, including Snow White. But she wasn't going for it. I'm the Wicked Stepmother, she said with an ineffable smile, I'm the one who offers the poisoned apple. But I, generous to a fault, insist on assigning her the role of heroine.

The day began gloriously, and the seven I picked (Snow White insisted on being the Wicked Stepmother and not giving up her own role; I insisted on calling her Snow White) were delighted to go out for a sail, with no demands, just to get a little tan, to kick back a little, practice napping, be somewhere else . . . That's what Snow White told them to bring them around. I only asked for a minute to pick up my things at the hotel. I didn't give up my room. I threw the few things I brought with me in my bag, making sure I had my shaving kit, my toothpaste and toothbrush, deodorant. The girls would look divine in the sunlight, despite a sleepless night and the dancing. I could tell I looked gray, unshaven, bloodshot, dry skin. The different drinks I'd had gathered into a fist inside my head, hammering at it. The girls saw me and probably said to themselves, We won't have any problems with this wreck. I barely had time to look at myself in the mirror. With repulsion, I thought about the coffee-colored receptionist in his guayabera. He wasn't there. How right they were to let him out only at night; sunlight would destroy him.

8:00

They may have begun to see me differently when I showed them how much I knew about handling a beautiful ketch with fixed stabilizer, twin masts, boom, and two jibs. Thirty-six feet long, a beam of nine feet, and a thirty-foot displacement, it cut a fine figure leaving the docking area on its way to the bay, running on the auxiliary motor, with my firm hand on the tiller to take it out of Acapulco. Then, leaving control of the helm, I passed it to Snow White, who almost fainted with shock, amid the giggles of her ladies-in-waiting, so I could raise the mainsail and then the mizzen, all with precise movements, tying cables, setting bitts to wind other cables around them, tying down the boom with a clove hitch and the jibs with a couple of half hitches.

I clamped down a cable that looked loose.

I made everything fast and shipshape.

The ketch was ready for any adventure. A sensitive craft, faithful, that followed every movement of the person who loved her and sailed her well, it was the most beautiful ornament of a splendid day, the kind only the Mexican Pacific knows how to give. Like a poem I learned as a child, anyone who's seen a sea like this and still wants to get married can only do it with someone like the sea itself.

Ireland boils in my veins. Even more the black Ireland of a descendant of Spain, a castaway it seems, Vincente Valera is my name, but my ambitions are much more modest than those in that poem of my childhood. Vincente Valera is my name, and the name of my ketch, to the boorish satisfaction of the hotel receptionist, is *The Two Americas*.

Snow White and her seven girl-dwarfs stare at me in admiration, and if I don't marry the sea, I'll have to settle for going to bed with them. All seven? Two Americas, one Apollo, and seven whores? What a salad!

9:16

I took the helm again. I think the girls had never seen one of their customers carry out maneuvers they'd only seen done by the boatmen in the port. The morning was cool and blazing hot at the same time: the brilliant, dry heat redeems everything in Acapulco—the ugliness of the buildings, the filth on the streets, the misery of the people amid the tourist boom, the blind pretense of the rich that there are no poor here, all inexplicable, all unjust, all, probably, after all is said and done, irredeemable.

In the eyes of the seven dwarfs, I saw something like an immediate admiration, which did not demand from the guy cast as the macho more than a series of strong, well-defined acts to take control of their feminine veneration. Of course, I tried much too hard. My head was splitting, I felt I needed a bath, an aspirin, and a bed more than I needed all this work; but when we were out to sea, far from the corrupt fingernail of the bay, the Sun and the Pacific, that glorious husband and wife team that overcomes all unfaithful storms and even the most hurricane-plagued divorces, embraced all of us, the eight women and me, in an irresistible way. I think we all had the same idea: if we don't give ourselves over to the sea and the sun this morning, we don't deserve to be alive.

The minibar on *The Two Americas* was well stocked, and there were also some platters of Manchego cheese and Spanish ham along with sliced jicamas covered with powdered chile. No sooner did the girls discover them than they devoured them, all feeding each other, while Snow

White shrugged her shoulders and poured some drinks. She came over to me, holding out a glass. I should have said no, but she insisted on drawing a face in the air, on top of my own, as if she'd guessed what my dream was, as if she were trying to hypnotize me. So I left her with the tiller again, whereupon she again became nervous. "Just keep going straight ahead. There are no trees on the road," I said laughing, both of us laughing, creating a strange link between the two of us.

I had an idea. I wanted to teach the girls something. I thanked my lucky stars that the hotel people had put a rod and reel on the ketch. I announced to them that I was going to teach them to fish. They all laughed out loud and began to make jokes. One after the other, they played word games, the custom in both Mexico City and Los Angeles, sister cities where language is used more for self-defense than for communication, more to conceal than to reveal. The wordplay digresses, camouflages, hides: from an innocent word you try to squeeze a filthy word, so that everything comes to have a double meaning or, if you're lucky, a triple meaning.

I say they laughed a lot and that their collective voice was like the sound of birds. But their jokes were crude, physiological, more suitable for vultures than for nightingales. The fishing rod was the object of myriad phallic metaphors; the hook became a dick, the bait a pussy, flying fish became flying fucks, and soon every squid, ray, oyster, or snapper in the vast sea metamorphosed into every imaginable sexual object and word. After a night of giving themselves over to the energy of their bodies, it was as if the girls had sweated out all their corporeal juices. Now their heads were lubricated, and they could dedicate themselves to the art of language. But it was foul language, which produced a chain reaction of hilarity among them and, at the same time, seemed to affirm the fact that they were in some way superior beings, owners of language as opposed to the owners of money, castrators of the "decent" language of the master, the boss, the millionaire, the tourist, the customer.

I should probably confess that my poor Anglo-Saxon similes, extremely brutal, were no competition for the metaphoric pyrotechnics of the gang of seven girls, loosened up in their collective giggle. Their camaraderie and their instant commitment to joking were contagious, but I stopped listening to them, oh my sad condition, your sad cuntdition? cunt, runt, grunt, cuntinue please, yes give me a hand here, a handjob here? a handkerchief? you need a fingerbowl, no, a fingerfuck, Dallas, Texas, not Dullass but good ass, good as gold, no Gold Finger, oooh! not a Cold Finger, oh oh seven, you mean up up six, six is a lot for a teeny little twat, well I give tit for twat. Not one pun unturned.

While they fooled around, I copped a few feels. The pretext, as I said, was to teach them how to fish, to use the rod and hook, and to do it, I stood behind each one and taught her to cast, carefully, so no one would get hurt. I hugged each one, sitting each of them on my lap, teaching them to fish, my hands around each waist, on each thigh, and on each and every sex, feeling in short order the excitement of my own when I dared to rub their nipples and then to slide my hand under their bikini top, or into the bikini bottom and put my finger full of their juices into the mouth of . . .

I began to sort them out, my seven dwarfs, as they began to get hot and asked me to teach them to fish: Now it's my turn; No it's mine, you cut in, bitch.

No. This one must be Grumpy because she resisted my advances, saying No, I'm not like them, now you've got me pissed off, get your hands off me. Another had to be Dopey because she only laughed nervously when I felt her up and pretended not to notice, without being able to control the comic movement of her ears. The third must be Sleepy because she pretended I wasn't touching her and acted the part of the tourist while I stuck my finger up her wet, excited vagina, as if that could tell me the temperature of the other six and announce the tidal wave of sex that was rolling in.

I had identified Doc, who simply looked very serious, while Bashful wouldn't come close, as if she was afraid of me, as if she'd met me before.

Sneezy was the one who drove me crazy, the first one to sink her nose into my pubic hair and begin to sneeze as if she were coming down with hay fever. And the seventh, who would be the most hardworking and careful, unbuttoned my shirt and stretched me out naked on the deck of the ketch that Snow White was steering in complete ignorance, without daring to ask: What do I do, now what do I do?

Without even daring to admonish her wards: You can look, you can listen, you can even sniff, but around here you can't touch anything.

They touched everything I had, the seven demonic dwarfs of Acapulco. The seven whores of the marvelous Apollo who had outdone himself, who had completely realized his capabilities in that moment when I lost the notion, which I'd just attained, of the individuality of each one of them. They were only what I had said they were: dopey, dreamy, sneezy, diligent, and wise, enterprise and sensuality. They were obscure angers and palpitating desires, all together. They lacked faces, and I imagined my own under the sun, under the shadows that covered me, naked on a ketch that was heading straight for the middle of the ocean, farther and farther (Snow White never changes course, doesn't protest, doesn't say a word, an argonaut, a whoronaut, an argoinvalid paralyzed by the sea, the breeze, the sun, the adventure, the danger, our increasing distance from terra firma), and I only know that seven eighteen-year-olds (on the average) are making love to me.

I see seven asses that sit on my face and offer themselves to my touch and my mouth. I want to be honored and to notice differences, to individualize. I want to glorify them in that culminating moment. I don't want them to feel bought. I don't want them to think they're part of a pack. I want them to feel the way I felt when I got the Oscar, king of the world, and they, my seven dwarfs, my queens. Asses as hard as medlars and smooth as peaches. Asses as vibrant as eels and as patient as squid. Asses that protect the dark essence, the smooth, slight hair of the Indian woman. The impossible protection of the wide hips, the impossibly slim waists, the thighs of water and oil that surround, defend, and protect the sacred place, the sanctuary of the vagina, my seven asses this morning which I smell, touch, desire, and individualize.

Seven cunts seven. Cunt the flesh of a freshly peeled papaya, rose-colored, untouched, like a carnivorous, perfumed pearl. Palpitating cunt of a wounded pup, just separated from its mother, pierced by the damned arrow of an intrusive hunter. Cunt of a pure spring, water that flows, without obstacles, without remorse, without concern for its destiny in the sea that will drown it like a salt gallows. Night cunt poised to spring in full daylight, kept in reserve for the weakness of the day, vaginal night in reserve for the day when the sun no longer shines and the woman's sex should occupy the center of the universe. Fourth cunt of the Acapulco girls, fourth, fortress, cunt like a furnished fortress, warm, inviting, expecting its perfect guest. Fifth cunt, the fifth the best, a metallic cunt with veins that refuse to be mined and give up their gold, asking the miner that he first die of suffocation in the heart of the tunnel. Glorious cunt of eucharistic libations, sixth, sexth, religious cunt, Irish, black, what would my waspish WASP wife Cindy say, whiteanglosaxonprotestant who tries to hand me her boring genealogical charts: You don't know how to enjoy yourself, Vince, unless you think you're sinning, miserable celluloid Apollo, inflammable, perishable, take me as a woman, as a human being, as your equal, not as a symbol of your spiritual odyssey, son of a bitch, I'm not your communion or your confession, I'm your woman, I'm another human being, why the hell did I ever marry an Irish Catholic who believes in the freedom of sin and not in the predestination of the flesh!

I flee from that: I want to enjoy the final cunt, the seventh seal, the cunt without qualities, the sexual purgatory without heaven or hell, but with my name tattooed on the entrance to the vagina, Vince Valera, conquered Apollo: the seven on my dick, the seven sucking me, one after another, one sucks, the next sticks her finger up my ass, the third kisses my balls, the fourth shoves her cunt in my mouth, the fifth sucks my tits, the sixth licks my toes; the seventh, the seventh rubs her huge tits all over my body, tells the others what to do, bounces her breasts in my eyes, drips them on my balls, glides a nipple over the head of my dick, and then each one sucks me. But not only them: the sun, the sea, the motor of *The Two Americas*—they all suck me.

The impassive stare of Snow White sucks me as she continues in her useless pose with her hands on the tiller. Uselessly, because all the rules of her kingdom are being broken and she can do nothing but stare at us with an indifferent absence which must be that of God Himself when He sees us revert to the condemned but indispensable condition of beasts.

Uselessly, because *The Two Americas* has already attained its inertia and only goes farther into the sea, just as my sex goes farther into just one, just one of the seven holes offered this morning to my absolute surrender, the demand that I be given everything, that nothing be held back, that I not find a single pretext to be here or flee, marry or divorce, sign a contract or aspire to a prize, impress a boss, smile to a banker, seduce a columnist as we have dinner at Spago's, nothing, nothing more than this: the simultaneous ascent to hell and heaven, the unleashed palpitation of my chest, the awareness that I drank too much, that I idiotically did not sleep, my heart gallops and my stomach twists, I haven't shaved, my cheeks scrape the divine ass of Dopey as the thorns scrape Christ's face, the sun falls on us like lead rain, the breeze stops, my pain becomes ubiquitous, the sound of the motor disappears, the sun goes out, my body runs out like water, the laughter of the seven dissipates, there are no longer seven holes, there is only one hole into which I weightlessly fall, there are not seven nights, there is only one night, I softly enter it without vacillation, predestined as my wife, Cindy, wanted, without a heart or a head now, pure erect penis, pure phallus of Apollo in the mouth of a bordello muse who caresses my face and whispers in my ear: "This is your ideal face. You'll never have a better one. This is the face for your death, Daddy-o."

12:01

I just died, when the sun passed its zenith. I just died screwing. I was just killed, aboard *The Two Americas*, by the biggest blow job in the history of sex.

12:05

"What are we going to do?" asks Snow White, her hands wrapped tightly around the tiller, as if our not capsizing really depended on it, not daring to sweat, her hands more rigid than my sex, which refuses to die with me.

My dick is still stiff, expecting the second coming, but in reality, I realize, it only predicts, with its excessive hardness, the total stiffness, the rigor mortis that will soon take control of my body, which is still limp, tanned, and unshaven. Is every man's secret dream to have a permanent erection, the thing doctors call priapism? Well, God's just given me one, as much an act of grace as giving military genius to a conquistador, a poetic star to a writer, a good ear to a musician, language to a translator . . .

The dream into which I sink tells me many things, and one of them is this: Vince Valera, you no longer have to prove your masculinity on screen. You've proven it in life. And now, in death, you are going to be the hardest, most unbendable slice of cold cuts that ever descended from an Irish mother. Only the worms from County Tyrone will be able to deal with you!

Shit, I tell myself, I'm talking about my body from the outside. The voice of the Lord is right. Inside, what's going to happen to me inside? Everything that happens to me is passive, a final consequence, a last sigh. My nails and hair keep on growing. This is the first thing I know for a fact:

I listen to it. The gastric juices flow, but the blood begins to stagnate, finding its eternal inlets and ponds. They are the puddles of eternity. I fear postmortem flatulence. I fear it, and, of course, I convoke it. There's nothing like thinking about a fart to make you fart. My dead body farts.

The seven dwarfs laugh, some openly, some in sorrow, with a hand over their mouths, others holding their noses, whew! anybody know what's wrong with this roughrider, his cattleprod's ready but his saddle's sure smelly, and you-know-who just sneezes and Sleepy stretches out next to me, cuddles with me awhile, and asks me if I'm sleepy, and another starts to play games, lullaby is fuckaby, gootchy-gootchy-coo is stick your fingers in my goo, maybe your baby needs a nice meat pacifier, well, cuddle or curdle, look at this guy, he gets it up even when he's sleeping, so what's so weird about that? Who says he's sleeping anyway, look at those big old eyes of his, he looks like an owl, he licks and you howl? No, sticks in a hole, is there room for one more? There's room for seven whores, get on the stick, Doris, they all shout at the one I called Doc, trot along my pony, up the prick and down, upupupupdowndowndown, I think when the Divine Doris got on my prick I came posthumously.

They all laughed when Doris dismounted, and their jokes chorused the contraction of my penis, the disinflation. "That match won't set off any dynamite now, looks like he's shot his wad." Then Doris started singing a belated reveille: "There's a monkey in the grass / with a bullet up his ass / getitoutgetitoutgetitout," provoking another chorus of laughter, except for the boss lady, Snow White, who looked at me and at them very seriously.

"What are we going to do?" she repeated, a look of controlled fear on her face.

"Let him take his siesta," laughed Doris Doc sympathetically.

"He's all tuckered out because he worked overtime," said Sleepy.

"Let's see if I can make him sneeze," said Sneezy, brushing her bush over my nose.

"My tickles are better, they can raise the dead," said big-eared Dopey, scratching the soles of my feet.

They all laughed and started scratching my ribs, my knees, my sex, and under my chin.

I didn't laugh. I swear I didn't. I didn't tremble.

The laughs and jokes began to fade.

Their hands got hotter and hotter. But they were touching a body that got colder and colder despite the midday sun burning through my open eyes.

"What's wrong with him?" asked Doris.

"No, what are we going to do?" repeated Snow White, as she had at the beginning.

12:20

As long as they don't throw me into the water. That's all I ask. That they don't toss me to the sharks.

12:39

"Never saw a dead man before?" Snow White shouted to them. And as if her words convoked all the powers in the world in order to make up for my sudden absence from life, the sun redoubled its energy and flowed over our heads like melted gold. The wind fell until it simply disappeared, forcing the women to pant instead of sigh as they assessed, awkwardly and with difficulty, their situation.

But if it was hard for them to breathe because the breeze died down, I gave thanks that the winds weren't threatening the ketch, although, as I already said, all nature underwent a brusque change the moment I died of ecstasy. The wind may have died with me, but in the far distance thunderheads were gathering. And the ocean, just when Snow White in a reaction of pure fear cut off the motor with a nervous movement, suddenly grew rough. I told myself that this was the natural result of a rapid suspension of movement. The boat began to roll with each new wave: the sea's turmoil seemed to rise from the deepest part of the Pacific, which is where we were, four hours after leaving the Yacht Club. We were surrounded by solitude but anchored in a turbulence that seemed dedicated only to us, to *The Two Americas* and her crew.

"Never saw a dead man before?" repeated Snow White with an exasperated tremor. "Think we're never going to die, that we'll always live happily ever after, that we, just because we're us, are the only ones who will never die?"

Captured in a silence and a calm more terrifying than any squall, the seven women said nothing, became pensive, and I, stretched out on the deck, really began to tell them apart. Did I have to die in order to individualize them, de-Mexicanize them, de-thirdworldize them?

I stared at them fixedly and almost came back to life in surprise: in death, I could clearly see the images that passed through the minds of the living. I understood it this way, directly and simply: This was my new, my real power. This was death's gift to me. Was its name immortality? Snow White asked her question—"Never saw a dead man before?"—and Sleepy metamorphosed into what her real name was when she awoke to life, María de la Gracia. And I, thanks to my new powers, saw in her eyes a dead child in a little box painted white in a shack where the candles were stuck into Coca-Cola bottles.

Bashful's real name was Soledad, and the death that passed through her eyes was that of an old man with open eyes who thanked her for accompanying him to the end, because dying alone is the most terrible thing in the world.

Doc in reality was Doris, and I recognized her death because it took place in the Mexican part of Los Angeles. Doris, a knapsack on her back, was walking along with a little girl more beautiful than a Diego Rivera drawing. She was holding the little girl's hand as they walked down a street lined with stone walls. Suddenly two street gangs started shooting at each other from opposite sides of the street. The knapsack and the books inside it saved Doris. The little sister—Lupe, Lupita, nobody sweeter—died instantly. In tears, Doris went down on her knees, and because of that the last bullet didn't blow her brains out.

Never saw a dead man before? Sneezy's name was Nicha (Dionisia). She grew up at her mother's side in a whorehouse in the port of Acapulco. There was a big, central dance floor, crummy little lights, and neon beer signs. All that passes through her eyes when Snow White asks them if they've never seen a dead man before. Nicha pushes the sight of death aside with a vision of tangled mangroves and burned-out lights. She relives a long wait in one of the rooms surrounding the dance floor. There are three smells. The natural smell of the tropics, which are eternally rotting, and the disinfectant spray used to clean the floors, bed, and lavatory. But the third aroma is that of an orange tree that miraculously grows outside the little room and tries to poke a branch, a perfume, a flower, occasionally a fruit through the window to overwhelm the smells of rotting and disinfectant. She already knows she has to hide under the bed when her mom comes in with a man. She hears everything. That is her image of death. The memory of the orange tree saves her.

On the other hand, big-eared Dopey from time to time recalls a girl with the improbable name Dulces Nombres de Cristo—Sweet Names of Christ—which is she at the age of ten. She's walking among unsleeping dogs and pot-holes filled with muddy water, among hundreds of buses standing like elephants in front of a river of cement, among hundreds of taxis that seem to besiege downtown Acapulco, duplicating the city with a squadron of motors. The taxi drivers wash their cabs at night for the next day's work, while Dulces's mother, drunk, her legs spread, laughs, sings, shrieks, and fans her cunt at the door to the cabaret.

What haven't they seen? No, Grumpy's mind is a blank. Through it pass only deaths in Technicolor, deaths I rec-ognize. Movie dead men, gangsters, cowboys, dead men covered with ketchup. Her name's Otilia, and she doesn't allow a single real dead man into her head. But the last one, Happy, the hardest-working, whose name is Dolores, offers me a long vision of rivalries, always two men killing each other over her, killing each other over her with pistols, knives, clubs . . . These rivals for Dolores's favor are buried up to the knees in the hard, imprisoning earth, the way the two men are in a famous picture by Goya. Where could Dolores have seen that picture? It seems inconceivable to me that she would have a Goya in her head. Could my vision be tricking me, am I fooling myself with everything I see? As if she obeyed an impulse from death (mine), the girl lights a cigarette with a match taken from a matchbox with the label "Classics" on it. She protects the flame with the box in order to light her cigarette. And there's Goya's terrible, black painting: on a matchbox. It's the portrait of the bitterest fatality.

In the afternoon

These memories took more time than you might imagine. The chronology of memory in death is different from what it is in life, and the communication between the two consumes hours and (I still don't know this) days. I'll miss, I'm sure of it, this pause in memory. Because now practical problems take precedence over everything else.

I'm dead.

They admit it.

The first item then is what to do with me.

Dulces Nombres de Cristo reveals her dopiness when she asks that I be tossed overboard. "That way," the savage says, "there won't be any evidence of what happened." I hate her and put a curse on her: I hope you're locked up in an English asylum and fed porridge until you rot, bitch.

Otilia agrees energetically. "What happens if they catch us with this dead guy? We're in the clinker, my dears. Nobody's going to ask how it happened. We're guilty. We were born guilty, don't be jerks."

A terrible murmur of approval grows. Dulces and Otilia grab my arms, and Nicha helps them out, taking hold of my ankles. Soledad joins in to speed up the operation. I feel the foam of the waves caressing my ankles.

Doris saves me. "Are you dumbbells or what? In a little while another boat's going to pick us up. They'll ask us what we're doing alone in a yacht. Then they'll ask if any of us know how to drive it. None of us does, right? Then they bring us back to Acapulco. They find out that the gringo hired this thing and hired us at the same time. Seven whores and their madam and a disappeared gringo, murdered or who knows what. That's about when they'll put us on ice, Otilia."

They don't drop me, either into the sea or back onto the hard deck, let it be said to their honor. They make me comfortable, with all due respect, on the bench that runs along the gunwale.

Snow White says Doris is right. Does anyone know how to drive one of these boats? Dolores asks if it's the same as driving a car.

Later on

No, it isn't the same. Stretched out on the bench, staring at the sky, I also see the trapeze of the boom sail set between the triangular sails of the jibs, properly raised, but which, because they're not receiving either attention or (more important) nautical *intention*, will soon sag and fall, prematurely aged, wrinkled. Because a good sail knows the intentions of the sailor. A good hull is ready to obey even the slightest wish of a wise sailor. The absence of that seems to discourage the sails, which communicate it to the mast, which in turn trembles down to its base, where it joins the keel.

In other words, they don't know what to do. The gasoline will run out. The boom sail and the jibs will be pushed by a soft tropical breeze. Each cough of the motor makes them shake with fear. Finally, when the sun disappears, the seven of them will huddle together. They will form a kind of medieval galliard dance (I made a costume movie in Italy about the plague in the thirteenth century), which will culminate with them hugging Snow White's fat legs.

With her eyes fixed on the darkened horizon, the owner of the Fairy Tale will not release the tiller of *The Two Americas*. Then the sun will sink into the sea, and the seven will whimper together, a deep, almost religious, wail.

I appropriate it. It's my responsory, my requiem.

The night fell

Now, at night, I think about the fact that barely twenty-four hours ago I was swimming in a pool filled with flowers in a luxury hotel, thinking about where to go to have some fun. With my chin leaning on the edge of the pool, I read and tried to memorize a poem by William Butler Yeats that evokes past softness and the deep shadows of my eyes. And if the great modern poet of my homeland were to see me now, would he weep? I actually think he foresaw my fate (according to Leonello Padovani, a great poem is prophetic and communicates what we are going to be) when he wondered about those who loved my moments of glad grace and my beauty, with love false or true, and added: How many were they, how many? How many eyes, how many platonic lovers does appearing on screen grant you, when you stand in for Apollo in the modern mythology proffered by movies? Does the poet answer? Does he say something more? I try to recall the end of the poem, but in death my memory doesn't respond. It's stubbornly silent. I'm encouraged. Does it mean that with the poem unfinished, I still have a destiny to live out, an unfinished margin of my own life in death?

I've fornicated. I've died. I've discovered that dying means reading the minds of the living.

But my professional (not to say artistic) appetite is not so easily satisfied. Is this my stellar role? My seven producers here will decide that for me. The night scares them. They're adrift. Both they and I know it. They're afraid that if they start the motor it will hurl them on an uncontrollable, catastrophic course. They could, as Doris suggested, start it and dash off into the four points of the compass. Which one—north, south, east, west—brings them to shore first?

I don't think that's their problem. I may spend the night floating and staring at the stars, but what they'd like is to disappear from the night: the women, the stars. Solitude adrift gives them an absolute night without a roof, one that doesn't belong to them, their usual lives. This night returns them to the helplessness they've only managed to escape through self-deception all through their short lives. Young and dumb. With just enough intelligence not to throw me to the fish. But without enough intelligence to let themselves be guided—not by the instruments that horrify them or the words of which they are ignorant (I look at them and think that thanks to these women technology once again becomes magic)—but by the stars they've never known anything about. Perhaps in immobility they may find their only security.

As if she'd heard me, Dolores says out loud: "We sure don't have a lucky star."

I'd like to know what species they really are. Machines and nature are equally alien to them. So for what purpose, for whom have they been created? Thinking about them from the perspective of death, I recognize and reconcile them. They are the children of artifice, neither nature nor technology. Do they have the power to re-enchant the world? Maybe they are only the energy of the artificial. How little there is of it, how intense it is, how useless is everything that happens to us.

Sunrise

Well, at least the sea behaved like a mirror. The ketch has the wind in its sails and is heading farther out to sea. The motor is still turned off. There are no birds in the sky. The women wake up. They shake off their sleep with sensual movements that I recognize and am thankful for. Sexy until death. They're hungry. It's written all over their faces. All that's left are bits of olives, cheese, and slices of jicama. Dulces Nombres grabs the platter as if it belonged to her and starts eating. The morning breeze arouses their appetites. Otilia pulls the platter out of her hands. The olives, uniformly perforated so the anchovy can be inserted, bounce over the deck. One of them falls, absurdly, between my lips. The two girls steal bits of the antipasto from each other, but their avid hands stop, confused and repelled, over my lips and the olive which now adorns them.

The base of the mainmast creeks in the mast hole. Doris quickly steps in and arranges things so that what's left of the platter is distributed equally. "Is there anything else to eat?" "Sure," laughs Nicha the sneezy. "The olive in handsome's mug." No one else laughs. No, there's nothing else but the platter. But there's stuff to drink: bottles of Campari, Beefeater, Johnnie Walker, Bacardi, ice, and mineral water. You won't die of thirst. Besides, I taught them to fish. I know it was only a pretext. I hope they think of it. There are bonito and hake to be had here.

They don't think about any of that. Two things happen. The dawn heightens the senses, especially smell. The night seems to stock up the smells of the world in order to set them free at daybreak, loaded with dew or sage, with mist and moist earth, with puppy skin and the sweetness of the beehive, with coffee beans and tobacco smoke, with cumin and wallflower. All that evokes daybreak, associating it with different places on earth. The Pacific, the sea of Balboa and Cortés, should yield its own strong, marvelous aromas torn from the bottom of the ocean and from nostalgia for the land. But grumpy Otilia can only evoke oranges; she says that ever since she was a little girl she's drunk orange juice as soon as she awakens. It was the only luxury in her home, in all the American movies they drank orange juice before going to work or school, but in this damn boat there is no orange juice, not even the smell of an orange. She begins to cry.

The truth is that only one smell takes possession of *The Two Americas*. It's the smell of my body. I've been dead for eighteen hours. I'm beginning to stink. Eight women with my rotting body. I read their eyes. What are they going to do with me? The waves begin to get rough. They don't know what to do. Snow White saves my life. Excuse me: she saves my death. She sees the same thing I do. The eyes of the seven dwarfs reflect more hunger than disgust. Snow White makes her play. She quickly starts the motor. They all turn to look at the new captain. The motor coughs, sneezes, spits, but doesn't start. Nicha catches the sneezes from the motor. We all look up at the spars to see if the mast and the booms are keeping the boom sail and the jibs tight and swollen.

Noon

I can't stand the heat. I beg them to do something, cover me with a canvas, for pity's sake, carry me down to the cabin and lay me out there. I'm good and stiff. Soon they won't be able to move me. I stink and I'm hot. I almost wish they would throw me overboard. I long for the coolness of a bath, the orange juice desired by Otilia. But the women think only about hunger, which is now surfacing in the looks they exchange among themselves and sometimes turn on me. They try to drown their hunger with rum and whiskey. They begin to get sick. Drunk and dizzy, Soledad and Nicha end up vomiting. Doris grabs them by the hair, pulls them around, and scolds them. Bashful and Sneezy cry in despair, "What are we going to do now? Everything was going so nice, the heat, the sailing around, the sex. Now just look, it's all fucked up." "Same as always," says Dolores. "Same as always. Damned life."

It must be three in the afternoon

The heat is unbearable. The sea is possessed by a calm that presages something bad. They don't know what to do with me. They don't want to touch me, true enough. I fill them with terror, disgust, compassion. They don't even dare to close my eyes. They haven't recognized my death. I've discovered that to die is to acquire, in a single instant, the ability to see the images that pass through the heads of the living. Through the heads of these women, like a movie running nonstop, run the same images of a little girl shot to death in Los Angeles or of a dead whore at the entrance to a nightclub with a fan between her legs. An old man thankful for the presence of a girl when he dies. Or a girl thankful that the branch of an orange tree defers the certainty of death. Should I be satisfied with last night's unconscious, spontaneous response provoked more by the end of the day than by my death? A little white box and four candles stuck into Coca-Cola bottles. To whom can I commend myself? María de le Gracia, all by herself, quickly pulls my pants up.

Now they don't look at me. They don't touch me. María de la Gracia falls asleep easily. She went into the cabin warning the others, "Girls, if we don't get out of the sun, it's going to peel our skin off. Who's going to hire us if we look burned, damn it." There are no hats. Some of them have draped their bikini tops over their heads. Others, the more offensive ones, have stuffed Kleenex into their nostrils. Only Snow White, uselessly, doesn't abandon her post. Like me, she's lived enough to know that this calm is not natural. She looks at the sails. Without real control, they're beginning to loosen, to snap against the wind, to give up . . .

Another sunset

Everything's going badly. Without proper control, *The Two Americas* is smashing her prow through the growing waves and is beginning to roll sharply. The girls scream and huddle in the back of the lavatory and the cabin. The wind gets stronger and then weakens; periodic gusts give way to sudden calm. The wind begins to blow from the stern, steadily now. The immediate reaction of the ketch to run with the speed of the waves forces the screw and the rudder to rise out of the water at the crest of the wave. I shout from the far shore of death, Tie back those sails, the jib has to go on the side opposite the boom, if it doesn't it will block the boom, tie it down with the jib boom, why aren't the sails reefed, why aren't the others stiff in the wind?

I'm talking to the wind. I'm speaking to the onset of night. Naturally the boat begins to luff, the angle of the prow goes into the wind. The girls scream. The mainsail begins to bend, parallel to the direction of the wind. It snaps back and forth, so hard that it almost throws me off the deck where, slowly but surely, I'm rotting, silent and hungry for the night to refresh my skin and, soon, my guts. I give up the olive resting between my purple lips. The boat is completely out of control. It goes where it pleases. It luffs more and more. The prow rises up and the jib boom extends along the boat's flank. Then comes a sudden calm, the wind stops blowing and the danger ceases.

I hear sobs. I read water, thirst, images of water flooding the previous images of death. Everything begins to calm down. Long nails begin to claw me in the darkness.

Another Dawn

The sun strikes me in the eyes, but I need something. Something I miss because it was part of my body. I don't want to imagine it. I look for the women's eyes. First I see their faces, more and more peeled by the sun. I try to penetrate their minds. This is the privilege of my mortality. Doris is thinking about a man I don't know. María de la Gracia is a void; she's still asleep. Soledad has a swimming pool filled with blue, clean, fresh water in her head. Nicha thinks only about bottles and more bottles of sunscreen. Otilia has a big orange dripping sweet juice in her mind. A man other than myself has gotten into Snow White's head. Otilia imagines a mirror. And in Dolores's head I find my testicles.

Noon?

They exchange looks. The sun addles their wits. They can't think. They can't act. Have to wait for afternoon to come. I would like to touch the place where my balls used to be. Snow White takes the rod and casts the hook into the sea.

4:33

They've come to an agreement without speaking. María de la Gracia is still taking refuge in sleep. There she is neither thirsty nor hungry. She always dreams of a child who died of diphtheria at the age of three. She thinks that if he'd lived, her little boy would have saved her from this life she doesn't love. Why? she asks herself. Wouldn't the kid have been just one more burden, one more mouth, forcing me to do something worse than what I do innocently, which is to dance naked, protected by the lady who doesn't let anyone touch us? It isn't bad. The thing is, I have no one to go home to. Nobody's waiting for me when I get back. So I sleep, I sleep a lot so I don't remember that I could be cooking his food or sending him to school, scolding him if he gets bad grades, helping him with his homework, learning with my son what I never learned by myself. That's what I need. To go home and find something. Where is my son buried? What's the name of the town I left dead with grief and as beautiful as a wounded jaguar at the age of fifteen, no threat to anyone? Oh God, I just sleep. And I want to dream about my son and can't because I sense that something bad's going to happen to me, that all my friends here are closing in on me, saying

All she does is sleep all the time, she won't even know when . . .

"Who's going to touch her first?"

Snow White shouted: "A fish bit the hook, a nice hake, isn't there anything to cook with on the boat, no kitchen? Okay then, grouchy Otilia, damn you, get out your box of Classics, take off your panties if that's all we have, set them on fire, and be careful not to burn down this goddam thing 'cause then we'll really be fucked up."

Warm silent night

From the shore of death, you can see the stars better. They're the map of heaven and their lines tell me we're being dragged north after drifting out of control to the west. Maybe we're getting close to land, but these women don't know it. If we continue in this direction, we'll hit the tip of Baja California, Cabo San Lucas, entering the Sea of Cortés between the coasts of Sonora and the peninsula, which is longer than Italy, where the desert and the sea meet: huge cactuses and the transparent sea, the sun as round as an orange. What the conquistador told his sons, if he had time to talk to them, I don't know.

Columbus never knew he'd discovered America, and Cortés never knew Baja California was a peninsula. He thought it was an island that led to the prodigious land of El Dorado. If the women don't die of hunger and thirst, we'll enter the Sea of Cortés like helpless explorers, but soon we'll reach Mexico's armpit, the salty mouth of the Colorado River, Terra Firma . . .

How far away we are. At the same time, on this warm, quiet night a ship in full regalia, full of lights and noises, from which the insistent rhythms of mambos and guarachas reach us, passes in the distance. Its lights shine, more than in the night, in the eyes of Snow White and her seven dwarfs. They all wave their arms, call out, scream while the white cruise ship goes off without seeing us. Not reluctantly, Dulces Nombres sings the tune the night is broadcasting:

> Mexican girls dance the mambo
> so very pretty and tasty

and the others join in, united in hope, fear, and frivolous joy, all at once:

> like Cuban girls they shake their hips
> they're gonna drive me crazy.

A different dawn

They've eaten. They wake up María de la Gracia to offer her a slice of half-raw hake, what can we do. Dolores is just about to make a joke about a dish of mountain oysters, but she stops herself just in time. She laughs; at least it's something to sink your teeth into. She goes on laughing like a fool, and her laughter spreads to the others, just like last night when they all sang the mambo together, just like that, the way it happens sometimes, you laugh, I laugh, we all laugh, even if we don't know why. Maybe it has something to do with that old saying: A full stomach means a happy heart. They laugh, their mouths stuffed with half-chewed fish. But they don't see the shoreline. They look at Snow White who uselessly scans the horizon, and their joy fades. The mambo ship was an illusion, its lights a mirage.

But since their energy's been renewed, they decide to use it. It's as if they have to live the morning that each one of them lives—and I die—because of my presence. They have to live it with more fury, more intensity, more defiance than ever. They start making puns again to lighten up the situation, then they start to exchange recriminations, men one stole from another, clothes they stole from each other, Why did you copy my hairstyle, shitass? and Who wore that red skirt first, huh? Who gets more money stuffed into her shoe when she dances, and who's got more in the bank, and which one is going to quit this life first, who's going to have her own house, who's going to have things turn out for her like Julia Roberts in *Pretty Woman*, bring on my Richard Gere, here Dick, who's going to get married and with what kind of macho, macho, macho . . .

Suddenly they all repel me. I try to close the curtain of my death over their vulgar film, their vile mess, so I can enter my own film again, the film Italy and Leonello Padovani gave me, far from my own messes made in California, near the Sea of Cortés . . . Padovani didn't hide, in fact he exaggerated his status as aristocrat and homosexual. It was a splendid defiance of his heritage while fashionable at the same time. Member of the Communist Party, he would dare anybody to say that a person's social origins determine his political participation. Not all rich people are reactionaries; not all workers are progressives. Sometimes the bourgeoisie carries out the revolution, while the poor support fascism . . .

Supremely knowledgeable about the female heart on the movie screen—Alida Valli, Silvana Mangano, Anna Magnani were brighter stars than ever when he directed them—he challenged every convention by understanding the souls of women without ever touching their bodies. They said he transposed and sublimated in his heroines his own sordid adventures with low-class masculine lovers, in whom he found, often to excess, the characteristics of sexiness and ingratitude, cheap self-interest and bestial passion. He treated me with the utmost respect. He was the first to see me and deal with me as a human being. With him, I dared to talk about things that were forbidden in Hollywood ... How could I remember an Ireland I abandoned in childhood but that returned, violent and beautiful, perfumed and savage, to my dreams? Why, in my unconscious memory, did there appear so many tall reeds, so many hazel forests, so many silver trout and white butterflies which only fluttered around at night? Why so much dew drowned in dew? Did I know all that, did I remember it and live it only because I'd read Yeats?

"No." Padovani smiled. "Perhaps you know it because before you read a poet you were one."

I told him I was barely the Apollo of B movies, as my wife calls me.

"Apollo is light," Padovani told me, he and I sitting in the solitary Lido in Venice one November afternoon. "He's associated with prophecy, archery, medicine, and flocks. His sister is the Moon. Thanks to her, he triumphs over the deities of the dark night.

"I love Yeats's poem where a man grows old and dreams about the soft look your eyes had once. He asks himself how many loved his moments of glad grace, how many loved his beauty with love false or true . . ."

Padovani's eyes abandoned mine to look for a sign of life in the Venetian afternoon. He admitted that at times he felt lonely and missed the kind of company that all the caprices and all the glory in the world couldn't get him. If I read Yeats, he knew Rilke well and recalled the verses about an Apollo with a shadowless gaze, a mouth that was mute because it had still not been useful for anything but had insinuated the first smile.

"Someone," Padovani concluded, "is transmitting him his own song."

Then the light reveals the stain of dry blood around my open fly. The women all look at each other. Suddenly they love each other, Oh sister, look we're together in everything, just like we are on this boat, how are we ever going to be apart, guys? Sisters to the death, they hug each other, cry, remember—the man, the son, the parents—they share a past they invent in order to be sisters. Now they invent a future in which each one helps the others, things will be terrific because the first to make it will scatter her gold and share her success with the others, of course, of course . . .

Only two of us keep our distance while the tears swell, the hands are joined, the hugs go around, the tremors, the sweats.

Snow White, because she knows them all too well and simply, says, "Bunch of assholes."

And I, I envy them because I don't remember in my profession or my life a comparable fraternal experience.

What time is it?

The boat follows its own whims; it's uncontrolled, and responds to the heavy seas we've encountered. The current drags us along like a magnet toward the Sea of Cortés, whose very name the women are ignorant of, but which I imagine transparent and sown with jewels: Didn't the poor conquistador scatter all his wealth on the bottom of lakes and seas—Moctezuma's gold in the swamps of the Sad

Night when he fled Mexico City losing almost everything, the emeralds of the conquest in a naval battle at Algiers? What kind of treasure does an adventurer like that leave to his posterity, the conqueror of an empire equal to the sun? My sister the Moon answers me tonight, this dawn, this afternoon of a moon appeared out of time, I no longer know, but the Moon answers me that perhaps he leaves nothing more than the name of a sea, a testament of water, a fame of salt and wind. I'm dead, and I see only a gigantic, trembling spiderweb at the bottom of the sea.

The ketch luffs again, the prow rises and the jib boom hangs to one side, sinks and begins to drag the boat. There is no hand on the tiller; the amount of sail dragged by the boom overwhelms the tiller. We are adrift, and in that precise instant all appetites, memories, and fears fuse into one fearsome object, which is I myself. What remains of me understands and trembles in knowing it. I am to blame for the situation, guilty of having abused them, guilty of being an American, rich, famous, of being everything but what they don't know, because I already said it, they know nothing about the stars and don't know how to read the heavens or, for that matter, the compass. I am an actor, goddamn it, I'm a frustrated actor, doomed equally for habitual mediocrity and exceptional success. Yes, I'm guilty of many things, of my profession, my wife, my associates, my fellow workers, who are the people I remember. And suddenly, dead here and rotting under the Pacific sun, losing my features little by little but instantly, I think about the statues of Apollo that only count old age in terms of centuries and never count death. I try to save my responsibility by assimilating myself like the statues, joining with the poets and artists, embracing my vanished sister the Moon, draping over my temples the laurels of the names that are the princes of languages and vision: Yeats, Rilke,

Padovani, Turner and the sea, Géricault and the raft of the Medusa, everything I learned in my childhood and didn't find again until a certain afternoon on the Lido in Venice. But I am guilty about an Indian housemaid who stopped to look at me in the gardenia-filled pool with the bottles in her hand; I am guilty that a boy resembling me guided me to the garden illuminated by Chinese lanterns where I found these women. I am guilty for another boy I didn't know who saved himself from death because an orange tree in bloom perfumed the bedroom where his mother screwed with men she didn't know. I am, finally, guilty for a poor sixtyish gringa I offended by confusing her with my wife, Cindy, and slapping her in public . . .

In all of their eyes, I saw a time which disregarded my individuality. Above all, I saw those Mexican children and felt afraid of escaping from my own more or less protected individuality, constructed with a certain care and lots of patience so I could face a helpless humanity in which circumstances neither respect nor distinguish anyone.

I realized what had happened. In death, I had become a Mexican.

At noon

The coast guard boarded us amid the confused joy and fear of Snow White and her seven dwarfs. We'd reached Barra de Navidad, a good distance from the Sea of Cortés. Well, death is a disorienting experience. Excuse me. The nearest port was Manzanillo. The sailors covered their noses with handkerchiefs before coming aboard. The captain quickly inspected and quickly questioned them. "He died of a heart attack," said Snow White. The girls said nothing. "So who castrated him?" asked the captain, pointing to my fly. "All of us," shouted María de la Gracia. Dolores was about to shout, I was hungry. Snow White spoke up. "He was a pervert. He was a gringo. He tried to take advantage of my girls." The coastguardsmen laughed at her. "All right then," said Snow White. "I did it. I was hungry. Don't you like to eat mountain oysters? That's how you get started. But anyway, we're Catholics and Mexicans."

The next day, every day

They towed the ketch back to Acapulco. No one could identify me. There was nothing left of my more or less famous features. The Yacht Club said I paid in cash and in advance without leaving my name. That wasn't true. The hotel arranged for the service. But no one wanted to get involved in such a strange case or involve anyone else, the hotel didn't want to involve the club, and the club didn't want to involve the hotel. While the investigation went forward, María de la Gracia confessed I was her boyfriend and the father of her child. She claimed the body. Just to get rid of it (I mean of me), they gave it to her. I mean, they handed me over.

She put me in a box and spoke to me very softly, thanking me because thanks to me, she said, she'd remembered the name of her hometown and her son's grave.

They carried me in a bus to a nameless village along the Costa Chica in the state of Guerrero. My presence was celebrated by the other passengers.

When we got to the town, the carpenter recognized María de la Gracia and gave her a coffin.

She thanked him and buried me next to her son, in a cemetery where the crosses are painted indigo blue, vermilion, yellow, and black, like birds, like fish. The grave is next to a tall orange tree, about eighteen or twenty feet tall, which seems to have achieved its full height. Who could have planted it? How long ago? I wish I could know how much history will protect me from now on. Do I lie in the shadow of history?

When the hotel receptionist, the little man covered with coffee powder and sporting a thin mustache, said he was the only person to see me, he lied. The Indian chambermaid saw me floating in the pool reading a wet book of poems. Only now do I remember that line: "But one man loved the pilgrim soul in you, / And loved the sorrows of your changing face." Now I remember that verse when I think about a young illiterate Indian girl who didn't even speak Spanish. The little man in the guayabera wanted to save his skin but follow the story in the conspiracy. He said that it was true, he had registered me, that he had seen me, but that I'd walked away without leaving my name. The bill had been put down to the name on my American Express card.

The investigation centered on me and if in fact some people did deduce that I was the corpse found drifting with seven Acapulco whores and their madam in the Pacific near Barra de Navidad in a ketch named *The Two Americas*, no one would think of following a poor being as humble as María de la Gracia to her small village on the Costa Chica. And besides, Snow White was nervous about having cut off my balls but proud as well for having saved the girls. Everything is forgotten. Clues disappear. The possibility of my strange death merited a small obit in the *Los Angeles Times*. *Time* magazine didn't even bother to note it. In the transitions column of *Newsweek*, this is all they printed:

PRESUMED DEAD. Vince Valera, 55, bushy-browed hero of
B movies, graced with a certain Irish charm, winner of

the only Oscar given to an American actor for a European film (*The Long Night*, directed by Leonello Padovani, 1972). Disappeared in Acapulco.

Cindy inherited everything and no longer wanted to find out anything.

Dead, I would like to add something, much more, to that brief biography. I dream of other destinies that could have been mine. I imagine myself in Mexico conquering Great Tenochtitlán, loving an Indian princess. I imagine myself in jail, dreaming about my dead, abandoned mother. I imagine myself in another century, amused, organizing toasts and serenades in a baroque city I don't recognize. Opposite another unknown but ancient city, I imagine myself dressed in black standing before an army in mourning, determined to win in a battle against pure, invisible space. In a long night of fog and mud, I see myself walking along a river holding a child by the hand. I've saved her from prostitution, sickness, death . . .

I dream about the orange tree and try to imagine who planted it, a Mediterranean, Oriental, Arabian, Chinese tree, in this distant coast of the Americas.

Since my face disappeared because of the seawater, the sun, and death, María de la Gracia took a papier-mâché mask she bought in the village market and put it over my face before burying me.

"This is your face. Your face for death."

That's what the girl said, as if she were intoning an ancient rite.

I've never been able to see that mask. I don't know what or whom it represents. You see: I've closed my eyes forever.

Acapulco–London, May 1991–September 1992

The Two Americas

TO BÁRBARA AND JUAN TOMÁS DE SALAS

*. . . to give an account to the King and Queen
of the things they saw, a thousand tongues would be insufficient;
nor would the author's hands suffice to write about
them, because they seemed enchanted . . .*
—CHRISTOPHER COLUMBUS,
Journal of the First Voyage, from the extract made by Bartolomé
de Las Casas

Fragments from the Diary
of a Genoese Sailor

TODAY I landed on the enchanted beach. It was hot and the sun rose at an early hour. The radiance of the water was brighter than the light in the sky. No sea is more translucent, as green as the lemon juice my sailors craved, ravaged as they were by scurvy during the long voyage from the port of Palos. You can see all the way to the bottom, as if the surface of the water were a sheet of glass. The bottom is white sand, crisscrossed by fish of every color.

The storms shredded my sails. On August 3, we crossed the Saltes bar, and on September 6, we saw land for the last time when we left the port of Gomera in the Canaries. There were three caravels, but all that remains is the ship's boat I managed to save after the mutiny and massacre. I am the only survivor.

Only my eyes see this shore, only my feet walk it. I do what habit orders me to do. I get down on my knee and give thanks to a God who is certainly too busy with more important matters to think about me. I cross two old branches and invoke the sacrifice and benediction. I claim this land in the name of the Catholic Kings who will never set foot on it, and understand why they showed such magnanimity when they granted me possession of everything I might discover. They knew very well that without resources I couldn't dominate anything. I've reached these shores naked and poor. But what will they or I possess? What land is this? Where the hell am I?

• • • • • • • • • • • • • • •

Back in Genoa, my mother would say to me while I helped her stretch the huge sheets out to dry—while I imagined myself, even then, carried along by great sails to the far edges of the universe—"Son, stop dreaming. Why can't you be happy with what you can see and touch? Why do you always talk about things that don't exist?"

She was right. The pleasure of what I'm looking at should satisfy me. The white shore. The abrupt silence, so different from the deafening clamor of Genoa or Lisbon. The mild breezes and weather like Andalusia's in April. The purity of the air, with not one of the foul odors that plague the thronged ports of the Tyrrhenian Sea. Here only flocks of parrots darken the sky. And on the beaches I don't find the shit, the garbage, the bloody rags, the flies, and the rats of all the European cities. Here I find the snowy white horizons of purity, pearls as plentiful as the sand itself, turtles laying eggs, and beyond the beach, in successive ranks, a thick forest: palm trees near the beach and then, rising toward the mountains, thick groves of pine, oak, and strawberry trees. It's bliss just to look at them. And, on the highest peak in the world, an extremely high mountain crowned with snow, dominating the universe and exempted—I dare say it—from the furies of the universal flood. I have reached—can there be any doubt? —Paradise.

· · · · · · · · · · · · · · · ·

Is this what I wanted to find? I know my plan was to reach China and Japan. I always said that in the end we discover what we first imagine. So getting to Asia was only a metaphor for my will, or, if you prefer, of my sensuality. From the cradle, I had a carnal impression of the roundness of the earth. My mother had two glorious breasts that I was so good at sucking that they quickly ran dry. She said she preferred washing and hanging out sheets to feeding such a voracious baby. One after another: that's how my Italian wet nurses came, each one milkier, rounder, than her predecessor, enjoyable, with their breasts capped off with delicious tips which for me came to represent, clearly, my vision of the world. Breast after breast, milk after milk, my eyes and my lips overflowed with the vision and savor of the globe.

First consequence: I always viewed the world as a pear, very round except where it comes to a point, where it is highest. Or like a very round ball, but, instead of a ball, like a woman's breast, with the nipple being the highest part and closest to heaven.

Second consequence: If someone told me I was insane and that an egg can't stand on its end, I would win the argument by smashing one end of the egg and standing it up. But my mind, in reality, was thinking about biting a nipple until the breast was empty of milk, until the wet nurse shrieked. In pleasure or in pain?

I'll never know.

• • • • • • • • • • • • • • •

That childhood of mine had a third consequence I'd better confess right now. We Genoese are not taken very seriously. In Italy, there are different levels of seriousness. The Florentines give us Genoese no credence. Of course, they see themselves as a nation of sober, calculating people with a good head for business. But the citizens of Ferrara view the Florentines as sordid, sinister, avaricious, full of deceit and tricks they use to get what they want and justify themselves in some fashion. The people of Ferrara prefer to be fixed and aristocratic, like classical medals and just as immutable and refined. Because they are (or feel) so superior, they do nothing to betray the image of their nobility and quickly fall into despair and suicide.

So, if the Ferrarese scorn the Florentines, and the Florentines scorn the Genoese, there's nothing left for us to do but despise the loudmouthed, scummy, frivolous Neapolitans, who, in turn, have no way out but to heap filth on the sinister, murderous, dishonest Sicilians.

I want the readers of this diary, which I will soon toss into the sea, to understand what I've just said so that they will also understand my dramatic decision. A man of my country and my era had to suffer as many humiliations as he inflicted on others. As a Genoese, I was considered a visionary and a fraud in every court in Europe to which I brought my knowledge of navigation and my theories about the planet's mammary circumference. Fast-talking and proud, more full of fantasy than facts. That's how I was treated, whether in Paris, Rome, London, or the ports of the Hanseatic League. That's how Ferdinand and

Isabella—I was told by the ubiquitous gossips—talked about me after my first visit. Which is why I moved to Lisbon: all the adventurers, dreamers, merchants, money-lenders, alchemists, and inventors of new worlds congregated in the Portuguese capital. There I could be one among many, be anything I wanted while I learned what I had to learn in order to embrace the round world, grab the universe by the teats, and suck its nipples until there wasn't a drop of milk left. I had a costly apprenticeship.

· · · · · · · · · · · · · · ·

Yesterday I was approached by the first men I'd ever seen from these new lands. I was sleeping on the sand, exhausted by the last days of my voyage in the ship's boat, alone, guided only by my excellent knowledge of *the stars*. In my dream, actually a nightmare, appeared the terrible scenes of storms on the high seas, the despair of the sailors, scurvy, death, the mutiny, and finally the vile decision of the Pinzón brothers to return to Spain and abandon me in a boat with three casks of water, two bottles of spirits, a sack of seeds, and my trunk filled with curiosities: trumpery, red caps, and a secret compartment with paper, quill pens, and ink. They left me in dire straits: yesterday I dreamed their toothless corpses passed by on a raft made of snakes.

I awaken, my lips covered with sand, like a second skin granted by the deepness of my sleep. First I see the sky and the fugitive procession of ravens and ducks, instantly blocked out by the circle of faces the color of the natives of the Canary Islands. They speak like birds, in a singsong, high-pitched language, and when they rise to take me by the armpits and stand me up, they reveal themselves totally naked before me.

They gave me water and led me to tentlike buildings

where they gave me food I didn't recognize and let me rest.

Over the course of the following days, cared for and protected by these people, I regained my strength. I was amazed by these men and women unsullied by the evil of war, naked, very gentle, and without weapons. Their lands were extremely fertile and very well watered. They led peaceful, happy lives. They slept in beds that swayed back and forth like cotton nets. They strolled through their villages carrying smoking coals they sucked with as great satisfaction as I had sucked breasts. They made very beautiful dugouts ninety-five palms long out of a single trunk that carried as many as one hundred and fifty people, and thus they communicated with other islands and the mainland, which they soon brought me to see.

Yes, I had reached Paradise, and I had only one problem: Should I communicate this discovery to my illustrious European patrons or not? Should I remain silent or announce my feat?

· · · · · · · · · · · · · · ·

I wrote the appropriate letters so the astonished world would honor me and the monarchs of Europe would bow at my great deed. What lies didn't I tell? I knew the mercantile ambition and the boundless greed of my continent and the rest of the world, so I described lands full of gold and spices and mastic and rhubarb. After all, these discovery companies, whether English, Dutch, Spanish, or Portuguese, were paid to put salt and pepper on the tables of Europe. So I wrote that gold nuggets may be gathered like grains of wheat. King Solomon's mountains of gold are to be found here, safe from the waters of the flood, tall and resplendent, as if they were the breasts of creation.

Also, I was not ignorant of my contemporaries' need for

fable, the metallic wrapping that would disguise and make palatable their lust for gold. Gold, yes, but hidden in deep mines by cannibals and fierce beasts. Pearls as well, but revealed by the song of sirens, sirens with three breasts—three. Transparent seas, but plied by sharks with two phalluses—folding phalluses. Prodigious islands, defended by amazons who receive men only once a year, who allow themselves to be made pregnant and each nine months send their male children back to their fathers, keeping only the girl children. Implacable with themselves, they cut off one breast, the better to shoot their arrows.

• • • • • • • • • • • • • • •

Now, I must admit that both my mythical outlandishness and my very solid appreciation of the nobility of these savages masked the most painful experience of my life. Twenty years ago, I joined a Portuguese expedition to Africa, which turned out to be an infamous business of capturing blacks and then selling them. No one had ever seen greater cynicism. The black kings of the ivory coasts would hunt down and capture their own subjects, accusing them of rebellion and desertion. They would hand them over to Christian clergymen who would convert them and save their souls. The clergymen, in turn, would entrust them to the kind care of the Portuguese slavers, who were to teach them trades and transport them to Europe.

I saw them sail from the ports of the Gulf of Guinea, where the Portuguese traders would arrive with shiploads of merchandise for the African kings, to exchange for their enslaved population—redeemed, of course, by religion. The ships would empty of silks, percales, thrones, dishes, mirrors, views of the Ile de France, missals, and chamber pots; they would fill up with husbands separated from their wives—the women sent one place, the men elsewhere, their children similarly divided, and all thrown into crowded cargo holds with no place to move around, forced to shit and piss on top of one another, to touch only what was near them and to speak to others, mortally embracing them, who understood nothing. Has there ever been a race more humiliated, despised, subjected to the pure whim of cruelty than they?

• • • • • • • • • • • • • • •

I saw the ships sail out of the Gulf of Guinea, and now, here in my New World, I swore it would never happen again.

This was like the Golden Age the ancients evoke, which is how I recited it to my new friends from Antilia, who listened to me without understanding. After all, I was describing them and their time: first came the Golden Age, when man governed himself with uncorrupted reason and constantly sought the good. Not forced by punishment, not spurred on by fear, man used simple words and possessed a sincere soul. There was no need for law where there was no oppressor, no need for judges or courts. Or battlements, or trumpets, or swords to be forged, because everyone was ignorant of these two words: *yours* and *mine*.

Was it inevitable that the Iron Age come? Could I put it off? For how long?

I had reached the Golden Age. I embraced the noble savage. Was I going to reveal his existence to Europeans? Was I going to deliver these sweet, naked people, devoid of malice, to slavery and death?

I decided to be silent and to stay among them for several reasons, using several strategies. I don't want the reader to think he's dealing with a fool: we Genoese may be liars but we aren't idiots.

I opened my trunk and found the hats and beads. It

gave me pleasure to give them to my hosts, who enjoyed themselves immensely with the trinkets. But I asked myself: If my intention was to reach the court of the grand khan in Peking and the fabulous empire of Japan, whom did I think I was going to impress with this junk I picked up in the Puerto de Santa María market? The Chinese and the Japanese would have laughed at me. So, within my mammary, unconscious zone, I knew the truth: I would never reach Cathay because I didn't really want to reach Cathay; I wanted to get to Paradise, and in Eden the only wealth is nakedness and unawareness. Perhaps that was my real dream. I carried it through. Now I would have to protect it.

I was helped by the most ironclad law of Portuguese navigation, the law of secrecy. The sailors who left Lisbon and Sagres had imposed a policy of secrecy at all costs, ordered by their Sebastianist, utopian monarchs. Any Portuguese captain (to say nothing of common sailors) who revealed the routes or the places they'd discovered would be hunted to the ends of the earth and, when found (which they would be, don't doubt it for a second), would be drawn and quartered. The heads, feet, and hands of traitors had been seen all along Portuguese routes, from Cape Verde to the Cape of Good Hope, from Mozambique to Macao. The Portuguese were implacable: if they encountered ships intruding in their sea-lanes, they had standing orders to sink them immediately.

I am availing myself of that absolute silence. I turn it inside out like a glove and use it for my own advantage. Absolute silence. Eternal secrecy. What became of the talkative, fantastical Genoese? Where did he really come from? Why, if he was Italian, did he write only in Spanish? But why doubt he was Italian when he himself (that is, I myself) wrote: I am a foreigner. But what did it mean in those days to be a foreigner? A Genoese was a foreigner to a Neapolitan, as was an Andalusian to a Catalan.

As if I had foreseen my destiny, I sowed minuscule confusions. In Pontevedra, I left a false archive to drive the Galicians insane. No matter, their heads are a muddle of realism and fantasy. On the other hand, in Estremadura, where they never dream, I convinced people that I grew up in Plasencia, when in fact it was Piacenza. As for Majorca and Catalunia, well, I gave them the flesh of my flesh: my last name, that of the Holy Spirit, which abounds on those coasts. Corsica, which as yet has produced no man of note, could claim me because of a lie I told to two drunken abbots when I passed through Bastia.

I fooled no one. The only thing about myself I put down in writing clearly is this:

At a very tender age, I became a seafarer and have continued to be one until this very day . . . For more than forty years I have been doing this work. Everything that until today has been sailed I have sailed; everywhere I have traveled. I have had business and conversation with wise folk, churchmen and laymen, Latins and Greeks, Jews and Moors, and with many others of other sects.

My country is the sea.

. . . .

I threw the bottle with its pages of legend into the sea —all the lies about sirens and amazons, gold and pearls, leviathans and sharks. But I also told the truth about rivers and coasts, mountains and forests, arable land, fruit and fish, the noble beauty of the people, the existence of Paradise.

I disguised it in a name I heard here and created a

special identity for it. The name was Antilia. The identity was intermittence; that is, the isle of Antilia would appear and disappear. One day, the sun would reveal it; the next, the mists would blot it out. It floated one day and sank the next. A tangible mirage, a fleeting reality between sleep and wakefulness, this land of Antilia was only visible, ultimately, for those who, like me as a child, could imagine it first.

I tossed the bottle with the legend into the sea, certain that no one would ever find it. If someone did, he would read in it the ravings of a madman. Led by my sweet friends to the place that would be my permanent residence, I told myself a truth that only now I can put on record.

This was the place: a freshwater gulf into which seven rivers emptied, overwhelming the salt sea with their fresh force. A river is an eternal birth, renovation, perpetually renewed cleanliness and spirit, and the rivers of Antilia flowed into the gulf with a delightful, constant noise that dispelled the clamor of the Mediterranean alleys with the din of their peddlers, children, doorkeepers, rogues, street surgeons, butchers, trinket sellers, knife sellers, oil sellers, tinkers, bakers, skinners, and barbers. It also banished the silence of the night and its fear. The silence of imminent death.

Here they assigned me a hut and a hammock (the name of their woven beds). A tender woman, eager to please. A canoe for my little trips, and two young oarsmen to accompany me. Plenty of food, dorados from the sea and trout from the river, deer and turkey, papaya and custard apples. Out of my sack I took orange seeds, and together we planted them along the valleys and hillsides of the Gulf of Paradise. The trees grew better in Antilia than in Andalusia, with shiny leaves and fragrant flowers. I never saw better oranges, oranges that so resembled the sun they made the sun envious. I finally had a garden of perfect breasts, suckable, edible, renewable. I had conquered my own life. I was the eternal owner of my recovered youth. I was a boy without the shame or nostalgia of being one. I could suck oranges until I died.

That's right, paradise. So I stayed there, liberated above all from the horrible need to explain a different reality to Europeans, a history for them inexplicable. How could Europe understand that there is a history different from the one it made or learned? A second history? How will Europeans accept that the present is not only the heir of the past but the origin of the future? What a hideous responsibility. No one could stand it. Especially me.

I would have enough trouble eliminating all the lies about me and admitting that I'm not Catalan, Galician, Majorcan, or Genoese. I am a Sephardic Jew whose family fled Spain because of the usual persecutions: one more, one of so many, not the first and not the last . . .

• • • • • • • • • • • • • • •

The reader of these notes dedicated to chance will no doubt understand the reasons behind my silence, my abstention, my staying in Antilia. I wanted to attribute the care with which I was treated to my personal charm or to my empathy with those who received me. I paid no attention to the rumors that transformed me into the protagonist of a divine legend. Me, a bearded white god? Me, punctually returning to see if mankind had taken care of the earth I'd given them? I remembered the breasts of my wet nurses and took a big bite out of the orange that's always at my side, perennially renewed, almost my scepter.

From the top of my high, whitewashed belvedere, I see the length and breadth of the lands and the confluence of the rivers, the gulf, and the sea. Seven rivers flow down, some calm and others torrential (including one waterfall), to fill the gulf, which, in turn, gently opens on to a sea protected from its own rage by coral reefs. My white house, cooled by the trade winds, dominates the orange groves and is defended by dozens of laurels. Behind me, the mountains whisper their names: pine and cypress, oak and strawberry. Royal eagles perch on the white summits; butterflies descend like another waterfall, half gold, half rain; all the birds in the world meet in this immaculate air, from cranes, macaws, and owls wearing black glasses to those I identify more by their looks than by their names: birds like witches with black ears, birds that unfold what look like huge parasols, others dressed in the red of princes of the Church, others with plantlike throats, woodpeckers and squirrel birds, birds with red beaks and doves with short beaks, birds that sound like trumpets and others that sound like clocks, jacamars and ant-eating birds who live off the abundance of those they consume. The permanent cry of the caracara bird presides over all: my earthbound falcon that has never flown but which, dragging itself over the earth, devours waste and in so doing redeems life.

Beyond the visible life of my earthly paradise is what sustains it, the minutiae of invisible life. The richness of animal life is obvious, and the crow, the ocelot, the tapir, and the ounce mark their paths through the jungle or the forest clearly. They would get lost without the guidance of the living odors that are the routes of the silence and the night. The araguato monkey, the armadillo, the jaguar, and the iguana are all guided by millions of invisible organisms that purge the water and the air of their daily poisons, just as the caracara falcon does it right before our eyes. The aroma of the jungle is dispelled by millions of hidden little bodies that are like the invisible light of the forest.

They await the night to move around and learn things. We wait for the dawn. I look at the enormous, downy ears of the gray-brown wolf that comes up to my door every night. Blood rushes into those ears and allows heat to escape. It's the symbol of life in the tropics, where everything is arranged for living well, provided we want to prolong life and respect its natural flow. But everything turns against us the instant we show hostility and try to dominate nature by harming it. The men and women of my new world know how to care for the earth. I tell them that from time to time, which is why they venerate and protect me, even if I'm not God.

I compare this life with the one I left behind in Europe and shudder. Cities buried in garbage, redeemed from time to time by fire, but immediately drowned in soot. Cities with visible intestines, crowned with feces, along whose gutters flow pus and urine, menstrual blood and vomit, useless semen and dead cats. Cities without light, narrow, cramped, where everything wanders, ghostlike, or nods off like a succubus. Beggars, thieves, the insane, multitudes talking to themselves, skulking rats, runaway dogs that return in packs, migraines, fevers, vertigoes, tremors, hard volcanoes of blood between the legs and in the armpits, a black pattern on the skin: forty days of abstinence did not prevent forty million deaths in Europe. The cities were depopulated. Bands of looters came in to steal our possessions, and animals took over our beds. Our eyeballs burst. Our people were accused of poisoning wells. We were expelled from Spain.

Now I live in Paradise.

For how long? Sometimes I think about my family, about my scattered people. Do I also have a family, a wife, children here in this new world? Possibly. To live in Paradise is to live without consequences. My loves pass over my skin and my memory like water through a filter. What's left is more a sensation than a memory. It's as if time hadn't passed since I reached these lands and took up residence in the white mansion with the orange trees.

I cultivate my own garden. My most immediate sensual pleasures occur in the orange grove—I look, touch, peel, bite, and swallow. So do the oldest of sensations: my mother, wet nurses, breasts, the sphere, the world, the egg . . .

If I want my personal story to have a collective resonance, I'll have to go beyond the breast-orange to the two memory objects I've always borne with me. One is the key to the ancestral house of my forefathers in the Toledo ghetto. Expelled from Spain by persecution, we never lost the language of Castile or the key to our home. It's passed from hand to hand. It's never been a cold key despite being made of metal. Too many Jewish palms, fingers, and fingertips have fondled it.

The other thing is a prayer. We Sephardic Jews all travel with it and nail it to the door of our closets. I do the same thing in Antilia. I've improvised a clothing chest that holds, like mementos, my old doublet, my jerkin, and my breeches—my New World friends have taught me to wear linen, smooth and soft, white and airy: a shirt and trousers, sandals. To the chest I've nailed the prayer of the Jewish émigrés, which goes like this:

Mother Spain, you have been cruel to your Israelite children. You have persecuted and expelled us. We have left behind our houses, our lands, but not our memories. Despite your cruelty, we love you, Spain, and we long to return to you. One day you will receive your wandering children, you will open your arms to them, ask their forgiveness, and recognize our fidelity to your land. We shall return to our houses. This is the key. This is the prayer.

I recite it, and, almost like a satisfied desire, a memory returns to me of my disastrous arrival, shrieking like a caracara bird. I am sitting on my balcony at the first hour, doing what I do best: contemplating. The earliest breezes are blowing. The only thing missing is the sound of nightingales. I have recited the prayer of the Sephardic return to Spain. I don't know why, but I'm thinking about something that never worries me because I'm so used to it. Antilia is a land that appears and disappears periodically. I haven't discovered the laws that govern this mutability, and I prefer not knowing them. I'm afraid that knowing the calendar of appearances and disappearances would be something like knowing the date of our death beforehand.

I prefer doing what nature and the real time of life ordain. Contemplation and enjoyment. But this morning, surprisingly, a white bird flies by carrying the stalk of a bulrush, the kind of bird sailors see with pleasure because it doesn't sleep at sea; it's a sign land is near. The trade winds blow and the sea is as flat as a river. Crows, ducks, and a gannet pass over, fleeing to the southeast. Their haste alarms me. In a rare gesture, I stand up with a start as I see a kite floating high in the sky—a bird that makes gannets and other birds of prey vomit up their food and then eats it. It's a seabird, but doesn't land on the water, and never goes farther than twenty leagues out to sea.

I realize I'm looking at an event from the past. This is what I saw when I first arrived here. I try to dismiss this mirage and see what's happening today, but I can't distinguish between the two events. Another bird becomes visible in the sky. It comes closer, first barely a dot, then a brilliant star, so brilliant that it blinds me when I compare it to the sun. The bird descends toward the gulf. From its belly emerge two feet as huge as canoes, and, with a horrifying grunt that silences the terrified shrieking of the caracara, it settles on the water, raising a cloud of foam.

Everything becomes calm. The bird has doors and windows. It's an air house. A combination of Noah's ark and the Pegasus of mythology. The door opens and there appears, smiling, with teeth whose shine darkens that of the sun and of metal, a yellow man, just as my predecessor Marco Polo describes them. He's wearing glasses that add to the glare and is dressed in a strange fashion: he carries a small black case in one hand and wears crocodile-skin shoes.

He bows, boards a roaring boat lowered from the flying ship, and comes toward me.

· · · · · · · · · · · · · · · ·

Nothing surprises me. From the beginning, I disabused those who wanted to see in me a kind of garrulous, ignorant sailor. God gave me intelligence, and it flourished in the sailing world; of astrology it gave me a sufficiency, as it did of geometry and arithmetic; and ingenuity enough in my soul to draw spheres, and within them the cities, rivers, mountains, islands, and ports—all in their proper place.

Even if I possess these talents, I've grieved deeply (while never admitting it) because I suspect I never reached Japan, as I'd wanted, but a new land. As a man of science, I had to confess its existence; as a political man, I had to deny it. Which is what I did, but that fatal morning in my story, when the small man in the light-gray suit as brilliant as the bird that brought him to me, with his black leather case in his hand and his crocodile shoes, smiled and introduced himself, I discovered the terrible truth: I hadn't reached Japan. Japan had reached me.

Surrounded by six people, four men and two women, who worked all sorts of contraptions, compasses perhaps, hourglasses, calipers, or chastity belts for all I knew, and who pointed disrespectfully at my face and voice, my visitor introduced himself simply as Mister Nomura.

His argument was direct, clear, and simple:

"We've been attentively and admiringly observing your custodianship of these Lands. Thanks to you, the world possesses an immaculate reserve of rivers, forests, flora and fauna, pristine beaches and uncontaminated fish. Congratulations, Cristóbal-san. We have respected your isolation for a long time. Today the moment for you to share Paradise with the rest of humanity has come."

"How did you find out . . . ?" I stammered.

"You did not reach Japan, but your bottle stuffed with manuscripts did. We are patient. We've been waiting for the right moment. Your Paradise—do you see?—would appear and disappear very frequently. Expeditions sent out in the past never returned. We had to wait for a long time, until we perfected the technology that would fix the presence of what we agreed to call the New World, locate it permanently, despite its random, ultimately deceptive movements, despite the appearances and disappearances. I'm talking about radar, laser, ultrasound . . . I'm talking about high-definition screens."

"What is it you want?" I managed to say, in spite of my growing confusion.

"Your collaboration, Colombo-san. Be a team player. We only work in teams. Cooperate and everything will turn out fine. Wa! Wa! Wa! Conformity, Don Cristóbal," he said, prancing a bit and then standing on tiptoe.

He smiled and sighed. "We meet at last. Well, better late than never."

I signed more papers than I had during the Santa Fe capitulations with Ferdinand and Isabella. Nomura and his army of Japanese lawyers (the gulf filled up with yachts, ketches, and hydroplanes) forced me to cede the beaches of Antilia to the Meiji Company which in turn subcontracted their development to the Amaterasu Company which in turn ceded construction of hotels to the Minamoto Corporation which contracted to buy tablecloths from Murasaki Designs, all towel-related items from the Mishima Group, and soaps and perfumes from the Tanizaki Agency, while foodstuffs would be supplied by Akutagawa Associates in combination with the Endo Group insofar as imported products were concerned and with the Obe Group insofar as domestic products were concerned, all of which would be processed on the island by the Mizoguchi Corporation and transported to the hotels by Kurosawa Transport Corporation. All of it would be procured by local employees (what term do you think we should use for them: "aborigines," "natives," "indigenous peoples," "Antilleans"? We wouldn't want to hurt anyone's feelings) who will prosper with the influx of tourists, Columbus-san, and see their standard of living go through the roof. We need tourist guides, drivers, bus lines, car rental agencies, pink jeeps, and pleasure boats for the hotel guests. Which in turn will require highways and everything tourists need strung out along them: motels, pizzerias, gas stations, and recognizable trademarks to make them feel at home, because tourists—it's the first thing you should know as Admiral of the Ocean Sea and president of the Paradise Administrative Council Inc.—travel to feel they haven't left home.

He offered me some bitter tea: "Accordingly, we've given concessions to very familiar trademarks. You should sign—right here, if you don't mind—private contracts with each one to avoid difficulties that might arise out of the antimonopoly law of the European Economic Community, which, I add to relieve your conscience, would never have accepted something as greedy as the 1503 Casa de Contratación in Seville."

Dazed, I signed the various contracts, including clauses relating to fried chicken and soda water, gas stations, motels, pizzerias, ice cream parlors, picture magazines, cigarettes, tires, supermarkets, cameras, cars, yachts, musical instruments, and a list of etceteras longer than the list of titles belonging to the monarchs of Spain for whom I had embarked on my voyage of discovery.

I felt my new world had been covered over by a spiderweb and that I was the poor fly captured at the center, impotent, because, as I've already said, living in Paradise was living without consequences.

"Don't worry. Work with the team. Work with the corporation. Don't ask who is going to be the owner of all this. No one. Everyone. Trust us: your natives are going to live better than they ever did. And the world will thank you for the Last, the Supreme, the Most Exclusive Resort on the Planet, the New World, the Enchanted Beach Where You and Your Children Can Leave Behind Pollution, Crime, Urban Decay, and Enjoy a Pure Earth, PARADISE INC."

· · · · · · · · · · · · · · ·

I want to shorten this. The landscape is changing. Night and day, an acid smoke flows down my throat. My eyes tear, even when I smile at the hyperactive Mister Nomura, my protector, who has placed at my service a team of

samurai who guard me against the people who have threatened me or organized unions and protests. Not long ago
they were my friends.

"Remember, Don Cristóbal. We are a corporation for
the twenty-first century. Speed and agility are our norms.
We avoid offices and bureaucracies; we have no buildings
or staff; we rent everything, and that's it. And when reporters ask you questions about the real owner of Paradise
Inc., just say: No one. Everyone. Team spirit, Cristóbal-
san, company loyalty, yoga every morning, Valium every
night . . ."

Nomura pointed out that, far from being a restricted
place, Paradise Inc. was open to all nations. It's true: I felt
nostalgia looking at the old flags I'd left behind as they
arrived on the airships with a horde of tourists eager to
enjoy our immaculate waters and our pure air, the whiteness of our beaches and the virginity of our forests. TAP,
Air France, Iberia, Lufthansa, Alitalia, BA . . . The colors
of their insignia reminded me, with sweet bitterness, of
the courts I'd wandered through, begging support for my
enterprise. Now they were like the coats of arms decorating
a herd of Pegasus in the field of the Pleiades.

Thousands and thousands of tourists came, and on Oc-
tober 12, dressed in my fifteenth-century clothes, I was
paraded around on a float brought from the Carnival of
Nice, surrounded by naked Indians (male and female).
Now, it's hardly worth saying, all my clothing comes from
Banana Republic. No one bothers me. I'm an institution.

But my nose vainly tries to sniff the invisible highways
of the night, when thousands of hidden organisms used
to perfume the air to guide the tapir, the deer, the ocelot,
and the ounce. But I don't hear them anymore, don't
smell them either. Only my gray-brown fox with pointy
ears stays close to me. The heat of the tropics escapes

through those palpitating white ears. The two of us look toward the orange groves that surround us. I wish the fox would understand: the grove, the animal, and I are survivors . . .

They don't let anyone near me. They've forced me to become fearful. From time to time, I exchange glances with a lanky, dark-skinned Indian girl who fixes my pink-sheeted bed and waters the orchids before leaving. Her eyes are not only wary but hostile and something worse: resentful.

One night, the young Indian maid doesn't show up. Annoyed, I'm just about to protest. I realize a change has taken place. I become intolerant, comfortable, old . . . I open the netting that protects my hammock (I've retained that delightful custom from my original astonishment) and find stretched out in it a slim young woman the color of honey: stiff as a pencil, only the swaying of the hammock softens her. She introduces herself with verbal and gestural intensity as Ute Pinkernail, native of Darmstadt, Germany. She tells me she's managed to sneak in by taking the maid's place, that I'm very protected and don't know the truth. She stretches out her arms, wraps them around me, and whispers breathlessly, nervously into my ear: "There are six billion people on the planet, the big cities in the East and the West are about to disappear. Asphyxiation, garbage, and plague are burying them. They've fooled you. Your paradise is the last sewer for our narrow, packed, beggarly cities without light, without roofs, through which wander thieves, madmen, crowds that talk to themselves, skulking rats, dogs in savage packs, migraines, fevers, vertigoes: a city in ruins, submerged in its own sewage, for the majority; for the smallest minority, there is another, inaccessible city on the heights. Your island is the last sewer,

you've carried out your destiny, you've enslaved and exterminated your people . . ."

She was unable to go on. The samurai came in shouting,
jumping, brandishing submachine guns, violently pulling
me away. My veranda was shrouded in dust and noise;
everything was bathed in white light, and in one vast,
simultaneous instant, the flamethrowers burned up my orange grove, a bayonet pierced the heart of my trained wolf,
and Ute Pinkernail's breasts appeared before my astonished, desiring eyes. The girl's blood dripped through the
weaving in the hammock . . .

. . . .

To live in paradise is to live without consequences. Now
I know I'm going to die, and ask permission to return to
Spain. First, Mr. Nomura berated me: "You didn't act like
a member of the team, Cristóbal-san. Well, what did you
think, that you were going to be able to keep your paradise
away from the laws of progress forever? You've got to
realize that by preserving a paradise you were only mag-
nifying a universal desire to invade it and enjoy it. Try to
understand once and for all: there is no paradise without
a Jacuzzi, champagne, a Porsche, and a discotheque. No
paradise without french fries, hamburgers, sodas, and Neapolitan pizza. Something for everyone. You can't go around
believing in the symbolism of your name, 'Christ-bearer,
dove of the Holy Spirit.' Come back, fly away little dove,
and carry your message: Sayonara, Christ; Paradise, Ban-
zai! Wa! Wa! Wa! Conformity! The nail that sticks out
will soon be hammered down."

On the Iberia flight, I'm treated like what I am, a ven-
erable relic: Cristóbal Colón returning to Spain after a five-
hundred-year absence. I'd lost all notion of time and space.

Now, up in the sky, I recover them. Oh, how I enjoy seeing from up here the trace of my first voyage—in reverse: the oak-covered hills, the strawberry trees, the incredibly fertile soil all under cultivation, the canoes plying the gulf into which seven rivers empty, one of them in a smooth, milk-colored cascade. I look at the sea and the sirens, the leviathans and the amazons shooting their arrows at the sun. And flying over my burned-out orchard, I begin to sense the beaches with shit tides, bloody rags, flies and rats, the acrid sky, and the poisoned water. Will they put the blame for all this on the Jews and the Arabs before expelling them or exterminating them again?

I observe the flight of ducks and ravens, and I feel that our own ship is pushed along by soft trade winds on a variable sea—here it's as smooth as glass; there, when we're anchored in the sargasso, it's sometimes as stormy as it was in the worst moments of the first voyage. I fly near the stars and yet I see only one constellation as night falls. It's made up of Ute Pinkernail's magnificent breasts, the teats I was never to touch . . .

They serve me Freixenet champagne and they give me the magazine *Hola* to read. I don't get the drift of the articles. They don't mean anything to me. I'm on my way back to Spain. I'm going home. In each hand I carry the proof of my origin. In one hand, I clutch the orange seeds. I want this fruit to survive the implacable exploitation of the island. In the other, I carry the frozen key to my ancestral house in Toledo. I'll go back there to die: a stone house with a sagging roof, a door made of creaking boards that hasn't been opened since the time of my ancestors, the Jews expelled by pogroms and plagues, fear and death, lies and hatred . . .

I silently recite the prayer nailed to my chest like a scapulary. I recite it in the language the Jews of Spain kept alive during all eternity, so we would not renounce our home and house:

> You, beloved Spain, we call Mother, and during all our lives we will not abandon your sweet language. Even though you exiled us like a stepmother from your breast, we will not cease to love you as a most holy land, the land where our fathers left their families buried and the ashes of thousands of their loved ones. For you we save our filial love, glorious nation; therefore we send you our glorious greeting.

I repeat the prayer, I squeeze the key, I caress the seeds, and I give myself up to a vast sleep over the sea where time circulates like the currents, uniting and relating everything, yesterday's conquistadors and today's, reconquests and counterconquests, besieged paradises, pinnacles and decadences, arrivals and departures, appearances and disappearances, utopias of memory and desire . . . The constant element in this going back and forth is the painful movement of peoples, immigration, escape, hope, yesterday and today.

What shall I find when I return to Spain?

I shall open the door of my home again.

I shall plant the orange seed again.

London, November 11, 1992